THE WOLF AND THE MAN

OTHER FIVE STAR WESTERNS BY MAX BRAND:

Stolen Gold (1999); *The Geraldi Trail* (1999); *Timber Line* (1999); *The Gold Trail* (1999); *Gunman's Goal* (2000); *The Overland Kid* (2000); *The Masterman* (2000); *The Outlaw Redeemer* (2000); *The Peril Trek* (2000); *The Bright Face of Danger* (2000); *Don Diablo* (2001); *The Welding Quirt* (2001); *The Tyrant* (2001); *The House of Gold* (2001); *The Lone Rider* (2002); *Crusader* (2002); *Smoking Guns* (2002); *Jokers Extra Wild* (2002); *Flaming Fortune* (2003); *Blue Kingdom* (2003); *The Runaways* (2003); *Peter Blue* (2003); *The Golden Cat* (2004); *The Range Finder* (2004); *Mountain Storms* (2004); *Hawks and Eagles* (2004); *Trouble's Messenger* (2005); *Bad Man's Gulch* (2005); *Twisted Bars* (2005); *The Crystal Game* (2005); *Dogs of the Captain* (2006); *Red Rock's Secret* (2006); *Wheel of Fortune* (2006); *Treasure Well* (2006); *Acres of Unrest* (2007); *Rifle Pass* (2007); *Melody and Cordoba* (2007); *Outlaws From Afar* (2007); *Rancher's Legacy* (2008); *The Good Badman* (2008); *Love of Danger* (2008); *Nine Lives* (2008); *Silver Trail* (2009); *The Quest* (2009); *Mountain Made* (2009); *Black Thunder* (2009); *Iron Dust* (2010); *The Black Muldoon* (2010); *The Lightning Runner* (2010); *Legend of the Golden Coyote* (2010); *Sky Blue* (2011); *Outcast Breed* (2011); *Train's Trust* (2011); *The Red Well* (2011); *Son of an Outlaw* (2012); *Lightning of Gold* (2012); *Comanche* (2012); *Gunfighters in Hell* (2012); *Red Hawk's Trail* (2013); *Sun and Sand* (2013); *The Double Rider* (2013); *Stagecoach* (2013).

THE WOLF AND THE MAN

A WESTERN STORY

MAX BRAND®

FIVE STAR

A part of Gale, Cengage Learning

GALE
CENGAGE Learning®

Detroit • New York • San Francisco • New Haven, Conn • Waterville, Maine • London

LIBRARY OF CONGRESS CATALOGING-IN-PUBLICATION DATA

Brand, Max, 1892–1944.
    The Wolf and the Man : A Western Story / by Max Brand. — First Edition.
        pages cm
        "The Wolf and the Man first appeared as an eight-part serial by George Owen Baxter in Street & Smith's Western Story Magazine (3/4/33–4/22/33)"—T.p. verso.
        ISBN 978-1-4328-2762-5 (hardcover) — ISBN 1-4328-2762-6 (hardcover)
        I. Title.
PS3511.A87W65 2014
813'.52—dc23   2013038368

First Edition. First Printing: February 2014
Published in conjunction with Golden West Literary Agency
Published by Five Star™ Publishing, a part of Gale, Cengage Learning
Find us on Facebook– https://www.facebook.com/FiveStarCengage
Visit our website– http://www.gale.cengage.com/fivestar/
Contact Five Star™ Publishing at FiveStar@cengage.com

Printed in Mexico
1 2 3 4 5 6 7 18 17 16 15 14

ADDITIONAL COPYRIGHT INFORMATION

CHAPTER ONE

Gray Cloud had lived only two years, but since his ninth month he had made nearly every week a memorable one. It was in his ninth month that he discovered how neatly his fangs would cut the hamstring of a cow, or even of a full-grown bull. That ended all necessity of hard labor for him.

Other wolves had to work hard across the diameter of a hundred-mile range. But Gray Cloud took things easily. Winter or summer, he could always find beef when he wanted it. Since he grew to prefer it perfectly fresh, he had to kill more often, and since he killed more often, he had to lurk closer to the dwellings of man. The terrible scent of steel and gunpowder was seldom out of the far-drawn horizon of his scenting powers, and nearly always there was the trace of man himself in the air.

That taught him lessons all the faster. He was learning, as it were, with a gun at his head, in more senses than one. He was nipped half a dozen times by bullets, but he was never seriously wounded by any of the hundreds of shots that were fired at him. He had discovered that at any distance over four hundreds yards he ran little or no danger from firearms. He knew that in the open a horse could run him down, but for that reason he usually chose to hunt where there were rocky hills. In such going he could easily leave horses behind him, and dogs also dropped to the rear.

Yes, they had begun to hunt him with dogs when he was a scant year and a half old and was just putting on the last of his normal hundred and thirty pounds. He learned a great deal from the dogs. He found out that they were helpless, singly, that they were timorous even when they ran in pairs, but that in groups they would fight as savagely as cornered wildcats. However, the life was close to the surface in them. Henry Morrissey found that out.

When the price on Gray Cloud's scalp rose to $1,000, Morrissey brought down his pack of hounds, and they nailed Gray Cloud in a narrow little gulley at the third running of him. He was not really cornered, but he was tired of running away from the brindled leader. So he turned in the narrows of the little ravine, and when the hunters came up, they found five dead or dying dogs on the ground, while the others stood back and growled at a wolf that had disappeared again among the rocks.

Morrissey went back to the Purvis Ranch that night, and Gray Cloud followed him down. He killed a prize thoroughbred bull during the small hours of the morning, dined heartily, slept off the feast inside the Purvis barn while the dogs howled and raged on vain trails, and came out and nosed the poisoned carcass the next night. But he was not fooled. They had tried poison on him a hundred times; he knew all about it.

He was not really hungry, so he contented himself by drifting in on the dogs and cutting the throats of two more of them before he loped away into the brush. Morrissey came out and saw him in the moonlight, and thought he was as big as a grizzly bear. He fired five shots, and swore that three of them, at least, must have hit the mark.

People were always swearing that they had put a slug or two in Gray Cloud. But as a matter of fact, Morrissey had not even grazed him.

It was after this affair at the Purvis Ranch that the cattlemen got together in a special meeting, the first time in history that so many prominent men had gathered to talk about any animal—that is, since the days of dragons. They agreed that a wolf that killed from two to four cows in a month was worth a price. They laid $2,500 on the head of Gray Cloud, and thereby they turned him at a stroke into something that was both history and legend.

You can still read the accounts of that meeting in a fine and flowing hand, written upon slightly yellowed paper, and signed by the clerk *pro tem.*

Morrissey, not so much for the money as for the sake of his honor, rebuilt his pack, bought four Russian wolfhounds, and tried again.

His Russian wolfhounds were faster than the rest. They were so fast that they outdistanced the pack and came up neatly, in pairs, perfectly matched, one on each side of the monster. In Russia they had been trained to close at the same instant on the quarry. They tried the same trick on Gray Cloud, and although he only killed one of the four, the other three were ruined for their business thereafter.

Morrissey gave up the job and returned home, without glory. And the Gray Cloud problem became a burning question. He had been lifted to the dignity of newspaper follow-ups—that is to say, the journals of the surrounding towns carried items about him every day, mentioning the last slaughters attributed to him, and always winding up, of course, with the amount on his scalp. It was the hard cash that made him the good news.

As a matter of fact, hardly a week went by without revealing, to some hungry cowpuncher or trapper, a sight of the great wolf.

Sometimes Gray Cloud was gliding off among the rocks. Sometimes he came up to the verge of campfires to study his enemies at close hand, as it were. He was always known, after his going, by the size of the prints of his enormous paws. Their dimensions were etched upon the memories of every boy and man on the entire range.

Still, he continued to grow wiser and safer, and safer and wiser. He knew as well as you do the difference between a gun in the holster and a gun out of it. He knew, if they were to windward, whether men had guns or not. He nearly paid for his life with that knowledge, for Buck Wainwright, of the Harry Smith ranch, got a rope on him one day when he ventured too rashly close, and might well have dragged the famous beast to death, except that the teeth of Gray Cloud were too sharp for the strands of the rope.

That was another lesson, and he could be trusted to remember it.

Yet, for all his past, he went far down into the grasslands hardly a month later for no other reason than because he was a little bored with the ease of his life. He wanted adventure, and he got it in the most unsuspected way.

It was a rabbit that started the trouble. Gray Cloud, drifting cautiously over the ridge of a hill—for he knew the danger of showing himself against any skyline—first made sure that there was not a sign of a human being in the wide hollow. Next, he saw a rabbit a hundred yards away, and the rabbit saw him. With the folly of its kind, it ducked down behind a tuft of high grass that grew up around a small stone, and there it waited, with the quivering tips of its ears plain to see. Upon the folly of jack rabbits most Western beasts of prey make their dinners. And Gray Cloud started to stalk. It was not that he wanted the dinner, but that he wanted the game.

A wolf that can catch a rabbit can also catch an antelope now and then, and Gray Cloud loved venison even more than he loved beef. So he went down the slope into the hollow as softly as a silver cloud draws down the soundless blue arch of heaven. He came near to the tuft of grass. He gathered his legs under him. Through his limbs ran an iron tremor of strength; he was just ready for the spring that is the chief delight of hunting when the rabbit happened to poke its silly head above the tuft of grass and saw fate smiling at it with a capacious set of white teeth.

The rabbit and the wolf leaped at the same time. The side slash of Gray Cloud missed its mark; he turned and rushed after the dissolving streak of tan. It was not that he had the least hope of overtaking that little flash of dim lightning; it was merely because his muscles needed the tuning of a bit of hard running. Also, he was irritated.

So he sprinted a furlong, losing about as much distance as he covered, and then found himself flung heavily to the ground. His own weight and the force of running half stunned him. Then he dragged himself to his feet and found the rigid teeth of a trap had closed over a hind leg. He lay down and thought the matter over, occasionally studying the scent of his own blood. It was oddly like the smell of other blood.

He was afraid, dreadfully afraid, not because of the pain, not because of the inexorable hold of the steel teeth, but because this gift had come to him from man. He recognized the present; he recognized the state of war. He had preyed on man and the things of man most of his life. Now man would take a hand in the final session.

He had seen others of his kind, and many a coyote, standing helpless till a bullet knocked them over. Instinct told him that he could bite off his foot below the trap's teeth and then pull out the mangled leg. It was better, first, to see if he could not draw out the leg without resorting to this desperate means. He stood up tentatively, then heavily strained at the trap, his lips furling back with a grin of agony. And as he put down a forepaw for a second effort, another trap closed over it with a clank.

He was stretched out to the full beneath the pair. He could not move. Therefore, after blinking his yellow eyes a few times, he lay down and waited for remorseless fate to overtake him.

He lay there for two days, burned by the terrible strength of the sun. On the first day three coyotes stopped by to visit him. They could see, clearly enough, that he was helpless, and they would gladly have tasted his blood. But when he lifted his great head, they leaped away and fled, their tails down. Instinctive terror was greater in them than knowledge.

On the second day a pair of buzzards began to circle in the blue above him. By midday they were wheeling low down, and he could see their naked, ugly heads. He understood that, also. What beast in the wild does not recognize those living graves that float forever in the thinnest of the air?

It was early afternoon, when he had done studying the buzzards, that he noted something else—a taint of smoke and an increased heat coming down the wind. It was a grass fire. That grass was not the crisp yellow that it would be a month later, but it was dry enough and long enough to feed a hot blaze. The loose skin along his back puckered. He turned over on his belly and snarled. It was better to die in any way, better to die under the tooth, even, than to endure fire.

The heat, the smoke, increased momentarily. The sun turned a dull red. Tired of this, he closed his eyes and thought back to happier days—to the day when the wolfhounds had closed on him in the throat of the gulley, and had met the deadly flashing of his teeth.

When he looked out again, the sun was quite blocked away by the head and shoulders of a man.

Chapter Two

The horror that came over the wolf was greater than Gray Cloud would have felt had the red rim of the running fire topped the line of hills at that instant. Fear does not depend upon reason, but upon instinct. And the instinct of Gray Cloud taught him that nothing in the world, not the puma, not the grizzly bear, is to be dreaded half as much as man is to be feared.

The other looked over his shoulder toward the direction of the fire, frowned, shook his head, and then raised and pointed the rifle in his hands.

By making an effort, the lobo could barely manage to stand, and this Gray Cloud did, his short, furry ears pricking. He knew perfectly well what happened on occasions like this. The brief thunder spoke; the animal dropped; the end had come. But the quickest way was the best way.

Big Dave Reagan lowered the rifle after an instant and shook his head again. "Game," he said aloud. "Dead game." He considered the bright, yellow eyes. Steadily they looked back into his. Then he looked again over his shoulder, and, as he did so, the prairie fire topped the horizon and dipped over the brow of the hill into the hollow.

Dave Reagan started. It was time for him to be on the move. And if he wished to have the scalp of Gray Cloud to show, and one of those forepaws to prove that he really had found the famous prowler, it was time to kill the wolf and use the knife with haste—the fire was coming fast.

But he was a simple soul, this Dave Reagan. His cousins, with whom he lived, called him a half-wit; nearly everyone on the range smiled and shrugged shoulders when his name was mentioned. At least, he was so simple that he could not pull the trigger on this beast, and he knew it. He had shot many another wolf in a trap, but this one was different. Perhaps Gray Cloud's fame changed his status and made his yellow eyes seem more fearless, more understanding, more human, as it were.

Instead of shooting, Dave Reagan made up his mind to another course, though he grunted and swore a little as he did so, knowing that he would be accused of folly. He took out a long cord, noosed an end of it with deft fingers, and flung the noose over the muzzle of the wolf.

Gray Cloud did not stir. He allowed the noose to be drawn tight while his gaze remained, fascinated, upon the approaching line of the fire. It had seemed to him, at first, that death by the hand of man was the most terrible of all. That was before man had come. Now, with an age-old dread, he watched the running line of the fire, and saw the flames toss up into high heads when they reached and consumed a longer and richer tuft than usual. It would be at him soon, eating his great body as it would eat a log of wood. The dread of it made his throat dry and puckered his eyes. He was almost unaware of what the man beside him was doing, until the noose was fast about his jaws and tied back around his neck to hold it securely in place.

Then Dave Reagan sprang the jaws of the locks with the might of his hands, picked up his prize as shepherds pick up a lamb, and slung the heavy burden over his great shoulders.

The fire was not twenty yards away, running fast. Hardly another man on the range could have endured the blast of heat and smoke as long as he had already endured it. But now he bowed his head so that the wide brim of the hat might offer some protection to his face, and ran forward straight toward the line of fire, but at its thinnest and lowest point. He closed his eyes. Flames gushed up around him. He ran on, paused, threw the wolf to the ground, and beat out the fire that had started in his trousers legs.

He would be reproved for that, he well knew. When another garment had to be provided for him, the whole family always looked upon him with savage eyes.

When he recovered himself, he was amazed at two things— first, that the captive had not taken this moment to make off, and second, that Gray Cloud had not put his teeth in his benefactor while he was being carried—for the cord had already been slipped from the muzzle.

The first problem was easily solved. The traps had been fixed in the fore and hind leg on the right side. Had they been alternate, Gray Cloud might have hobbled away at a staggering lope. As it was, he could not move without falling down. He was barely able to stand, shifting his paws a little as the heat of the ground burned his pads. The matter of his failure to flee was settled, then, but why had not Gray Cloud used his teeth on a human enemy? That was a greater mystery.

Dave Reagan had no solution for it. But, as a matter of fact, he was accustomed to being bewildered; he could merely let his mind leap forward to a definite conclusion. Gray Cloud thought that he had met a friend. Dave stepped closer. The wolf did not snarl or snap. Instead, Gray Cloud turned his head and looked after the line of the retreating fire. A miracle had been performed for him. It would be hard to say that there was really gratitude in his heart, but at least he knew that he was still helpless. He might sink his teeth in the leg of the man, but he could not leap as high as the soft throat, where the human life lay— not from those crippled legs of his. So he endured.

He was shuddering in every limb at the closeness of the human scent, and the smell of steel and gunpowder was rank in

15

his nostrils. But he had learned the philosophy of the wilderness. When death comes near—well, it has long been known; it is a familiar thing. The caged lion is as fierce in its instincts as when it was roaming through the jungles, but in the cage it knows its helplessness, and allows itself to be whipped and prodded around the floor.

So Gray Cloud stood still.

The man reached down and laid a hand on his head. It was not such a fearless thing as it seemed. Those jaws might be swift to turn and snap, but the hand was swift, also. And if the jaws were strong, there was crushing power in the man's fingers.

Gray Cloud could not know that, but he could recognize fearlessness. It is the first of all qualities that appears to beast or to the human mind. Besides, he was helpless.

It was by no ordinary process that Dave Reagan reached his next conclusion. To kill the trapped wolf had seemed murder of a special sort. To kill the animal after he had, in a measure, risked his own life for that of the beast, was tenfold murder. Besides, suppose that he could walk into the back yard of the house of his cousins with that famous captive? That would be something worthwhile.

He was rarely able to make them exclaim, except in disgust or in contempt. They called him fool and half-wit to his face. No labor was sufficient to win praise from them. Whatever he did was wrong, and his happiest days were those on which the fewest words were addressed to him. But now, if he returned with the equivalent of $2,500, could they keep from praising him?

He smiled with a strange eagerness, as wistful as an unhappy child.

He could lash the jaws of the wolf securely this time, but, on the other hand, half the glory would be gone from him if he came in with a victim helplessly tied. The miracle was, in his case, to keep those famous jaws inactive, but not by sheer force.

He leaned lower. Gray Cloud did not stir. His yellow eyes turned green, but that was all. His teeth were not showing.

Nothing can be done without risk. That was an early lesson in the hard life of young Dave Reagan. In a moment more he had caught up the wolf like a sack and had the animal over his shoulders again.

He had steeled himself to feel the slash of the teeth, but there was not so much as a growl. Gray Cloud submitted. He had been carried once before in this manner, and taken through consuming fire. Other strange things might happen. Besides, this was no time, obviously, to translate thought and fear into tooth-work.

It was four miles to the Reagan house, and Gray Cloud weighed a hundred and thirty pounds, though there was hardly an ounce of fat on him. Yet the man carried that burden the entire distance, only resting twice on the way.

And each pause was memorable to Gray Cloud. For he was placed on the ground beside a brook the first stop, and there he was allowed to drink to his fill. Now and then, guiltily he jerked up his head and looked into the face of the man, but danger was not threatened. And the water slaked such a thirst as he never had known before—more than two days of dreadful famine. He lay down, his eyes closed, panting. He rose and drank again. When he was sufficed, he rested once more, and now the man, the familiar, the ancient enemy, washed the fever from the trap wounds and tied up the hurts with bits of rag.

Gray Cloud lowered his head and sniffed at the process once. Then he drew himself back into his attitude of calm indifference. Miracles were still happening. He could not understand, because nothing like this had ever happened to his ancestors except, far away in the past, certain strange events with Indians. Some of these, perhaps, moved faintly in the current of his blood, not coming into the mind, but helping to control his actions.

He was lifted again onto the shoulders of the man, and the powerful muscles worked and stirred and slid like snakes beneath him as Dave Reagan stepped on.

The second halting place was at another brook. Gray Cloud drank again, luxuriating in the cool of the water. Most of the pain had left his wounds.

And again he was lifted, and carried straight on to the house of the man. As it rose out of the trees, a single tremor ran through him, yet his body remained limp. Then dogs rushed out, half a dozen of them, and made straight for them. He started to struggle, but a terrible roar came from the throat of the man, and the house dogs slinked away.

The wolf settled down on those competent shoulders. There was much to fear, of course, but in one thing there could be placed some trust—this strange creature that stood like man, walked like man, and carried the scent of humanity, plus steel and gunpowder. Yet there was a difference. In the profound depths of his mind, Gray Cloud registered that difference, and found his mind overwhelmed.

Chapter Three

In one corner of the corral stood the little shed in which was housed the forge, and the anvil, with a few tools and hammers hanging from the walls or leaning against it. That shed was the only heaven that the young man knew, except for the days when he was allowed to hunt on the range. Recently he had been given more and more of those days, for, as Cousin Bush Reagan was fond of saying: "The kid, he's so dog-gone' close to an animal, that he knows their ways. He'll turn up a deer pretty near anywhere." But aside from the hunting, the forge was the heaven of the young man. It was the one place where he could shape things with his hands, make things out of his imagination. As a rule, there was simply sheer drudgery.

For he was the plowman, the reaper, and it was he who mowed the hay, cared for the driving stock, caught up horses that others would ride. His own riding was confined to the breaking of new colts from the pastures, or newly purchased wild mustangs. Otherwise, he was never in the saddle. It was only three miles to town, and the half-wit could walk perfectly well. And as for the riding on the range, could that be trusted to him? No, only in the bitter winds of January and February. Then he might be given the worst horse for a day and sent out into the blizzard.

Only drudgery was given into his hands, and it was simply because the sharpening of plowshares, or the welding of a break, or the fashioning of ironwork of any sort was considered drudgery by his cousins, that he was allowed to do these things. In slack times he was allowed to go to the village and hang about the blacksmith shop to pick up what information he could. The time came when Bush Reagan could collect a dollar for every day that Dave worked in that shop, therefore the days increased in number, and the mist that hung over his brain in other things did not seem to interfere with his handicraft.

"That's where he's got all of his brains . . . in his hands, and in the broad of his back," Bush Reagan used to say.

In the little blacksmith shop in the corral, now, the young man halted, laid the wolf on the floor, and spent half an hour turning an old section of a leather trace into a collar. To this he attached a chain, and the chain he fixed around one of the posts that upheld the roof of the shed. Even the teeth of a wolf could not crack that chain, so Dave went contentedly on toward the house.

He looked back, and saw that the dogs were gathering around the shed, sniffing, howling softly and plaintively. But he smiled at this, for he knew that it was not in their mongrel hearts to come to grips with that formidable stranger.

When he walked into the house he found Bush Reagan seated in the dining room, playing the card game called pedro with his two sons, Hank and Pete.

"Hey, back so soon? Get us a deer?" asked Bush Reagan.

His two sons looked with mingled contempt and expectation on this provider of meat for the family.

"I didn't shoot a thing," said the young man.

Bush Reagan stared through the window and saw the height of the sun above the horizon. "Then," he roared, "what you mean by comin' back at this time of day? You dummy, what you thinkin' of?"

A mild warmth of satisfaction spread around the heart of the young man. The bitterness of persecution now would make the sweetness of praise all the pleasanter later on.

"G'wan out and try again," commanded Pete Reagan angrily, lolling in his chair and thrusting his thumbs into the armholes of his vest. "I ain't had a decent venison steak for a 'coon's age. G'wan out and try again!"

"I brought back something else," said Dave. And he smiled upon them diffidently.

"You didn't shoot nothing, but you brung something back, eh?" snapped Hank Reagan. "Whatcha mean by that, eh?"

"You'd better come and see," said the young man. He stepped back and opened the door to the back porch for them, still smiling.

"What's he think that he's gone and done?" Bush Reagan asked, scowling. "What fool trick's he up to now?"

"We can stretch a leg, anyway," said Hank. "I'm tired of that game. I never see no cards."

"You see plenty of cards, but you play 'em like a blockhead," said his brother.

"Shut yer face, will you?" asked Hank. "Your brains is all in the end of your tongue. Talking don't make no money for you, though."

With this pleasant badinage they walked past their cousin onto the back verandah.

"Out in the blacksmith shop," Dave said.

"What's out in the blacksmith shop?" asked Bush Reagan.

"You'll see," he assured them. He walked behind them down the path, two boards wide, toward the corral gate. He hoped to win from the moment to come more happiness than he ever had gained through his cousins in the years he had spent with this family.

Even from the first he had been an outsider. It was not only that the mist was over his mind, but that from the beginning he had noticed vast differences. So long as his father and mother lived, they had been his universe. And when he came at the age of eight years to this rough tribe, his only kin in the world, he had been oppressed by the sense of change. No matter what happened, therefore, he clung to the past. The few books he had brought with him from his first home, he had read over and over, not because they meant a great deal to him at first, but because they were of sacred origin. He had them still, thumb-worn, but matters of holy importance.

In his habit of speech, too, he harked back to the older days. It was one of the things that made him so silent—the fact that the language of his cousins was not that to which he had been accustomed in his real home. And when he did say anything, from the first the model that he used was the old one. He used to have to squint his eyes and look vainly, hopelessly back down the years, trying to remember how his father or his mother would have expressed themselves on any subject. But he never picked up the oaths, the slovenliness of tongue that distorted the talk of the new household.

Perhaps that was the chief reason for his backwardness in mental development. That and a certain quality of deliberation, of fumbling toward a subject with instinctive rather than intellectual understanding that had been the greatest characteristic of his mother.

To Bush Reagan, Dave's coming had been the most golden bit of luck that ever befell him. With an invalid wife, rapidly failing, two growing boys, and only a small patch of range, Bush had had to hire himself out as a day laborer and turn his hand to anything that would bring in a penny. After the coming of Dave this was changed, for Dave had a handsome patrimony in hard cash, a clean $100,000, so left to him in the care of his guardian—Bush—that the latter could invest as he pleased. He pleased, so long as the invalid wife lived, to put something more than half of the fortune into land and cattle. After she died, he

took a trip East and came back with the remnant of cash spent—
"On bad investments," he used to tell his neighbors at home.
There remained the ranch and the cattle, and the new buildings
that he had erected. But the cattle did not prosper. Bush Reagan was always what he himself termed an "unlucky" man,
though some of the hard-working and intelligent cattlemen of
the district could easily have suggested other terms for him.

That was not all. As the number of his cattle diminished,
Bush Reagan lost all concern for the rest of his property. He allowed the whole place to run down, and began to lead a rather
wild and careless life, fishing and hunting for the meat they
needed, and finding with increasing difficulty means to get the
money necessary to provide the other items for his family.

His two sons grew up like their father—rough, heedless, indif-
ferent to the slovenliness of their life. All three understood the
greatness of the wrong that had been done to Dave, their cousin.
And therefore all three joined in hating him and despising him.
The banker in town, who was the only soul able even to suspect
the extent of the wrongs that had been done to the youth, was a
very close-mouthed man, but yet he had dropped a few phrases
here and there that were filled with meaning, and a vague rumor
attached itself to the family. It was too vague to do more than
win for slow-minded Dave Reagan a sort of nebulous pity. Men
were apt to say: "There's reasons for him being backward."

One reason was that undoubtedly he was always the last in
this family of the Reagans. He was the last to sit down at the
table, because he was generally the one to serve the food. He
was the last to turn in at night, because his duties included
cleaning the dishes after supper, and last he was, now, in walking down the board path toward the corral.

Bush Reagan kicked the corral gate open, and it bumped
from hand to hand until it crashed shut behind Dave, pulled by
the weight that was attached to it.

"Hey, Dave, how many times I told you to ease that gate? Wanna have it battered to pieces?" demanded Bush Reagan.

"I'm sorry," Dave said with honest regret.

"Yeah," said his older cousin, "you're always sorry, but you never do nothin' about it, is what you don't do." He added: "That's the trouble with you."

"That's only one of the troubles, though," commented Hank.

And the three of them laughed.

They came to the blacksmith shop. They pulled the flimsy door open, and then there was an exclamation that turned into a shout from Pete.

"Look what he is! Look what he is!"

"Why, it's a dog-gone' gray wolf," said his father.

"Yeah, but what wolf? What wolf?" demanded Dave.

"What wolf is it?" asked Bush.

Hank Reagan found the answer, half by instinct and half by knowledge.

"By the jumpin' thunder," he shouted, "it's Gray Cloud!"

CHAPTER FOUR

Gray Cloud, stiff with his wounds, stood up and glared at them, and the deep-throated snarl that meant *Man!* formed and issued vibrantly.

The three instinctively stepped back from the monster.

"Hey, look at," said Pete Reagan.

"Look at what?"

"Look at the marks of the teeth of the trap," Pete said. "Got 'em on two of his legs."

"Look at twenty-five hundred dollars, is what I say," said Hank. "The only time that a piece of wolf ever meant twenty-five hundred bucks, I guess."

"Shut yer mouth," advised his father bluntly. He looked meaningly toward his son.

And the son, with instinctive quickness on a subject about which the entire family was unusually understanding, glanced toward Dave and nodded a little—as much as to say that if the dummy, as they were fond of calling the young fellow, did not know the cash value of that lobo, there was no use informing him. Certainly not a penny of that money must come to his hands.

"What trap you get that lobo out of, young man?" Bush Reagan asked sharply.

"You know that line of traps I put up?" said Dave.

"Catch him in one of your own traps?" snapped his older cousin.

"Two of 'em," Dave answered.

"A mighty lot of time you've wasted on them traps, away from your proper work on the ranch," said his cousin.

Hank winked at Pete, and Pete winked in return. They were dark men. Most of the Reagans, in fact, were swarthy, but Dave had his mother's red hair and steady gray eyes. Bush Reagan, on the contrary, was even darker than his sons. They had inherited from him their complexions, and each had the large mole that appeared on the left side of their father's face. Now they winked with a good deal of sympathy, for they recognized the favorite family sport—that of putting Dave in the wrong, no matter what he accomplished.

"Kind of wish you'd never put out them traps, it's taken so much of your time away," Bush said, frowning and clearing his throat, but also winking at his sons.

"Well," said Dave, "you've had a good lot of coyote skins out of those traps, and several wolves, too, and any number of wildcats. You remember the stack of pelts that you carted into town a month or two ago?"

"Aw, they didn't amount to nothing," said his uncle. "What would they amount to altogether?"

"Why," Dave said, "they didn't amount to anything as far as I'm concerned. I didn't get a penny from 'em."

He laughed a little as he said this; he intended no sting in his remark, but Bush Reagan flushed darkly, and his face contracted.

In the worst of us, conscience has power at times and will find the soul with a shrewd thrust. It found the very heart of Bush Reagan at this moment, and for an instant he lost sight of even the wolf, and considered the wasted years of his life and his crimes against this youth. Those recollections were so painful that presently they hardened him more than ever. He could not endure the compassion that he felt toward his cousin, therefore he shrugged it away.

"You never got nothin' from the traps that would pay me back for the time that you've wasted from the ranch to tend that line," he declared. "I dunno that even havin' Gray Cloud makes up for the difference."

He winked at Pete as he said this, and Pete winked back instantly, keeping the rest of his face as immobile as though it was carved out of wood.

Hank, venturing too close, drew a snarl and a leap from the monster. The leap fell short because the chain brought Gray Cloud up short and tumbled him on his side. But even so, his bone-breaking fangs had clashed a scant inch from Hank's leg.

"Hank, don't you be a fool," said his father angrily. He had drawn a revolver as he spoke. He was always armed. He was one of those who feel that the dignity of every Westerner can only be secured if he carries a gun. "We might as well put a bullet through him right now," he said.

This was not heard by Dave. At the fall of the wolf, as Gray Cloud struggled for an instant to regain his feet, and vainly because of the constriction of the chain and the hampering effect of the wounded legs, Dave stepped forward and leaned to help up the animal.

"Keep back, you dummy!" yelled Pete.

It was much too late for a warning to have been useful. The snaky head of the wolf turned like a flash and caught the forearm of Dave in the yawning mouth.

"Shoot, Pa!" Hank called out, seeing this.

"Don't shoot!" exclaimed Dave.

For the knife-like teeth had not cut through the skin. A last touch of instinct had kept the big wolf from biting home to the bone or even through it, as Gray Cloud so easily could have done. He crouched, ears flattened, eyes green, for an instant. Then he knew perfectly the scent of the man who was *not* man,

27

because he had saved a wolf from death by steel and death by fire.

Gray Cloud released the arm of Dave. With troubled eyes, he stared at the face of the young man, and saw the hand run back over his head. He lowered that head to escape from the touch. And yet it was not entirely unpleasant. A strange electric tingle ran through every fiber of his great body as he received the first human caress of his existence.

"Look at," muttered Hank. "Nobody'd believe that, would they?"

"What you doin' to that man-killin' wolf?" Bush Reagan demanded. He stepped a little closer. A chill of mystery struck through his body. The one standing excuse for his wastage of Dave's money was that the youth himself was so weak in the mind as to be worthless. And every hint that he might be something else was terrible to Bush.

"I'm only making friends with him a little," Dave said, looking up with a smile.

"I want to know how you muzzled him, and how you drug him in?" said Bush Reagan.

"I didn't muzzle him," Dave responded. "He worked the muzzle off. And I didn't drag him. I carried him on my shoulders."

"You mean that you had that mug full of teeth on your shoulder, next to your throat . . . all of four miles?"

"He was all right," said Dave. "I worried a little about what he might do at first. I don't suppose that I would have tried carrying him at all, but while he was in the traps a grass fire came zooming along, and I had to move fast to get him out of the way."

"Why didn't you shoot him and take his scalp and his paws?" asked Pete. "That'd have been proof enough."

"I wanted to shoot him," Dave said, running his fingers

deeply into the mane of the lobo. "I wanted to shoot him," he repeated, "and then something stopped me . . . something about his eyes."

The little shop filled with braying laughter from the three.

"Ain't that like a dummy, to work it out like that?" Bush Reagan demanded triumphantly. *If only the entire world could hear a remark as foolish as this,* he thought, *it would understand what I have had to put up with from Dave during these many years. Not a good influence on my own boys, for one thing. It's just the same as having a human animal around the house.*

Gray Cloud, under this new caress, lifted his head slowly and looked into Dave's face. The latter, enchanted, smiled down at his captive. "Look," he said. "Look at that, will you?" He laughed softly. "He sort of understands."

"That's a sight more than anybody else can do for you," snarled Bush Reagan. "Now, you back away from that wolf and I'll put a slug through him and take him in to claim the reward. The boys are goin' to open their eyes a mite when they see what I bring in today." He added: "Back away from that, Dave."

The latter looked with puzzled frown toward his older cousin. A handsome face he had, perfectly regular in contour, though perhaps the features were a little too thick and the brow too fleshy.

"Why would you shoot him, Cousin Bush?" he asked.

"Why? Because I'm goin' to do it, is enough reason for you!" exclaimed the other.

His sons looked on with a grin and a nod. They knew the vast strength that was locked up in the frame of their cousin, and it was always amusing to see him submit to such a check as this.

Dave stood up from the wolf and stepped back, shaking his head.

Bush Reagan poised his gun. Gray Cloud stood up and

silently bared his teeth to face execution.

Then Dave stepped to his cousin and pressed up the barrel of the gun.

The latter yelled out: "What you mean by touchin' my gun, you half-wit?"

Dave stood between him and the target. "Don't shoot Gray Cloud," he said quietly. "I couldn't stand it."

"*You* couldn't stand it?" shouted the other. "And who are you? And what difference does it make what *you* can stand? There's a price on the scalp of that wolf, and I'm goin' to collect it."

Still with his hand under the gun, Dave stared with his baffled eyes at Bush Reagan. Never in his life had he dared to check that formidable authority. But now he said: "I caught him in my own traps. Nobody has a right to shoot him. I don't want to see him shot."

Sudden awe struck the other three silent. A wild cry of rage burst from the throat of Bush Reagan as the spell dissolved.

But his son Hank took him by the arm. "You come outside with me, Pa," he said.

CHAPTER FIVE

Bush Reagan was obeying that impulse that was drawing him outside the blacksmith shop for the good reason that he felt that the world had come to an end. Never before had Dave dared to stand up to him. He could not understand this occasion.

Pete followed them out, and Hank was saying, quietly, as he led his father away: "Look here, Pa, there ain't any sense raisin' too much trouble about it. He don't want the wolf killed. But that's all right. I'll sneak out here tonight and put a slug through the head of the wolf. That's all right. You gotta remember . . . when you get started on the rampage, you say a lot of things. You might be firin' him, and then where would we be?"

"A sight better off than we are now," blustered Bush Reagan. "Better than havin' a half-wit around, disgracin' us, wherever we go."

"Wherever we go, we don't take him," Hank said. "All he does is to do the chores . . . the plowin', the cookin', the dishwashin', the house cleanin', and the range ridin', when the weather's too mean. He breaks the rough hosses, and he hunts the meat for us. There ain't any three men on the range," he added with a sudden afterthought, "that could do as much as he does, and as well. He mends every saddle and bridle, and he fixes up the wagons, don't he? Why, if we was to turn him loose, somebody else would get him, and they wouldn't know how we come to call him a dummy, hardly."

His father roared out: "He ain't got a brain in his head!"

And Pete broke in: "Well, he's got enough brains to do everything that a cowpuncher needs to do on a range, or a blacksmith, or a hunter, or a trapper. Some folks might say that that's enough brains for anybody to have."

"Any fool could beat him at a swap. He ain't got the brains to sell a dozen eggs, or a skunk skin!" exclaimed Bush Reagan.

"Yeah," said Pete, "but we can do that for him, pretty good. I ain't sayin' that he's got any brains, only he can do a lot of things. And he don't cost nothin'. What does he cost?"

"Look at the years I been raisin' him!" the angry Bush Reagan shouted.

"Yeah, but he worked his way from the start," said Pete. "Didn't he work his way from the start? When he was eight, he was as big and strong as being twelve. When he was ten . . . you remember when he was ten . . . he rode that buckskin five-year-old, and broke it, and got throwed a dozen times in an hour, and kept on ridin'? Yeah, I guess that he's worked his way right from the start, and he don't cost nothin'," he repeated.

His father started to make an answer, but Hank broke in: "The way you was workin' up yourself into a temper, you'd have been firin' him, pretty quick. You wouldn't wanna fire him." He added his brother's argument: "He don't cost nothin'. He shoots ten times more than even he can eat. He turns in enough pelts to buy twenty or a hundred times more clothes than we ever give him. Why, if he was a slave, he'd be worth a mint of money. Don't you get too rash with him, Pa."

Pulling at his mustaches, Bush Reagan said: "You got something in what you say, but I tell you, I know how to handle him. When they begin to talk back, they gotta be handled mighty sharp and quick. The first thing you know, he'd be askin' for rights, around here, wouldn't he? Yeah, that's what he would. Look at him havin' the nerve to stand up and say that *he* trapped that wolf and that wolf was *his*. He wouldn't have it shot, he wouldn't. Why, damn him, I'm goin' to teach him a lesson that'll last him the rest of his life."

"Yeah, you go on and teach him a lesson," said Pete. "But take it easy, will you? It ain't so bad to have somebody to cut the wood, and make the fire, and cook the breakfast, and take on a frosty morning in the winter. That ain't so bad, is it? You go easy, Pa. I'm goin' to take a ride into town and tell 'em what we're bringin' in tomorrow. I guess there'll be a lot of talk goin' around when the boys hear that."

"I'll go along with you," said Hank.

"You two stay right here on the place," said the father. "I'll do my own talkin'. . . ."

"It ain't your talkin'," Pete said. "I guess that Dave belongs to us as much as he does to you. And we get our split of the twenty-five hundred bucks, too, and don't you forget it. I'm goin' to buy that bay mare of the Shevlins, with part of my share, is what I'm goin' to do."

Angered to silence, but not really surprised by this outburst, the father stared at the pair of them as they started off to catch horses in the pasture beyond the barn, which had been built with a portion of the patrimony of Dave Reagan.

Bush, looking after them, realized that he might have acted in the same way, at that age, with his own father. He was angry, but also he respected his own blood, and his own ways of life. They would be hard on him, that pair, if he lived into the sere and yellow leaf—they would be hard on him, as he had been on his father, in the old days. Yet, as he looked after them, his smile grew more, and his wrath grew less. It is only our own kind that we can understand, or love, unless we are great of heart.

He went to the front verandah and sat half in sun and half in shadow throughout the rest of the afternoon, smoking his pipe, his legs crossed, and one foot swaying in a rapid rhythm up and down and up and down, while with dreaming brown eyes he looked into the future and figured out the ways in which the money could be spent.

It was not like the joyful time when he had taken some $40,000 East with him and spent it in one long, riotous party. He never had regretted the spending of that money. It was to him a proof of the gentility of his blood. No man could so enjoy the better things of life unless there was blood of the right sort in him. He, Bush Reagan, had the right sort of blood—$40,000 worth, in three months. That was the sort of blood that he had.

He pulled his mustaches, and refilled his pipe with sweet plug tobacco, and tamped it well down, and drew the thick smoke into his lungs.

He had the blood in him.

As for the $2,500, it was too bad that his sons would force him to cut it three ways. But, after all, it proved that they were coming to be men. And their maturity increased his pride. He was a man, was what he was.

After a time, as the dusk began, he heard the door of the barn slam.

That would be Dave, feeding the stock. Another comfort. After all, the boys had been right about the folly of discharging Dave. When one came right down to it, he was the major source of their income. The pelts from his traps supplied a great part of the handy ready cash; the meat he shot supplied the table, and the truck garden that he cultivated offered potatoes, and greens of various sorts, to say nothing of the berries in their season.

Yes, Dave was worth two men, if not three. From the time when he rose in the morning to the time when he went to bed, late at night, every step he took, every move of his mighty hands, was useful.

This thought had hardly died away in the mind of Bush Reagan, when he heard the ringing strokes of the axe behind the house. That would be Dave cutting the wood for the stove. And how he could swing an axe. He had hammered out for himself an axe of his own, with a longer handle than usual, and with at least three times as much weight, of the finest steel in the head of it. For an ordinary man, the weight of that steel would have been a crushing thing to wield for five minutes, but in the ample grip of Dave, it was a trifle. In long and slashing curves it revolved around his shoulders, their inexhaustible strength keeping the tremendous tool in play. And at every sure stroke, something was accomplished.

Yes, he would have been a fool to speak out all that was on his mind to the youth. Besides—as Pete had said, or was it that clever Hank—they could pistol the wolf in the middle of the night, and there make an end.

He heard a rattling of the stove in the rear of the house. That would be Dave, again, building up the fire and preparing to cook supper. As a cook, he was the equal or the superior of anyone on the range. To be sure, they had put him through a severe schooling, and, to this very day, hardly a meal passed without calling forth from one of them a few severe criticisms. Bush had set them the example in this, for he believed that no tool is so excellent that it may not be improved by constant sharpening. He chuckled, as this thought recurred to him. No, he and his boys had certainly not spoiled Dave with too much commendation.

The aroma of cookery came floating out to him. Supper would be ready, before long, and it was time for the boys to come home. But, for that matter, he could hardly blame them if they did not come until late. They were young. Young blood runs high and fast. And did they not have more than $800 apiece in prospect, for the morrow? Such a sum, in one lump, was not to be taken lightly.

He had reached this point in his reflections—he was wondering whether among the savors from the kitchen he had detected the sweet smell of baked cornbread—when a buckboard drew up at his gate, and the driver got down, fastened one of the leading ropes of his team, opened the gate, closed it gently behind him, and came striding down the dusky path.

It was Tom Williams who came up the front steps to the verandah. Bush Reagan rose in some haste as he recognized his visitor. For Tom Williams, though a neighbor, was not a neighborly man. He was one of those strict, stern men who are valued to work on committees when the cattlemen are in trouble. He was one to make up a posse—and actually catch rustlers with it. He was, in short, the sort of a man who everyone respected and would have voted for as sheriff, but who had few intimates.

He stood in the dusk of the day and said: "Hello, Bush."

"Why, Tom Williams," said the rancher.

"I dropped by to tell you that there's trouble in town," Williams announced. "There's trouble in town for you. Sam Weaver was jumped by your two boys in Pendleton's saloon. He's gone home, and the whole Weaver tribe is going to come in, I guess. Your boys have too much whiskey aboard, and they swear they won't leave the saloon. If I were you, I'd do something about it. Good night."

He turned, and strode off down the path.

CHAPTER SIX

The daydreams of big Bush Reagan disappeared like so many bright and foolish bubbles. For a moment, he stood gazing after the messenger of ill tidings, feeling a vague but deep resentment. It seemed exactly the sort of news that Tom Williams would bring him—there was almost spite behind it, he thought.

Then he turned and hurried back through the house to the kitchen. Big Dave Reagan—how comfortable a thing it was to note his size—looked up from the opening of the oven door, while a cloud of steam and smoke rushed out around his shoulders and face.

"Pete and Hank are in trouble in town," said Bush Reagan. "They're in Pendleton's saloon, and the whole Weaver tribe is goin' to come down on 'em."

"What did they do to the Weavers?" asked Dave.

"Nothin'!" exclaimed the anxious father. "No matter what they did, it ain't a time for you to stand, you half-wit. Go out with me while we catch up a couple horses and saddle 'em. We gotta ride hard to get to town."

Pendleton's saloon was not like other saloons in Rusty Creek. It was rather a town institution. It had rooms to accommodate guests, and Ray Pendleton always had a small but selected list of articles to sell in his store. The best rifles, revolvers, ammunition, knives, traps, and various other odds and ends, were always to be found in his storeroom. In addition, he was the one to buy an extra fine pelt, any day, and out in his pasture there were nearly always half a dozen or more horses of a superior grade.

He would pay a fancy price for anything on four hoofs that pleased his fancy, and it took a still fancier price to get the prize away from him. But just as men came now and then to buy an extra-fine rifle, or an ornamented shotgun of the best make and the finest steel, or a richly decorated Mexican saddle, so they would come to buy a horse, too, now and then. When a man from Rusty Creek had made his strike, on returning home, he was sure to visit Ray Pendleton's and carry away some expensive prize.

Pendleton himself was a tall, angular man of fifty, with a face so thin that the whole bony structure underlying it showed through. One could tell how his skull would look after death had worked its season on him.

The silence that now filled his barroom was an appropriate atmosphere for him to move in, and thick was that silence, and made all the thicker by the occasional murmur that fell from the lips of one of the men. For there were at least forty people in the long, narrow room. The cause of the silence was not the presence of the young Reagans but what their presence was apt to cause in the future.

They stood about midway down the bar, half faced toward one another, and pretending to pay attention to their whiskies. But whiskey was not their thought. It was not the thought of anyone else. What occupied all attention was the coming of the Weavers.

It was some miles out to the Weaver place, and some miles back again, so that Sam Weaver, riding home for help, would have to use up time. But the longer the coming of the Weaver tribe was delayed, the more formidable would be their onset, for they were fierce men, and the two thirty-year-old twins, Doc and Jim, were famous men because of their guns and their hands.

Thinking of them, the sons of Bush Reagan seemed particularly young and helpless. On the whole, they were winning admiration. If they had played the parts of bullies in jumping young Sam Weaver together, they were being more or less heroic in standing their ground now. They were very pale. Now and then one could see the bulge of the muscles at the base of the jaw, as they set their teeth harder, but they were enduring this silence of expectation in cold blood, and that endurance was worth admiration, and received it.

Now the swinging doors were pushed open and most unexpectedly old Silas Weaver came into the room. Old Si was of the true pioneer stock, the sort of a man who may be bent, but never broken. Years were gradually doubling him over and fixing his eyes more and more firmly on the ground that must before long receive him. He had to cock back his head with a painful effort to look up into the face of a tall man. But at the same time, he had strength and activity remaining. He could still ride all day long, and he was not the least valued hand at a roundup.

He came stumping and scuffing into the room on old, heavy, cowhide boots whose discolored finger grips of canvas stuck out above the leather. The heels of those boots were worn down on the outside because the legs of Si were widely bowed out. He came to a halt, just inside the door.

"Them Reagan kids in here?" he asked.

Pete Reagan kept facing the bar and the mirror behind it. But his brother Hank slowly turned.

He nodded. Then he found his voice. "We're here," he said quietly.

The quietness with which he spoke was the final assurance to everybody in the room that blood would be spilled. Men who speak quietly in time of danger are apt to be men who fight to the death.

Old Si scuffled up to the young man who faced him and crooked his neck so that he looked up into the face of Hank. "You aimin' to wait for my folks to arrive?" he asked.

"That's what we're aimin' to wait for," said Hank.

Hoof beats, at this point, were heard pouring down the upper end of the main street. Were those the Weavers coming in mass formation?

"Look here," said Si Weaver. "There ain't any reason why this here saloon should be all messed up. I got my two boys, Jim and Doc, outside in the street. There's some mighty fine starlight out there, and the moon's beginnin' to show. They'd be mighty pleased to see you there."

There was a pause. The two Reagans looked at one another, paler than ever, and found no answer. They had been braced to wait for trouble. They were not eager to go searching for it.

Then said Ray Pendleton: "Shootin' in the dark is murder, Weaver."

The old man looked hastily around the room. No one spoke to him, but all eyes were brightly upon him. It was wonderful to see his matter-of-fact manner in this crisis.

"Well," said Si Weaver, "insults is insults, and has gotta be treated like such. And two on one ain't a fair fight. Two on one never seen the day when it was a fair fight. I didn't wanna get your place all messed up, Ray, was all."

He went shuffling out of the saloon, and hardly had the swinging doors begun to batter back and forth after his departure than they were thrust open again and in came Bush Reagan, and behind him the six foot three of his young cousin Dave.

A decided murmur of disapproval ran through the barroom. A battle between pairs was still a duel. Four on a side made murder. The rule is rather vague, but it is felt all through the West. Clan wars are always frowned upon.

"What's this goin' to be?" demanded the clear, cold voice of Ray Pendleton. "A massacre, or something?"

Bush Reagan went up to his two sons. Their color had been restored by the sight of that familiar face. Even death would be easier to accept, somehow, now that he had come.

Dave Reagan remained in the background, his handsome face darkened, a frown puckering his rather fleshy brow. He looked mildly around him, as if for an explanation. In the center of the room there was a stove around which clients used to sit in dense rows, when the cold of the winter came. There was a table beside the stove that was heaped with old newspapers from all sorts of places, even from abroad. Englishmen, even Frenchmen, could find familiar news familiarly written, in some of the journals that were heaped upon this table. To the edge of that table big Dave advanced, and stood there, leaning against it. His air was abstracted, as though his thoughts remained occupied elsewhere.

He heard Bush Reagan saying to Ray Pendleton: "This ain't goin' to be a massacre. But I heard from Tom Williams that the whole Weaver tribe was likely to come down on my boys, here. That's why I rode in."

"You goin' to have *him* take a part in it?" Pendleton asked in a significant voice.

The abstracted eye of Dave clearly saw a side wag of the head in his direction, but what the meaning was, he could not make out.

"He came in here with me, free and willin'," said his older cousin. "Dave, didn't you come in, free and willin'?"

Dave turned a baffled eye on the bartender, and then he nodded.

"It's an outrage!" exclaimed someone.

Dave looked to identify the speaker, but his mild eyes could not find the man. He heard his cousin saying: "He's a Reagan, ain't he?"

Someone said clearly, but not too loudly: "The more's the pity."

Dave wondered, when he heard the remark. It seemed both crass and unnecessary. But then there were many things that happened in the speech of other men that he could not understand. He was used to being mystified.

"He's a Reagan," said Ray Pendleton, "but we all know what else he is, poor feller."

Dave flushed a little. He could understand that last stroke. He was not quite so clever as other men of his age. He was not so quick in the wits, so subtle. Humiliation overcame him. He wished, profoundly, that he could be back there in the little blacksmith shop, with the wolf. He could be happier with the lobo than with the sharp tongues of other humans around him.

He heard Bush Reagan saying excitedly: "I know what you mean, but you're wrong. Dave can make up his mind same's you and me. Dave found Gray Cloud, to-day, is what he found. And carried him all the way to the house, on his shoulders, with no muzzle on him. Dave tamed Gray Cloud in one day. What one of the rest of you could do as much?"

CHAPTER SEVEN

"It was *him* that caught Gray Cloud, was it?" said Ray Pendleton. "That didn't come out before. You say that he carried Gray Cloud all the way back to the ranch . . . without a muzzle? Hey Dave, is that right? You foller what we been sayin'?"

"It sounds like a lot," Dave said, abashed when called upon to speak before so many. "But it was mostly luck, or accident. There was a grass fire coming along when I found him in the trap, and he was simply more afraid of the fire than he was of me. You see? That was what tamed him."

Before Pendleton answered, Dave heard someone murmur: "Talks sometimes like he had all his wits about him, don't he?"

Ray Pendleton said: "You may call it luck, brother, but I don't want that kind of luck on my shoulders for a four-mile hike. Not me."

There was general chuckle of agreement as this remark was made. And then the swinging doors were abruptly cast wide by a long arm, and through the opening came Jim and Doc Weaver. They were formidable fellows, and they looked it. They were as tall as Dave Reagan, and as heavily made, though perhaps their weight was not gathered with such consummate skill around the shoulders and arms as his was. But they were famous for their strength and their bulldog tenacity in a fight.

They stood side-by-side at the door, each, in entering, having made a stride away from it, and halted.

They seemed, to the enchanted eyes of young Dave Reagan,

the most magnificent and the most formidable pair of men he ever had laid eyes upon. To be sure, he had seen them before, and that naturally meant seeing them together, since they were inseparable. But at other times it had been like seeing wolves in cages. Now they were stepping abroad, looking for prey, and ready to use their fighting forces upon it.

A very different matter, indeed, from an ordinary day.

Old stories rushed through his mind, stories he had found in his books about princes, about giants. These were like giants— great in strength, that is to say, and dreadful without being kindly. It was said of Jim Weaver that he had entered a cave and killed a mountain lion with his bare hands. Aye, they were mighty men.

And he looked from them to Bush Reagan, growing gray and somewhat thin with years, and his two sons, who looked fragile. It was unfair, such a fight. It was terribly unfair. Bush and his two boys were not exceptionally good shots. They did not have practice enough to make them good. Their case was not like his—who was sure to have a dressing down unless he returned home with at least one head of game for every two cartridges expended. To shoot a deer was not enough; it must be dropped dead in its tracks.

That was the school in which he had learned to shoot with a rifle. And then, many a time, out of mere cruelty and casual desire to torment, Bush Reagan had given him a revolver only, to take out on a hunting expedition. That meant infinitely careful stalking, but when the range was short enough, he could make a revolver kill even more surely than a rifle. He had an instinct for it.

The gun that was given him was always the same, and Bush Reagan had armed him with it on this occasion. It was an old-fashioned single-action Colt, with the sights and the trigger filed away—a gun to be fanned with the thumb. But familiarity had made it precious and unfailing in his grip.

All of that training, he felt, was a vast advantage, in such a time as this. The Reagans, his cousins, had not had it. The Weaver twins distinctly had. They had been great hunters for many years. And the list of their battles with men was very, very long.

So it was that the sense of unfairness rose higher and higher in Dave's heart, like a black cloud.

He heard Jim Weaver say: "Pete and Hank . . . you Reagan, there . . . stand out of that, will you?"

Every man in the room had drawn back against the wall. Only Ray Pendleton stood behind the bar, tall, narrow-shouldered, his arms folded over his hollow chest, his colorless eyes flashing this way and that. He, Pendleton, would enjoy the battle, no matter how it turned out.

The three Reagans at the bar turned as one man. The glance of Bush Reagan fell like a whiplash on Dave, to bring him into action.

"Four of you, are there?" asked Doc Weaver. "Four . . . if you count the dummy, there. Is that the way that the Reagans fight?"

"Go get two more of your gang, and be damned," said Bush Reagan.

Dave was amazed to hear his voice, so high was it and so unnaturally thin.

"We'll get two more, and *pronto*," said Jim Weaver, "only I wouldn't wanna have *that* on my conscience." He pointed a thumb in contempt and disgust toward Dave Reagan, as he said this.

Dave stepped forward. He was angered, a passion that he rarely felt. It was not the contempt leveled toward himself that he now resented, but rather the fact that his cousins, comparatively inexperienced in the use of weapons, should be called upon to fight for their lives in this manner. So he stepped forward with a step that was long and wonderfully light. For he felt very much as he did when he began a stalk that had to be both rapid and silent.

The two Weavers glanced toward him without interest.

He stopped very close to them, and said: "It's not right, Jim and Doc."

"What ain't right, kid?" asked Doc Weaver. His upper lip lifted a little, as he spoke. The man was a wolf. His teeth gleamed beneath the furling of the lip.

Dave frowned at him with a suddenly increased distaste. That expression on the face of Weaver sent a tingle from his brain down to his fingers, and made them contract a little. "You and Jim are good fighters," Dave said. "My cousins are not very good shots. And they're not strong, the way you are. A fight like this wouldn't be fair."

"What're you whinin' about?" demanded Doc Weaver. He made a half step closer to the boy and drew himself up, but he could not make himself taller than young Reagan.

"I'm not whining," said Dave. "It's all right for me. I'm strong enough, and I'm a good shot, too. I've had more practice than they've had."

"You get out of the way," said Doc. "You get out. We don't aim to plant any lead in half-wits like you, if we can help it."

The word brought the stinging blood into Dave's cheek. "You oughtn't to talk like that," he said—words that were to be remembered long in Rusty Creek. "You're calling me names."

"Oh, get out of the way," Doc said, losing patience, and he cuffed the face of Dave with the back of his hand.

It would have been easy enough for big Reagan to avoid that blow. But something rose up savagely in him and made him actually lean forward to meet it. It stung his face. It lacerated his upper lip a little on the inside. His mouth was numbed by the force of it, and the taste of his own blood was instantly on his palate. Then, and only then, he acted. He hit Doc Weaver with a lifting fist that lodged in the small ribs of that man's side and buckled him over like a piece of rusty wire. He was knocked sidelong into his brother, and Jim Weaver, as he whipped out a revolver, went crashing to the floor. As he fell, he fired the only shot of the battle, a shot that knocked a hole in the board ceiling—it is still pointed out in the saloon.

It was the only shot because Dave Reagan stepped on the fallen arm. The bone snapped under the weight of his body. He plucked the gun from the nerveless hand, threw it on the floor, picked up the struggling, cursing bulk of Jim, carried him lightly to the door, and with a swing of his body hurled Weaver into the street.

He returned.

Doc Weaver lay writhing on the floor, gasping in the effort to regain his wind. He also had drawn a gun, but he was too blind with pain to try to use it. It was kicked from his grip. Then he was raised as his brother had been, and carried to the door, and hurled swiftly with the same powerful swing into the darkness.

Distinctly the men in the saloon heard the impact of Doc Weaver's body in the dusty roadway, his curse, and his groan as he struggled to his knees.

Dave turned back to his three amazed cousins. He was dusting his hands. "We'd better go along," he said.

He was not even panting, Ray Pendleton averred, afterward. Perhaps that was not the truth, but it was clear that he was not excited. It seemed to Dave Reagan that a marvelous thing had happened, but the miracle to him was not his own strength, but the weakness of the others. He explained it to himself very simply. A lucky blow had disabled Doc Weaver. And then Jim Weaver, with a broken bone in his arm, his gun hand, at that, had been practically helpless. Yes, luck had accounted for the whole battle, as far as Dave was concerned.

He repeated to the stunned face of Bush Reagan: "We'd better go along, Bush. Everything for supper will have to be all warmed up again. It's a lucky thing that I hadn't made the coffee, isn't it?"

Those words, also, were long remembered. They would have been the sheerest affectation coming from any other person, but from Dave Reagan they could be believed.

"We'll wait a minute, Dave," said Bush Reagan. "The Weavers, they might decide that they'll come back inside, ag'in. Wouldn't wanna disappoint 'em, if they did."

"No," Dave said seriously, "I don't think that Doc and Jim will come back."

A sudden gust of laughter broke and roared about his ears. Men surged around him, still laughing, patting his shoulders, probing at the thick cushions of muscle that explained the things that they had just seen performed, and Ray Pendleton was crying: "Here's where everybody liquors on the house!"

CHAPTER EIGHT

Dave Reagan did not drink with the others. In the first place, he never had formed a taste for whiskey—largely because such an expensive drink was never offered to him at the house. Now he took advantage of the confusion to slip out through the swinging doors, as the others poured up to the bar.

Standing in the starlight and in the dim moon shine that filled the street, he could see a number of riders mounting horses. Those would be the Weavers, of course, he thought. One man was being helped up to the saddle. He ran hastily toward them and stood in front of the leader of the party, old Si Weaver, bent almost double in the saddle. Angry voices muttered, and the mutter threatened to grow into a roar.

Young Dave Reagan held up his hand. "I wanted to tell you fellows," he said. "I just wanted to say that there's no hard feeling, far as I go. I hope that there'll be no hard feeling with you, either. I wouldn't want the Weavers to feel hard toward the Reagans on account of anything that I did."

A snarling voice broke from the throat of Si Weaver. "Get out of my way, or I'll ride over you."

Actually he spurred his big horse straight ahead. The shoulder of the lurching beast struck Dave and hurled him back against the wall of a building. As his eyes cleared after the shock, he saw the cavalcade rushing past him down the street. And yet he was bewildered, and could not quite understand why seven mounted men should have acted in this manner.

He was still staring after them, when three blanketed Indians stepped from somewhere out of a shadow and walked down the street.

As one man they raised their hands. As one man they uttered the greeting—*"Hau."*—and passed on, while he was barely able to make the response.

He could still remember how the three pairs of eyes had gleamed at him as they went by with their salutation. But it meant little to him. There might have been recognition, hostility, anything in those glances.

He returned to the hitch rack before Pendleton's place, and, untethering his mustang, he jogged it back toward the house.

Perhaps it would be some time before his cousins returned to the place. In the meantime, it came over him, with an overwhelming wave of remorse, that he had not offered Gray Cloud a single morsel of food.

He kicked the mustang to a canter, the horse grunting a little at every stride, because of the weight of its rider, but though Dave was generally the height of tenderness with the horses on the ranch, tonight he felt that the roan mustang could suffer a little, in order to bring help more quickly to the wolf.

There was an odd mixture of emotions in him—regret for the fighting that had taken place; the usual bewilderment that came to him after all his contacts with his fellow man, and above all a sense of joy that, like a voice about to sing, swelled his throat. He could not understand his happiness. He would have been astonished to have been told that it was the aftermath of the fight itself. And, looking up to the sky, where the bright moon was putting out the stars in myriads, he told himself that the beauty of the night was working in him.

A lonely beauty it was for him. The desire, that often swept over him, for some close human companionship, now almost mastered Dave Reagan. But he felt that that was an impossible desire. His mind was slow, very slow. He was handicapped in the presence of others. At the house he had been called, familiarly, fool and half-wit and dummy, ten thousand times. But on this night he had heard the same words used by people who were strangers to him.

It was plain that he was far beneath the glorious intellectual heights on which the other men of Rusty Creek lived. And the surety of this conclusion made him sigh deeply. He was not bitter about it. It was a thing that he had long half known. Now he accepted the grim fact. He was a useless thing, a mere machine that could walk and labor and hunt game. There his significance ended.

He was still under the cloud of this sorrow when he reached the ranch house. He put up the roan, fed it, and hurried to the blacksmith shop in the corner of the corral.

When he opened the door, a frightful growl rose out of the blackness and seemed to spring at him, so loud was it. He spoke. The growl ended, as if cut off by a knife stroke. He walked boldly in, but slowly, speaking as he went, and putting tenderness into his voice. He leaned. His hand touched fur, and a strong, edged vise gripped his arm and threatened to bruise the flesh to the bone. But the snap of the wolf was not driven home.

Triumph went rioting through his heart. Among men he was a fool, but the beasts knew him. Perhaps that was because he was a little better than a beast, poor half-wit that he was.

And yet the grief was less in him as he strode back to the house. He had made pets of horses, calves, dogs, before this, only to see them sold from under his hands when he had trained them, or raised them to maturity. But this was different. The wolf was a companion of a different nature. Who would take Gray Cloud from him?

Then Dave remembered, when he was in the meat house, cutting from the venison in the cooler a large slab of meat that weighed several pounds. He remembered that there was a high price upon the head of Gray Cloud—$2,500. Why, that was enough to buy a whole plow team, and a pair of plows, and the harness for the outfit, and a couple of wagons, and a buggy, and a span of fast trotters to pull it—it was enough quite to change the face of the ranch, as a matter of fact.

He trembled for Gray Cloud as he thought of this.

One thing he would have to do—to beg, to pray that they would not sell the wolf for the sake of the reward. Perhaps they would be kinder, considering that he had been of some service to them this evening.

That thought released him from some of the strain of anxiety.

He lit a lantern, and with it carried the meat to the blacksmith shed. He had put in a tin of water earlier in the day, and now he squatted near the great gray-furred beast, and offered the meat.

Gray Cloud extended his nose, shuddered with the strength of famine and desire as he sniffed the meat, found it reeking with the scent of man, and reared his head again to the dignity and indifference of his former attitude.

Dave frowned. He pulled up a box, sat on it, cross-legged, close to the head of Gray Cloud, and offered the meat again.

Again Gray Cloud sniffed it; again he reared his head with cold indifference.

"He smells man on it," Dave said to himself. "That's a taint that he can't stand." Suddenly his thought went dashing on, at lightning speed, toward new regions.

It was the taint of man that made life a weary thing for him, also. At his work, in the fields, or in the truck garden, he could be happy—so happy that oftentimes great, wordless music burst out from his throat. But it was the necessary return to man that blighted every day. And so it was with the wolf.

Dave tore a fragment from the rest of the meat and offered it a third time.

Curiously, with eyes squinted almost shut, as though in order to throw more responsibility upon the powers of the unaided sense of smell, Gray Cloud sniffed at the morsel. His long red tongue issued, and licked it. Then he jerked back, shuddering.

But nothing had happened to him. Nothing evil seemed to be taking place in his belly after the taste of the meat. And as for the scent that overlaid it, to be sure it was the scent of man, but of this man, only—this man who was not as the others of his kind.

Hunger helped. With a desperate snatch, Gray Cloud took the chance, and bolted the fragment. The taste of it let loose the devils of desire and greed. In an instant, he had bolted down the rest of the lump of venison and lay licking his lips, with fear and contentment mingled in his soul.

The man remained close to him, speaking gently, running his fingers through the dense mane.

The pangs of hunger were subsiding, were vanishing, as Gray Cloud's stomach contracted on this meal and set to work upon it. A cloud of contentment increased in his mind. He lowered his head upon his paws, and the hand of the man continued to pass down his neck, and the voice of the man continued to make, in his ears, the strange, new music that spoke to something in the soul of Gray Cloud that never had been touched before. The message was very new. It was telling him, in vague hints, that in this savage world of eye for eye and tooth for tooth, there nevertheless is mercy to be found, and gentleness, and unearned kindness that may be loosed in a flood.

Thinking of these matters, Gray Cloud closed his eyes. None of his thoughts were as clear as human words, but perhaps every emotion in a beast is more profound than the emotions of man, for the very reason that they are not bounded and limited by expression in sound. And the roots of a new instinct began to thrust down into the nature of Gray Cloud. That instinct embraced a single object for affection—this man, separated from the rest of his species, this man who had in the course of one portion of one day given life, water, food.

For a long time, Dave sat there. Finally, by his breathing, he knew that Gray Cloud had fallen asleep. Dave rose carefully. Gray Cloud did not stir. His eyes remained closed. Stealthily Dave Reagan went from the shed back toward the house, and, as he went, he smiled, like a mother that has seen its child asleep.

Men, as he knew them, were brutal creatures. It seemed to Dave that he had just crossed a vast horizon and had a glimpse of another world in which no word is spoken, but there may be happiness beyond all words.

CHAPTER NINE

Dave had barely reached the house when he heard the beat of the hoofs of horses. The three Reagans came swarming into the house in high feather.

"Trot out some chuck, Dave!" shouted Hank. "Whatcha been doin' all the time? Why ain't supper hot? Hurry it along, will ya?"

"I didn't know when you'd be back," apologized Dave, and rushed to build up the fire.

Pete came into the kitchen to overlook proceedings. He heard Hank say to his father in the next room: "You better go out and do it now. Get it over with."

"We better put it off to tomorrow," suggested Bush Reagan.

"Nope. You go on and do it now, Pa. It'd come better from you. You better do it now, and get it over with."

"Yeah, and maybe you're right," Bush said.

The screen door slammed, and Hank joined his brother in the kitchen where he leaned against the sink and also looked on at the work of warming up the already prepared supper. Neither he nor Pete knew what it was to work in the house. Their cousin was too ready a servant at hand.

"Where's Bush gone?" asked Dave.

"Aw, he had something to look at in the barn," said Hank. "Ain't that coffee hot yet? Hurry it up, Dave."

"That was a good sock that you hit Doc Weaver in the ribs," said Pete. "You sunk your fist into him up to the wrist. That was a good hearty sock, all right. I bet that jarred him."

"A pair of stuffed shirts is all they are," declared Hank. "Look at the way they both dropped."

"No wonder they dropped, the way Dave socked Doc," said Pete. "Where'd you learn to punch like that, Dave?"

"Lawler teaches me a lot about boxing and wrestling, when there's some spare time," said Dave. "He knows a good deal besides blacksmithing."

"Sure he does. Wasn't he in the ring once?" asked Pete.

"I don't know," Dave answered.

He did, in fact, know perfectly well, for many a time Lawler had told long stories of his conflicts—in those earlier days before every bone in his hands had been broken. But ordinarily Jud Lawler avoided speaking of those famous and strenuous times, and therefore Dave felt that he must not repeat what he had heard.

"Look at his hands, if you don't know. Look at the ridges of the busted bones across the backs of his hands," said Hank. "That's enough to show you he's been in the ring. The trouble with you, Dave, you dunno how to use your eyes. You take and use your eyes, and you'd learn something. You'd be different."

Dave said nothing. Studiously he built up the fire, and put the food back in the oven to warm. The coffee pot began to steam.

"Look at Dave here," Pete said to his brother. "He don't tell us much about what he does. He don't talk at all. All these years, he's been tryin' out with the gloves, down there at Lawler's, and he don't say a word about it at home. You put it over Lawler with the gloves, Dave?"

"He's smaller than I am, and he's older," Dave said, frowning.

"Yeah, but he can fight still," said Pete. "If his hands was good, I reckon that he'd still be in the ring."

Dave looked up with an embarrassed laugh. "When we first put on the gloves," he said, "I could hardly touch him. He's fast as lightning, and he knows all the tricks. I could hardly touch him." He laughed again, and shook his head.

"Can you touch him much, now?" asked Hank eagerly.

"Oh, yes," said Dave. "Oh, yes. I can touch him now. But he's quick. He's like a cat, when it comes to wrestling."

"I know what he done to big Steve Western," Pete said. "He throwed Steve clean over the wheel and into his buckboard . . . and Steve didn't try to climb down again. Can you throw Lawler?"

"Why, I'm younger than he is," Dave said, frowning as he was pressed to admit his prowess.

"All I mean to say," Pete continued, "is this . . . can you as much as get a grip on that slippery snake of a Lawler?"

"Oh, I can get a grip, all right," Dave said thoughtfully.

He was remembering a time, only the week before, when the groaning voice of Lawler had made him break off the wrestling bout, and how he had lifted the blacksmith into a chair, and how Lawler, with a white face and fallen head, had grunted out: "Don't you ever put your strength out ag'in, kid. Not unless you wanna kill somebody."

He had not put out his strength, as a matter of fact, even upon that occasion; it had seemed to him that he had hardly exerted that great engine of which he was aware, pulsing and throbbing and moving in him, ready for all demands that might be made upon him.

"I wouldn't want to hurt anybody," he had said to Lawler.

"Sure you wouldn't," said the blacksmith on that day. "You wouldn't want to, only you can't help yourself. That's the truth of it. You dunno what you got under the skin. But one of these here days, I'm goin' to tell you what you got, and you ain't got long to wait."

"He can take and beat Lawler, and he can take and put Lawler down," Hank said, gloating over the achievements of his cousin.

"I didn't say that I could do those things," protested Dave.

"Will you say that you *can't* do it?" asked Hank.

Dave hesitated, looking for a way out of the difficulty, without stating facts that might seem like betraying a friend, and boasting over him.

"You know," he explained, "Jud Lawler is always teaching me how to take care of myself. It's not as though we boxed or wrestled to put the other fellow down."

Pete laughed in jeering triumph. "Why," he said, "I bet you could lick any man on the range, right this minute, once you got your hands on him. The way Doc Weaver dropped, I never seen anything like it. He lay there and kicked around. The whole Weaver tribe, they had enough."

Hank laughed in turn, adding: "When they seen their two best men knocked out and throwed out of the saloon . . . 'Hell,' says the Weaver tribe, 'if one Reagan can do this, what would *four* of 'em do to us?' So they got up and started home, is what they did. You're a Reagan, Dave, is what you are."

Dave smiled rather vaguely in appreciation of this compliment. "I don't like to think about what happened there in Pendelton's saloon, this evening," he said.

"Why not, old son?" asked Pete.

"Because it seemed to me that there was murder in the air."

"Murder? Listen at him," Pete said, sneering. "There was bullets coming, but every man you kill, that ain't murder. That's just self-defense."

"You shouldn't kill anybody . . . unless it's a war, or something like that," said Dave, bringing out the idea with care and some hesitation. "I felt that in Pendleton's, tonight . . . that there was a death coming . . . more than one, maybe. They were all waiting for it. Everybody was standing around waiting for it." He made a gesture of repulsion.

"Was you scared, Dave?" Pete asked, with animal-like and greedy curiosity. "Say, did it scare you?"

"It made me sick . . . it just made me sick," Dave murmured with the puzzled frown of distaste still on his forehead. "It seemed to me that you and Hank were standing there, waiting to be killed."

"Don't you be a fool," said Pete. "We were goin' to give 'em hell before they got us. It would take more than Weavers to get a coupla Reagans. *They* know that, now."

"Yeah," Hank averred, a little more honest than his brother. "Maybe you were glad to have the fight ahead of you. But *I* wasn't. And you looked kind of green around the gills, too, it seemed to me."

"Things are about ready," Dave interrupted. "When will Cousin Bush be in?"

"Aw, he'll be back in a minute," said Hank, "and we might just as well start in eatin', right now, because. . . ."

On the heels of this speech a wild cry came to them. The source was the direction of the corral, and the voice was human with such a thrilling power of agony in it that it might have been welling up in the next room.

A wild look passed between the brothers. All three, without a word, dashed from the kitchen, and headed toward the corral, their feet beating noisily along the wooden boards of the path that saved one from winter mud.

Bush Reagan, when he left the dining room to go to the corral, had taken from the wall his best rifle, because he felt that it was an occasion that was worthy of a shot from his best gun. He had shot grizzlies, in his time, but he never had brought down a prize worth $2,500. To be sure, on this occasion the game was haltered and chained, and could not escape, but nevertheless there was a certain importance connected with the killing of Gray Cloud.

That sense of importance swelled Bush Reagan's chest more than a little as he walked down the path, opened the corral gate, and allowed it to close softly from his hand. A faint tingle of guilty dread went up his spinal column when he thought of Dave, back there in the kitchen. Poor fool, he would be busily carrying on the kitchen work and never dreaming that his prize was about to be turned from a silver bolt of cunning murder into a limp fluff of fur and worthless flesh. However, no one but a fool would be bothered by the possible reactions of a half-wit. He, Bush Reagan, was above that sort of nonsense.

He cleared his throat, frowned, drew himself up to his full inches, as though he were about to address an assembly, and then marched deliberately forward to the blacksmith shed.

He had brought a lantern with him, but he did not light it until he came to the door of the shack. Three times imperceptible puffs of wind made the flame of the matches dwindle to blue and then go out. The fourth time, cursing softly, he succeeded in igniting the wick. The chimney was drawn down, making a loud screech that grated on his nerves and caused him to glance apprehensively over his shoulder. For at that moment he had a picture of his young cousin turned into an insensate monster of rage, and rushing upon him through the darkness of the night. Far better to stand up before the charge of a grizzly bear—as he had done himself in the old days—than to face such an enemy as Dave.

He had taken the young fellow too lightly, all these years. There was something to be done with such a power as was in Dave Reagan. Slow wit or not, no ordinary fellow catches Gray Cloud and on the same day, single-handed, routs the formidable faction of the Weavers. No, there was something in Dave.

And if he were roused?

Yes, that would be a picture worth seeing. He had not been roused this evening, for instance. There had not been a trace of ferocity in his face, for instance, after he received the blow from the hand of Doc Weaver. No exclamation had escaped from his throat. No fury had appeared in his eyes. He had simply leaned forward, as though Doc's blow had been a hearty handshake— and then, with perfect calmness and good temper, he had struck hard enough to break bones.

Aye, if such a power as that in Dave was transformed by the battle fury, he might go far indeed. And if he, Bush Reagan, could learn how to direct it, he and his entire family could profit. He would bend his mind upon the problem and finally learn how Dave's power could be used. Perhaps—who could tell?—he might be able to make a fortune for his entire family.

CHAPTER TEN

These considerations gave Bush a glow of virtue. He did not feel that he was being essentially selfish. For whatever was in a stupid fellow like Dave was, he thought, no more humanly to be considered than the strength of blindly running water.

He opened the door of the shack, and, as the light of the lantern flooded the place, the great wolf leaped up on all fours and snarled at him, with bristling mane.

"Hey!" Bush Reagan said, surprised and half frightened, taking a step to the rear. "You ain't a cripple no more, eh?"

As a matter of fact, half the lameness of Gray Cloud had been caused by the position in which the traps had held him for two entire days. And now, having had a chance to lick his wounds, they were recovering with wonderful rapidity. Gray Cloud could already walk; he would soon be able to use that long, effortless lope with which a wolf can cover untold leagues, smoothly as the wind.

Bush Reagan entered, closed the door behind him, and reconsidered the monster.

Now that Gray Cloud was planted firmly on all fours, with mane fluffed out with rage, he looked as big as a bear, and ten times more alert, more savage. In those green eyes, there were infinite capacities for slaughter.

A shudder went through Bush Reagan. He looked back at the door, for the wind had shaken it a little. He half expected that it would be flung open, with the enormous shoulders of Dave

Reagan looming there against the dark of the night. Better a wolf to face, aye, even such a one, and unchained, than the bare-handed wrath of Dave!

Bush picked up the rifle again, hung the lantern on a peg where it would throw light on the proper place, and raised the weapon to his shoulder. The report would not be loud. With the wind blowing away from the house, it was highly improbable that Dave would hear it at all. After a night's sleep, he would walk out feeling that his adventure with the wolf had been no more than a dream, and to find the animal dead would be only the slightest of shocks.

Yet Bush Reagan was not entirely sure. There had been something in the face of Dave, when he leaned over the monster so fearlessly, that Bush never had seen there before. There was something miraculous in the expression. As though the young fellow knew, for one thing, that he was safe from the teeth that had actually closed over his forearm.

Well, let the future take care of itself. For what was the dim future to balance against the immediate prospect of $2,500?

So Bush Reagan's eyes cleared, and he sighted down the rifle, and aimed straight between the big, green eyes of the wolf.

Gray Cloud crouched, and snarled again. He showed his long, needle-sharp fangs that could slide through the hamstring of a full-grown bull as if it were a shred of tissue paper. Plainly he knew what a rifle meant. Plainly he guessed what was coming to him.

So plainly did he show his knowledge, and yet so fierce and high was his courage to face death, that the man lowered the gun with an exclamation of amazement.

"You been here before, brother, eh?" Bush Reagan said.

Gray Cloud stood up the instant the gun no longer pointed at him. Silent, attentive, he cocked his head a little to one side and studied the face of the man, as though to read his mind, and find relenting in it.

Bush Reagan grinned with a cruel sense of power. "You're wrong, you cattle thief, you," said Bush. "I'm goin' to stretch you out and take your scalp and your paws, and I'm goin' to turn 'em into hard cash, too. Whatcha think of that?" He leered as he asked the question. He had had a trifle too much of the hospitality of Ray Pendleton, at the saloon, after the fight.

He had been called back for a final drink, as his sons were already getting on their horses. Ray Pendleton had poured him out a brimmer, and into his own glass only a few drops. He had said, leaning confidentially across the bar: "Now lemme tell you something, Bush."

"You go on and tell me something," said Bush.

"That kid, there's money in him," answered the saloonkeeper.

"Is there?" Bush remarked untruthfully. "Then you gotta show me where. He ain't been nothin' but an expense to me."

Ray Pendleton blinked two or three times and swallowed hard, but finally he was able to put down the ready retort that had trembled almost on his lips. He went on: "Dave is worth something. He'd be worth something in the prize ring for one thing."

"Yeah, maybe he might, if he got any sense into his head. It takes brains, though, to make a prize fighter."

The other half closed his sharp eyes and nodded, letting his head rock back and forth as though on bearings. "Maybe he's got enough brains, too," he said with a hidden significance. "Them that are simple ain't always the fools. Not if they got heart in 'em. And he's got heart. He's got the heart of a bulldog. He's got the heart," Ray Pendleton added, suddenly flashing a glance at the other, and tapping his long, bony forefinger on the bar, "he's got the heart of a thoroughbred."

"Him? Aw, he can last, all right. He never gets tired," said Bush Reagan.

The other had seemed bent on developing his words, but, when he heard the last remark from Bush, he seemed to change his mind. "Well, look at here," he said. "He'd be worth something to me here in the bar, and doin' odd jobs."

"Would he?" Bush Reagan said, squinting, ready for a bargain. He added, not realizing that his present words were a contradiction of what he had said not long before: "He's worth all of fifty dollars a month to me, clean profit, out there on the ranch."

Ray Pendleton lowered his head. Was it to hide an expression of disgust? "I'd pay you fifty dollars a month for him," he said. "And another fifty dollars to him."

Bush Reagan was amazed. "You'd pay that much?" he answered.

"He's a hoss breaker . . . he's a first-class blacksmith . . . he's a fine hunter . . . he never told a lie in his life . . . and when a rough crowd steps into the saloon and starts to breakin' things up, I reckon that he wouldn't have to more'n look through the door to quiet things down."

Bush Reagan stared. "Twenty-five a month is more'n the poor boy would know what to do with," he said. "And I could use seventy-five a month while he works for you. I'm his guardian. I been to the expense of raisin' him."

The other turned suddenly away. When he turned back again, it was with a fresh bottle, with which he brimmed the glass of his guest again. His mouth was still twisted, however, into a wry expression. "Well," he said, "I'll tell you . . . we'll talk it over. You come in tomorrow."

So Bush Reagan had come home with a good bit more whiskey under his belt than he was accustomed to carrying. It was this that made him a trifle unsteady, and caused the muzzle of the rifle to waver as he jerked the butt to his shoulder, and fired.

A tuft of fur flicked from the jowl of the wolf. Gray Cloud had dodged his head like a flash, and saved his life—for that instant.

"You tricky devil!" roared Bush. "Now I'm goin' to fix you!"

Rage and whiskey made him foolishly reckless. He was already close. He made a pace still closer, and raised the gun once more, and, as he did so, Gray Cloud threw himself out, and slashed at the man's leg.

Gray Cloud found his mark, and slashed the calf from the knee to the ankle, well-nigh.

Reagan, the rifle falling from his hands, staggered, dropped to the floor, and sent out that scream of rage and pain that had resounded in the kitchen of the house. His yell might have been cut very short, for, as he dropped, the knife-like teeth struck for his throat again, and almost reached it. But in dropping, he had had the instinctive wit to roll, and so a twist of his body brought him out of harm's way.

He was sitting up, holding his leg under the knee in a vain effort to stop the flow of the blood, when the three young men rushed into the shack.

CHAPTER ELEVEN

"Pete . . . Hank . . . kill that damn' wolf! It tried to murder me . . . I'm bleedin' to death!" growled Bush Reagan.

"I'll fix him!" yelled Pete.

"I'll get him!" shouted Hank.

Each of them drew a revolver. The life of Gray Cloud was a split second from extinction. But the two large and capable hands of Dave reached out and gathered in the guns. He took them from his cousins as though they were little children with no grip in their fingers.

"Hey, whatcha mean?" roared Pete. "Gimme back that gun! Don't you see Gray Cloud's killed Pa?"

He tried to grab his gun again. Dave pushed him away, and the violence of the thrust hurled Pete floundering back against the wall of the shed.

As for Hank, he, too, had moved forward with extended hands, but, seeing what Pete had received, he halted abruptly.

Dave sank on his knees beside the wounded man, and began to examine the wound.

"Don't touch me! Keep your poison hands away from me!" cried Bush Reagan. "They been handlin' that damn' wolf, that devil!"

Dave raised his head from the examination. He paid no attention whatever to the outcry of Cousin Bush. It seemed to Dave that a hand was closing over his heart, crushing out all the human kindness and leaving only bitterness. For he had guessed at many things, the instant that he entered the shop.

"Pete," he said "you'd better ride to town as fast as you can and get the doctor. This'll have to be sewed up. It's not very deep. But it will have to be sewed. Hank, will you bring out some cloth? You'll find a lot of clean rags in the lower drawer of the bureau in my room. They'll be good to make a bandage that'll stop the bleeding till the doctor gets here."

The two young men, amazed, overawed by these calm directions, stared once at their father.

"Kill that wolf!" he screamed at them, turning purple with rage and a sense of helplessness.

But they backed out of the shop. It was only too apparent that their cousin had spoken sense, and good sense.

"You brought home the death of me, Dave, is what you done!" raged Bush as his two sons disappeared. "You went and brought home the death of me. The wolf's killed me. There's poison on a wolf's tooth. I'll die of it. You're a fool, is what you are. You're a half-wit. You never been anything but a burden and a curse on my head. There ain't any Reagan in you . . . there's nothing but your half-witted mother in you. . . ."

A great hand closed on his throat. His breath was stopped. Staring in new dread of his life, he saw that Dave's gray eyes were as green as ever the eyes of Gray Cloud had been, as he had faced the rifle.

Dave Reagan released his hold with a gasp of horror. "I'm sorry, Cousin Bush," he said. "I didn't know. My hand just moved of itself, when you. . . ."

He paused, and before either of them could speak again, Hank came running in with the clean rags, and the big hands of Dave, with a wonderful dexterity, began to build the bandage to check the flow of the blood. It was natural that he should have some skill in such work, for since he was also the cook of the household, he had been used as domestic doctor, too, these many years.

The voice came back to Bush Reagan as the pain subsided, under that skillful touch. He roared out: "Hank, you know what? He tried to throttle me . . . him . . . Dave . . . your cousin, there . . . started into choke me . . . *woulda* choked me, if you hadn't come back. Him that I took in from the street. That didn't have a rag to his back. Him, that I raised careful and tender like a father, as good as you and Pete . . . him . . . wanted to murder me! That's what he wanted to do!"

"Hey, Dave," Hank said, not at all convinced, though he was much astonished. "You hadn't oughta do a thing like that."

The mildness of this reproof enraged the father more than ever. "A lot of difference it makes to you, Hank. You'd be glad to see me out of the way. You'd be glad to see me dead. The ranch is what you want, you and Pete. The slavin' that I've done for you, it don't count."

"Aw, shut up, will you?" Hank said angrily. "I know how much slavin' you done for us! The money you've blowed in on yourself woulda bought a coupla ranches like this. Where'd you get the money that you blowed in when you made that trip back East? Answer me that? Where'd you get it? Tell Dave, here, where you got it!"

The ground had opened under the feet of Bush Reagan as he heard this accusation.

"You fool, you," he gasped at Hank. "Whatcha mean? Whatcha thinkin' of, anyway?"

Hank glanced uncomfortably at Dave, but the head of the latter was bowed.

In fact, Dave had not been following the words very carefully. All, to his ears, was a confused roar, a horror that crowned the long wretchedness of his life with this family. That grim scene in Pendleton's saloon was as nothing, compared with this. Father against son, son against father, hatred, spite, malice—he wondered if all the families in the world were like this, filled with venom? No, there had been one that was not. Like a memory of heaven it opened upon his mind, and the two unforgotten, gentle faces that had made its happiness.

He finished the bandaging, and rose to his feet.

"You, you," Bush Reagan roared, pointing at him, "pick up that rifle and shoot that wolf! Shoot him right now . . . you hear? You hear me, Dave?" He trembled with righteous indignation.

Then balm came to his frantic heart as Dave did, indeed, lean above the bristling wolf, and place a hand on Gray Cloud's mighty shoulders, and then pick up the rifle, unharmed by the bared fangs of the monster. For an instant, he handled the gun. Then Dave Reagan said, without turning his head: "A bullet's been fired out of it, just a moment ago. What did you shoot at, Bush?"

"What business is it of yours?" shouted Bush Reagan.

Dave did not turn toward him. He merely stood straighter and more stiffly. He looked at Gray Cloud, and beyond the wolf at an ugly future, ever dominated by these same detested voices and faces. Perhaps it was true that there was little Reagan in him. His mother's blood was his, his mother's eyes, and that slowness of mind, perhaps, he had from her, also. But where there is affliction, why should men add to it with the bitterness of their tongues?

The heart of the young man was swelling. Carefully he looked down at Gray Cloud. A bit of fur was missing there, near the jaw. And the hair was a trifle singed.

"Up with that rifle, and put an end to him," commanded Cousin Bush Reagan, "or I tell you what . . . out you go into the street that I got you from. I'm goin' to show you who's the master here. I'm goin' to show you what's what." He rolled a little from side to side, drunk with whiskey and excess of brutal authority.

"You shot at Gray Cloud," Dave said.

"You lie!" shouted Bush Reagan. "And even if I did . . . are you goin' to shoot?"

"No," Dave answered quietly. He was not angry. He was merely sickened—far more than he had been by the nearness of death in Pendleton's saloon.

"Grab that rifle and kill that wolf, Hank!" cried his father.

"Gimme the rifle, Dave. Don't you be a half-wit all your life," urged Hank. His voice was almost tender, arguing.

"No," said Dave. He hardly knew where he found the voice with which he spoke.

"Then get out of my sight, and stay out, and a curse on you!" screamed Bush Reagan, beside himself. "I hate the day that my eyes first fell on your fool of a face. I curse the years that I have been slavin' and carin' for you. Out of my sight, you ingrate, and keep out! Get out of my house into the street, and never come back. I'm done with you. I wash my hands of you."

Dave had leaned forward. He straightened again with the chain loose in his hands.

The wolf, feeling freedom, bounded through the open door. Dave was dragged into the opening before he could check that powerful rush. Then he turned. "I'm going," he said. "I'll tell you, Cousin Bush, that I'm sorry to go, if I owe you anything. It seems to me that I've been doing a man's work for years, without pay. That's all right. I suppose that you've taken care of me. But I wouldn't take care of anything in the same way." His eyes were troubled, not angry. He added, to the stunned and silenced Bush Reagan: "I don't think that I would have taken care of a sick puppy, the way you've always taken care of me. I'd give it a little kindness, once a year, at least. But I'm going. For everything you've done for me, I'll try to repay you, someday. If ever I make any money, I'll try to repay you. Good bye, Hank. Say good bye to Pete for me, too. The wound will be all right, I think. It just needs to be sewed up."

He disappeared into the darkness. For a moment, silence remained behind him.

"Look what you've done, you blockhead, you fool," Hank snarled softly through his teeth. "You've kicked out our meal ticket."

"The fool'll come cryin' back and ask to be let in," muttered Bush Reagan, his eyes wavering.

"Not if anybody can find him, anybody on this range that knows him and how he can work. They'd rather have him than any two men, and you know it."

Bush Reagan suddenly weakened. "Go out and get him!" he gasped. "Go quick. Bring him back, damn him!"

Hank bounded out into the darkness, but he saw nothing. "Dave, Dave!" he shouted. There was no answer.

Chapter Twelve

The voice of his cousin had come clearly to Dave Reagan, but he had not stopped. His head was clearing, as though from the effect of a stunning blow, and he hurried with great strides, never looking back at the dark shadow of the ranch buildings against the sky. Gray Cloud hobbled beside the young man, every moment gathering strength and suppleness of limb, and keeping the chain taut as though he had been accustomed to running on a lead for many years.

Again and again, the voice of Hank shouted through the night, but more and more faintly, and when it died away, Dave felt that at last he could breathe freely. He paused, gripped a fence post, and stood there, panting, his eyes half closing and opening again with the depth of his breathing. He was free—he was out of harbor, at last—out of prison and in the open, rather.

Before him gleamed the lights of the town, but they had little meaning for him. It was not the society of other men that he wanted. It was to be alone. The solitary life that Gray Cloud had led would be the life for him.

He felt in his pockets. He had one handkerchief, but not so much as a pocket knife. He had not a match or a string. He had nothing to furnish him for the struggle with the world except his two naked hands. And he was glad of it. He almost wanted to throw off the clothes on his back, and so step forward naked, and diving into the next creek, cleanse himself of every contaminating contact that had made his years wretched.

If there was stain on his body, however, was there not a deeper one in his brain? He vowed, as he stood there in the moonlight, grasping the fence post, that in all his ways he would strive to be exactly opposite from his cousins, the Reagans.

That resolve strengthened and deepened in him. Then, looking down, he saw that Gray Cloud had squatted in front of him and was looking up into his face with pricking ears. He stretched out his hand. Gray Cloud leaped to a distance with such suddenness and strength that the chain was whipped through the hand of Dave to the last link. On that he gripped, however, and kept the wild animal in check.

He spoke gently. Gray Cloud sat down again, permitted himself to be approached, and yet there was a snarl rolling in his deep throat when the hand of the man stroked his head.

It was better so. Steel that is too readily tempered does not make the best cutting edge. It needs to be hammered and hammered, and hammered again. And he would use patience on the monster.

But where would he turn, and what would he make the goal of his journeying? He scanned the entire horizon. The dark, ragged line of the mountains lifting into the moon-flooded sky drew him irresistibly. That must be his goal, but, before he started in that direction, he had one obligation, one final tie in the town that he must discharge. After that was paid, he would be cut free from all humanity and he could plunge deeply and forever into the silences, where the hated voices of men would never be heard again.

So, not many minutes later, he stood at the door of Jud Lawler. Jud himself came, and pulled the door wide, and stood blinking into the darkness, a vast, shaggy, ugly man with the forehead and the jaw of a great ape.

"Who's here?" he asked, his little eyes not yet familiar with the shades of the night.

"Dave," said the young man.

"Hey . . . Dave Reagan? Why, I been hearin' about the hell that you raised up there at the saloon. I been hearin' about how you used the left on Doc Weaver, eh? It was the left you used, wasn't it?"

"Yes," Dave responded.

"You come in here and tell me all about it. You socked him in the short ribs, eh? I wish that I'd been there to see it. Come on in. Hey, Ma, here's Dave Reagan come to call. Come on in, Dave."

"I can't come in," said Dave. "I've got something with me."

"Whatcha mean you can't come in? Whatcha mean you got something with you?"

"Gray Cloud, here beside me."

"Great thunderin' Scott!" gasped the blacksmith, and, jumping back as he spotted the glittering eyes of the wolf, he almost closed the door.

"Bring Dave inside," said the kind voice of the woman inside.

"Keep back, Ma," said her husband, warning her off with voice and hand. "He's got a wolf out there."

"Moses!" Mrs. Lawler exclaimed.

"It's all right," explained Dave. "I've got him on a short chain. He can't get at you."

"Got a good strong muzzle on him?"

"No, he hasn't a muzzle at all."

"Hey, Dave . . . you crazy?" the blacksmith asked.

"He won't bite me," said Dave.

"Never knew you to do a fool thing like that before," said Lawler. "Take him back a mite . . . lemme see him. Jiminy, I never seen a wolf that shaped up like that. That's Gray Cloud, all right, the beef-killin' devil. Yeah, that's Gray Cloud. What a head on him. He could swaller a man whole, pretty near."

"I've come in to say good bye to you," Dave said.

"Tut, tut, tut," said Lawler. "What's the matter? What's the matter? Look here, kid . . . I could afford to give you a regular job at my place. I could afford to take you on steady . . . if you didn't want too much to start in with."

"Thanks," said Dave, "but I can't stay. I have to go."

"Why d'you have to go? What makes you go? Them heathen cousins of yours?"

"Oh, they're all right," Dave Reagan said, "but I've got to go. I have to get away from Rusty Creek."

"Done something? Oh, I foller you. You're afraid that the Weavers will start after you. Is that it?"

"No. I wasn't even thinking of them," confessed Dave.

"Then what should make you wanna leave? People ain't been too good to you, up to this time, Dave. But now they're goin' to change. Oh, they're goin' to change such a mighty lot as you wouldn't know em. They're goin' to be all new. Anybody that could handle the two Weaver twins with one pair of hands at one time . . . why, that's the sort of a fellow that people like to have around, even if you ain't the head of the class, Dave."

It was a long speech for Lawler. He panted a little at the end of it, but he continued briskly: "I'd miss havin' you around me at the shop. I'd miss the sparrin' and the wrestlin' . . . sort of keeps me limbered up and young in the brain, if you know what I mean. I'd miss seein' you swing that twenty-pound sledge that you made for yourself, too. A beautiful sight it is to see you sockin' into a big lump of red iron with that tack hammer, kid. What for would you be pullin' up stakes and leavin'? You tell me that?"

"I had some trouble with Cousin Bush," the boy said slowly. "That was all."

"What kind of trouble?"

"I can't talk about it."

"I can, though. I can say that Bush was a fool to have trouble

76

with you, a meal ticket like you. I tell you something else. You been a fool to stay around there all these years. They been makin' a sucker out of you. They been. . . ."

Dave held up a hand. "I don't want to hear any more about them. I want to forget them," he said, and spoke from the bottom of his heart.

"I reckon you do. And now, Dave, I'm goin' to tell you why you ain't goin' to leave Rusty Creek. You ain't goin' to leave it, because I'm the gent that's goin' to make you rich. And maybe you're goin' to make me rich, too. Understand?"

Dave waited silently.

"Maybe you wonder," went on Lawler, "why I spent so many hours workin' out with you at the gloves. Partly fun, but partly business. I'll tell you something. The first time we put on the gloves, you mind that I knocked you flat?"

"I remember," said Dave.

"And you mind that you got up and socked me on the jaw?"

"I remember hitting back."

"That sock was the hardest that I ever got in my life . . . bar one or two. And you only a kid of fifteen or sixteen, then. I says to myself that I got a thunderbolt workin' on roller bearings, and I'm goin' to work you up into something, if you got the sand and the speed. And you have. And a nacheral left. That's what binged me between the eyes . . . a nacheral left. A lovely right for a finisher, all right . . . but a beautiful left. Oh, what a beautiful left. I been groomin' it ever since. I been dreamin' about it. I been seein' it in the middle of the night. You know how I been seein' it?"

"How?" asked Dave.

"I been seein' it landin' on the mug of the champeen of the world, and I been seein' it make his knees sag, right in the first round. A fast right can be blocked, but you can't brush the poison off of a nacheral left. If I ever wanted one thing and didn't get it, it was a nacherel left. And you got it. And I been oilin' and trimmin' and hand-polishin' it all of this while, and now . . . now is the time to start it into action. We're goin' to go to the big towns, and get a few easy matches. I'll have you at the top of the ladder in a year. I'll have your picture in all the papers. I'll have the crowds crazy about you. I'll have you champeen of the world."

"Hush, man, hush," his wife insisted. "They'll all hear you, and somebody'll come and steal him away from you."

"We'll make a contract," said the blacksmith. "I'll be your manager. I'll give you a square break, too. Understand me?"

"Jud," said Dave, "I'm sorry. I came to say good bye. I came to thank you for being kind to me. But I wouldn't stay here in Rusty Creek for millions and millions and tons of gold." He held out his hand.

"Hey, wait a minute, kid!" exclaimed the blacksmith, taking the proffered hand and striving to step out onto the porch.

"Look out for Gray Cloud," Dave said.

The blacksmith leaped backward with a howl of alarm, and Dave went down the steps rapidly.

"Good bye, Jud!" he called over his shoulder.

"Wait . . . hey, Dave . . . hey, Dave! Wait a minute . . . I wanna tell you what you can make. I'm goin' to make you rich. . . ."

But Dave Reagan kept on traveling.

CHAPTER THIRTEEN

He walked all night long, with a smooth, sweeping stride that was natural to him.

And the wolf, before that long march was over, had learned perfectly to obey the lead. Moreover, the constant exercise had made supple Gray Cloud's wounded legs, and he moved with hardly a trace of a limp. Through the gray of the morning they marched on. And when the sun was well up, they had crossed through the hills, and over the first range of the mountains, the lower range. Above them towered the loftier peaks. And Rusty Creek was fully fifty miles away from them.

Dave sat down on the slope of a hill, with a brook sliding in one long saber cut around the side of the slope, and, putting his back to the trunk of a tree and dropping his chin on his breast, he slept soundly until noon.

He had twisted the end of the chain around his leg, but as long as he slept, the wolf slept, also, only now and again opening one eye and giving the landscape a glance. As for Gray Cloud's sense of smell, it worked constantly and with hair-trigger precision, whether he waked or slept, carrying from the wind in his brain a constant succession of messages. If an important message arrived, it was sure to rouse him instantly to a full wakefulness.

No messages of such importance came, and when noon arrived, the young man stood up, stretched, yawned, and the wolf beside him did the same thing.

They were in a hollow, the bottom of which was filled with hills as this one on which they stood. The outer rim of the bowl was composed of two sweeps of the larger mountains, and the pass through which they had come from the rolling lands around Rusty Creek lay just to the north and east of them.

It was a pleasant land. There were everywhere groves of trees, and fine open meadows, and a thousand rivulets were springing down to the creeks, and the creeks were rushing in musical haste to join the deep murmur of the river in its distant valley. It was an interlude, at this level, between the dark forests or the white eternal winter of the loftier mountains, on the one hand, and the bitter summer heat of the plains beyond. It was a region of quiet. It was such a place as a farmer would have found bewildering, for everywhere there were offered sites of wood and water and rich soil, as much as the heart could desire. It was an embarrassment of riches.

But to the cattlemen, it was a different matter, by far. All around it opened many passes into the inaccessible heights of the mountains. And when the cattle barons had driven their great herds into this pocket to fatten them in dry summers or to shelter them in bitter winters, the cattle rustlers came out from their lurking places and made off with the cows almost as fast as they could appear.

Two or three times the cattlemen had attempted to use this pleasant land. And having failed on each occasion, it was left to itself. Now and then hunters penetrated and found a happy hunting ground on earth, but they came only occasionally. On the whole, it was as lonely a paradise as one could wish for. And nearly all that afternoon, Dave wandered with the wolf beside him, casting about for a spot where he might settle down for a time, until someone drove him out.

It was nearly dusk before he realized that night would be on him before long, that he had not eaten during the entire day, and that, even if he were ten times hungrier, there was nothing for him to devour.

He made some small traps with twigs, withes, and grass triggers. He baited them with seeds that he stripped from the grasses, and set them on rabbit runs—a dozen of the most favored places.

Then he went off to set about making a fire. He got two hard pieces of rock, and knocked sparks off them in showers onto a handful of dry tinder that he had collected. But he failed to start a blaze.

The darkness came. He went back to the traps, and found that rabbits had actually been snared in two of his traps, even in this short time. He fed them both to the wolf, tore up some dead brush, laid it on the ground in a place where the trees offered him a natural windbreak and roof, and was soon sound asleep on this bed.

When he wakened the next morning, the song of the mountain night was still in his ears—the howling of a mountain lion, like the desperate sobbing of a child, and the prolonged bay of a lobo somewhere not far off, and the sharp cry of coyotes. There were bird calls, too, at the end of the old day and the beginning of the new one, and the hooting of owls that hunted by moonlight.

He had not eaten for over thirty-six hours, and his face was beginning to pinch in the cheeks. But he was happy. His hands were clean. There were no men about him. No one could give him orders or call him a fool. If only he could make fire, he would be able to live in some comfort.

He had a breakfast of the same grass seeds that he had used on the rabbits. He put a handful in his pocket and chewed them carefully and long, while he went about his preparations to make fire. It had always seemed a simple thing, before. Fire was the last item that even a poor man had to care about in this land where wood could be had for the cutting and the hauling.

He spent half that day thinking the problem over.

At noon he got three more rabbits from the traps—big, fat fellows. And the wolf ate them all, crunching up the soft, brittle bones and swallowing them with the flesh. The mouth of Dave Reagan watered. Certainly the Creator had given some advantages to the four-footed tribe.

By noon he had determined what to do, reaching far back into his memory and recalling what he had heard. A straight stick, spun in a hollow in a dry piece of wood, would eventually start smoke by friction, and then fire would follow.

He found a dead tree, broke off some of the outer rind, cleaned away the dead pulp that adhered to it, bruised a hollow in the fine, hard fibers of the outer shell that remained, and then cut a straight stick, and started spinning it between his hands. He raised some blisters, and got no other result. When he felt the tip of the stick and the wood it had been spinning in, he could feel only a mild warmth.

So he spent the rest of that day sitting with his knees in the embrace of his mighty arms, and thinking. He knew, from old experience, that he could get nothing from that slow mind of his by forcing it on, with haste. Neither could he think while he was walking up and down, as so many other men loved to do. The only way for him was to sit in perfect quietness and banish all things from his mind, while he concentrated upon the one object of importance.

The seeds that he had eaten nauseated him. That made an extra handicap for him to master. To be sure, the Indians could live for months on roots that they dug in the woods. But he was not an Indian and he could not tell which were the edible roots. He dug, here and there, and chewed what was tender enough to eat. As a result he secured to himself a very bad, gripping pain in the stomach and an increased nausea that tormented him all night long. In addition, the wind blew up, suddenly, iced from the snows on the upper mountains, and bitter torrents of rain swept down and found him, no matter where he moved for shelter.

He therefore fixed himself as well as he could, got Gray Cloud against his side for warmth, and then sat up through the night, making his mind conquer the weakness of his body, and concentrating on the problem before him.

By the morning he had not eaten for sixty hours, except things that had half poisoned him, and his knees were weak to sagging, when he stood up. Nevertheless, he rejoiced, because he had a new idea. He had dragged it out of the deeps of his memory during the night.

First he visited the traps and found more rabbits, and the wolf got them again. Gray Cloud was moving with scarcely a limp, and the green wildness no longer gleamed in his eyes when the master came near. A sharp, steady pain came into the stomach of Reagan as he watched Gray Cloud devour that tender meat. Dave was half blinded as he started in his day's work.

His straight stick and the dry rind of dead wood, he had kept sheltered from the rain with his own body, and now as the sun came blazing out, he dried them once more, and went down to the river's edge. There he found what he wanted—a number of long withes, growing on the bank, slender, and almost as tough as cord. For he had remembered that Indians used to whip a stick with the string of a bow, until its spinning back and forth set up enough heat to start fire at the point of the drill.

He cut another strong stick, slightly curved, fastened a withe to either end of it, allowing enough play to make a loop around his drilled stick, hollowed out another bit of wood to hold the revolving upper end of the drill piece, and then set to work. He tried and broke six of the strongest withes he could find. With the second one he actually worked up a small amount of smoke, rising out of the hollow of the lower piece of wood, but then the withe broke.

Withes would not do. He needed a cord, and a strong one. Before long, he would have to eat raw flesh. He could do that, and live, but he told himself that it would be making a beastly surrender, and that he must fight even the starvation to live like a man.

He sat down to meditate once more. The sharpening pain in his stomach made concentration difficult, but he had just brushed away that difficulty and begun his train of thought when, looking up, he noticed that a number of the bushes near him had trailing filaments that gleamed in the sun. They were the long hairs caught out of the tails of cattle or horses that had found shelter under the trees from the heat of the midday sun. These were elements out of which a tough cord could be woven.

He began to collect them, and when he had a sufficient quantity, he started weaving his cord. By evening it was of a sufficient length, and he tried it confidently in the same way he had tried the withes. This time smoke definitely rose from the hollow of the wood, but, just as confidence came upon him, the string snapped.

A cold sweat rushed out on his face. He sat for hours in the darkness, fighting down fear, fighting down the dizziness of exhaustion that was undermining the strength of his brain. His body was weak, too, and his heart seemed to be rising continually into his throat.

Then the moon rose, at the full, and gave almost the light of day through the pure, rain-washed mountain air. The next day, he would have to eat raw meat, and confess that the wilderness had beaten him.

But then a second thought came to him, slowly as ever, drawn painfully out of the depths of his misty brain.

A string made of sound horsehair could not have parted. Some of the hairs must have been rotten from exposure to the weather, one could not tell for how many years.

So he started by moonlight and began collecting the hairs, giving to each separate one a twitch with his fingers. Sure enough, most of them parted, but those that held, he retained in his pocket. It was hideously long work. His body began to feel tremors of weakness that shook him from head to foot. He could feel his cheeks sucking in against his teeth, and there was no moisture in his mouth. The pain in his stomach never left him.

The sun was up before he had enough horse hairs for his purpose. He started the weaving of the cord with flying fingers, but a bit of reflection taught him that a whole day of starvation would be better than the careless weaving of another string that might break. So he unraveled what he had done and recommenced it, working with care. The compression of his lips turned into an ugly grin of resolution. Between his eyes a straight, thin line was chiseled that would not completely disappear so long as he lived.

It was midafternoon before at last the cord was of a sufficient length. He closed his eyes, grasped it at either end, and tested it with a pull. Moisture stood out on his brow. He increased the power of the strain, and the cord endured it.

So he strung the bow stick and tried once more. In five minutes, the smoke rose. He hastily scooped little bits of splinters of dead, brittle wood into the hollow beside the drill point. Once more he worked the drill. The smoke began again almost at once. It thickened. It rose as a slender pencil, milky-white, twisting slowly around and around, as though in sympathy with the whirling of the drill. Then, looking down, he saw a red eye of fire glowing in the hollow. On this, with a trembling heart, he sprinkled more tinder, lay on his face beside it, and breathed gently. The red spot dwindled, the smoke increased. He thought the hope of a flame coming was lost, when he heard a light, snapping sound, like the crackling of a twig under the treading of a stealthy foot. And, the next moment, a tiny arm of fire thrust up before his eyes!

Flame had become his servant to help him in the wilderness.

CHAPTER FOURTEEN

For two days Dave ate roasted rabbit, and rested and recuperated, though, as has been said, the story of the long days of privation would never entirely disappear from his face. But he had gained something more than fire. He now had at his command a trust in his own resources as he never had dreamed of before in all the days of his life. It was true that he was slow of mind, but he could not be quite the fool that other men had made him out.

Then, on the third day, in the morning, it seemed to him that the collar was a little loose around the neck of the wolf. He unfastened it to adjust the leather one notch closer, and while the collar was still open in his hands, Gray Cloud made one of his sudden leaps. This time it was to the rear. His snaky head slid through the hands of the man, the soft fur acting like a lubricant to break his grip, and there stood Gray Cloud under the blaze of the sun, a free creature once more.

The heart of the young man stood still. He remained on his knees, not daring to rise.

"Gray Cloud, old son," he said, and stretched out his hand.

Gray Cloud lolled out a red length of tongue, then wheeled and loped contentedly off through the brush. The instant that he was out of eyeshot, he was out of earshot, also, traveling like a gray ghost, without sound.

The stunning shock kept Dave Reagan on his knee, motionless, for a long time. Then he arose, and looked around him on a landscape that had become suddenly empty and melancholy to him. He had not realized, before, what the companionship of the wolf had meant to him, but now he knew. He was being beaten. It was better to lack fire and gnaw raw bones like a beast of prey than to live alone in the wilderness.

In his bitterness, he cast up a look of mingled agony and defiance and supplication toward the sky, as men through thousands of years had done before him. His teeth were bared; it was as though the sky were to him a human face, and that of an enemy.

One thing was certain—he would not remain in the pleasant hollow among the hills. If he had to live alone, it would be better to go to a strange land, and not to stay here where the memory of the great gray wolf would haunt him, stretched out under so many trees, gleaming up from the face of so many streams.

So he gathered up his two sticks, his two bits of wood, filled a pocket with tinder, and others with the sticks of which he built those efficient little traps, and marched for the next pass.

He crossed it at midday, and saw before him a deep gorge down the sides of which no horse could descend. All the better, since man could not cross this wall to reach to him. In the bottom of the gorge there was a flat stretch a quarter of a mile across, filled with scattering trees and meadows, and with a winding trickle of silver passing through the middle of it. This was a smaller hunting ground than the one which he had just left, but no doubt he could make sufficient use of it.

So he clambered down the side of the wall, and looked around him with a milder eye when he came to the bottom. The fiercer winds would not be apt to enter this valley, and strangers were not likely to penetrate to the headwaters of such an obscure stream as this.

When he reached the valley floor, within a hundred yards, he crossed the sign of wildcats, rabbits, quantities of deer, and the huge track of a grizzly, like the print of a vast, misshapen human foot.

His heart lightened. There would be game here. There would be quantities and quantities of game, though it would be difficult to make traps for anything larger than the rabbits. If only he had as much as an axe. As for a knife, he could chip out tools from the hard rocks.

But secluded as this corner of the mountains was, before he had gone on for ten minutes, he discovered that men had pushed up the headwaters of this valley before him—men with wagons. For he found the ruins of two big prairie schooners, side-by-side.

They had burned. Perhaps in a high wind there had been some accident, and the gale had consumed them rapidly. He could not waste pity on the unlucky travelers. For to him, the iron of the massive tires, the iron of the great trucks and the chains was a treasure that meant more than gold. Gold, in fact, would have been a useless thing. But iron? That was more than bread.

Straightway he camped and fell to work. Thanks to the labored teachings of Jud Lawler, he did not need to flounder in the dark here. Of stone he built a forge. Of sticks and rabbit skins he made a bellows. The face of one mighty rock sufficed him for an anvil; other stones were his hammers, with sticks of wood lashed to them with seasoned withes. He burned wood for charcoal, and set to.

But the first thing that he made with these clumsy tools was a real blacksmith's hammer, and, once that was finished, he fell to work with renewed zeal. An axe was the next necessity, and that involved adding carbon to the wrought iron to make steel. But he understood that trick from Lawler's teachings. He hammered out the bit of the axe with care, ground it sharp on a rough stone, finished it off on a smooth one, and fitted a shaft of tough wood into the hole in the head of steel. The fashioning of that hole had been the hardest task of all.

With a good axe in his hands, a ponderous axe of a weight to suit the grip of his hands and the sway of his mighty shoulders, he fell to work in a fury, felling trees to build a lean-to and to make his traps for the larger animals.

After that, everything was simple. He needed only time, of which he had plenty, and strength, with which he was over-endowed. Every waking moment was filled with labor.

For the house, he selected as backing a cliff face of strong stone, deeply hollowed. Against this he erected his logs, laid over a roofing of poles, branches, twigs, and mud, put a thatching above all this, and erected a fireplace in the hollow surface of the rock that would be sure to give him warmth for the winter.

He made half a dozen knives of the finest steel that he could manufacture, extra axe heads, and half a dozen spearheads, a foot long and sharp as a needle. Almost more important than all else, he manufactured two spades, and a pair of picks, which were invaluable for the construction of the pitfalls that he needed.

Here and there, in appropriate natural trails, he constructed the pits and cunningly furnished and covered them. They brought him in deer, whose meat he jerked and whose skins he cured for clothes and moccasins. He caught no fewer than six good-size black bears, and one small grizzly. A real grizzly was caught in one pitfall, but the drop of the beam was not enough to cripple it, and it tore the trap to pieces and escaped.

CHAPTER FIFTEEN

The autumn was coming on, winter was not far away—the lonely winter. He heaped up quantities of dried venison, and from the creek he caught any number of trout, two- and three-pounders that he cleaned, opened, slit off the heads, and then smoked for winter use.

He was starving for two things—bread and salt. But he found a saltlick, and washed from it a good amount of salt that remained brown, but was perfectly good otherwise. Then he made a sickle and with it harvested quantities of wild oats from the meadows. He ground it up, when the grain was perfectly seasoned and cured, with a mortar and pestle, and so secured a sort of flour against the winter season. More of the grain he stored in sacks made of deerskin, which might as well be used for this purpose until they were needed for clothes.

The dread of the winter diminished in him, though the nights grew shorter, and cold increased. Finally the time came when there was always a frosty chill in the silver mists that were streaked through the wood, even in the midday. But he had deerskin, wolf-skin, coyote-skin blankets. That winter he would catch enough of the weasel family to make a robe fit for a king, so light and so warm. In the meantime, he was well equipped. All around the cabin, the walls were fortified with corded stacks of firewood, seasoned for use. He had found a small chalk cliff, got flints from it, and thereafter did not need to fear lest his fire should go out, for a stroke of steel on the hard rock would always bring out a shower of sparks to commence a new blaze.

He wanted soap. It was made with tallow and with lye from wood ashes, a soft soap that was not pleasant to handle, but that cleansed well. That inspired him to try his hand at a razor, and for the greater part of a week, he made experiment after experiment, until at last he was equipped with a real hollow-ground blade. It seemed to him, when he used it, with hot water heated in a heavy iron cooking vessel he had found near the burned wagons, that he had conquered the last difficulty in the wilderness.

And it was when his face was cleansed of the masses of ac-cumulated beard that he looked up from his pleasant labor and saw Gray Cloud lying on a rock, taking the sun at the edge of the creek!

The shock of pleasant surprise went tingling to Dave's very brain, and down again to the tips of his fingers. From man he felt that he was barred away by a mutual distaste. But some companionship was as necessary as bread and meat.

It seemed to him that Gray Cloud, with lolling red tongue, was laughing at him as he had laughed on the day of his flight. Dave went into the cabin, cut off several pounds of fresh venison taken from the shed where he kept his supplies, and, going out again, he threw it close to the great animal.

Gray Cloud lowered his head, sniffed the meat, and, without tasting it, returned to his daydream in the sun. Big Dave Rea-gan shook his head. With horses, cattle, dogs, he could get on very well, but not with men or wolves.

He went about his day's work, which was the beating out of a great sheet of iron into the rounded form of a pot, which was what he needed for making stews of all sorts. Already he had constructed a very fair Dutch oven, and the pot would make his culinary department quite complete. The whole of the day went to the labor at the forge and the anvil. He had a complete set of hammers now, and a real anvil that he had cast in a mold of sand and clay. He paid no more attention to Gray Cloud, who had disappeared into the woods.

But in the evening, the wolf came out of the woods again and stood at the door, watching the cooking of the evening meal and wincing away from the tremor and gleam of fire on the broad hearth.

Perhaps Gray Cloud could be lured in, and the door shut behind him, but Dave Reagan made up his mind that he would not attempt such a thing. An unwilling companion was a captive, and not a real companion at all.

He ate his meal at the table that he had made, the hewing of the planks for the top of it having been a hard task. But it had been finished, at last, and it was a great comfort. While he ate, he tossed bits of food toward the great wolf. Gray Cloud let the first few fall to the ground, where he sniffed them, and finally ate them. But presently he was catching them adroitly out of the air, and swallowing them with avidity.

He came in and sat down two strides from his old master, staring curiously at his face, and Dave Reagan talked to him with a calm content. It was a very strange business, this. He might quite easily cast over the head of the wolf the rawhide lariat that was at his hand, but what was the purpose in taking the creature by force? A prisoner was not what he wanted, but a friend. And with the intangible bonds of the mind, he was striving to reach to the dumb beast and draw Gray Cloud closer and closer to him. It was like striving to catch a wild bull with spider-web gossamer threads.

When he got up from the table, the wolf leaped ten feet away through the door, but then came back to watch the washing of the iron cooking and eating dishes.

Dave Reagan went to bed with the door open, though the night was cold. The fire went out in the middle of the night; he was half frozen before the morning came, but, when he opened his eyes, the first thing that he saw was the great ball of silver fur on the floor, with the fluff of the big tail thrown over the nose of Gray Cloud.

When Reagan got up, he closed the door, but since Gray Cloud at once began to run about the place like mad, the young man opened it again, and the wolf darted out into the ice-cold of the morning.

Gray Cloud was not gone far or long, but came back and sat down in the doorway, lolling his tongue. Once more he came in for tidbits. And then in a few tremendous, tearing bites he wolfed down several pounds of the delicious fresh venison steak.

He ate that meat from the hand of his former master. Fear, suspicion, almost hatred were green in his eyes, but he ventured, and received the prize.

It seemed to Dave that his nooses of guile were falling more and more thickly around the big creature; it would not be a matter of many days, perhaps, before he could make sure of the wolf.

As a matter of fact, when he went his round of the traps that day, Gray Cloud sneaked behind him, generally keeping out of sight. There were real traps, now, furnished with powerful if somewhat clumsy springs, and mighty teeth, capable of gripping and holding the leg of a bear. But there were no bears out, now. Snow was in the air, the sky was gray, and black bears and grizzlies had already holed up for the winter.

After that day, Gray Cloud was hardly a moment from Dave's side. It was only upon a very distinct basis, however, that the wolf would remain. When Gray Cloud wished to be off, he had to be turned loose. For instance, if he decided that he wished to leave the cabin, he scratched once at the door, and then turned his head to appeal to the man. If Dave Reagan failed to respond at once, Gray Cloud lifted his head and howled a complaint that fairly lifted the roof of the house. And when they were out hunting together, he would sometimes take brief excursions to one side or another. But these grew fewer and fewer, for those expeditions in search of game, the man and the wolf together, were more amusing than Gray Cloud ever had enjoyed by himself when he ran alone through the wilderness.

For instance, a man is useful when one comes to cross a creek too wide to be leaped and too dangerously rapid to be swum. For man will roll a few boulders into the torrent and make a stepping spot in the center. Or, more likely still, he will thrust out a fallen log until it makes a precarious bridge.

Again, if one passes through the woods, and with sensitive nose and with wise eyes discovers a row of mountain grouse sitting on a branch, huddled under lumpish-looking white shells of snow, man will reach up with a spear point on a long haft and spear the game, one by one.

Again, when one hunts with man, even after the grizzlies have holed up for the winter, were there not terrible enemies like the cougar that must be watched? No, not when man comes, for the scent of him clears the trails of all the great beasts of prey.

Trail problems, too, that even the brain of a wolf cannot solve quickly, are often looked through at a glance by man. He strikes ahead, this way or that, and with a soft whistle, hardly heard through the woodland murmurs, he calls, and one may take up the scent freshly.

Besides is there a greater pleasure than to see man, with a thread mysteriously slender, draw up the shining beautiful tasty trout from the stream?

Gray Cloud always had his portion. In all things he always had his share, and the life little by little exerted a magic over him.

To his young master he was invaluable, for he could do things in hunting that no human could rival. Besides, he knew this range from of old, and it was he who guided big Dave Reagan through the high-heaped snows of the midwinter to the yarding place of a whole herd of elk. There they had taken shelter in the late fall, and, working back and forth through the trees, through the brush, through the grass, they had kept the snow beaten down so that it could be scraped away easily, and they could get at nutritious food.

But what good was it to the wolf to stand on the outer bank of snow, a bank eight feet high or more, and look in upon these moving mountains of fat meat. Of very little use, indeed. Gray Cloud dared not venture inside among those hoofs, capable of cleaving the skull of a wolf with a single stroke, to say nothing of the horns. For the man, it was different. With the wolf he stalked, and from the edge of the snowbank hurled a ponderous, short-hafted eight-pound javelin most of whose weight and length was composed of the iron of the head. It sank into the side of a young stag, just behind the shoulder, and found the heart, and the buck died.

From that spot the elk fled madly, when they scented and then saw the man. But Dave Reagan descended, skinned, and cut up the kill, hoisted a great part of the meat into a tree, and with the rest loaded himself and the capable back of Gray Cloud. For he would carry a pack—yes, and on those broad pads of his and his crafty way of going, he could support almost as much as an average man could bear. He was used to carrying a pack now. He hardly minded the neat straps of the saddle that were secured on his back of a morning. No, he rather rejoiced in it, for it meant the glorious pleasures of the hunt during that day.

There was no question of teaching Gray Cloud lessons by force of hand, club, or whip. Rather, he bent upon the mutual problems all the force of an immeasurably keen brain, trained by all those years of foraging for himself. He learned to watch not for the voice of the man, but for other signals. A whisper could guide him, but there were many places where one could not venture so much as a whisper. And therefore a motion of the hand must be studied, to tell when to stop, when to go on, when to sit, when to crouch flat on the belly, when to swing right and left, when to come in, when to do all of these things with leisure, or briskly, or at full tearing speed.

A hunting dog can learn most of this by dint of whip and patience, but the wolf learned from sheer joy. Gray Cloud made the great discovery that in the face of the man there was something constantly happening. He learned what the signs meant, the frown, the open eye of surprise, the squint of one sighting danger. A sway of the head could mean as much as the motion of the hand. Yes, and if one were close enough to observe, the mere movement of the eyes was sufficient.

Gray Cloud was learning with a willing heart to perfect the partnership that existed between him and this mighty hunter, in whose companionship there were no lean days, there were no dull ones, there were no days of freezing, no nights of sleeping cold.

Was it not easy, when the man's glance went toward the open door, to go to it, pull down on the stout leather thong attached to the latch, and close the door, thereby shutting out the bite of the wind? A glance toward the bottom of the bunk probably meant the moccasins, toward the top of it indicated that a blanket was wanted, toward one corner, and the snowshoes were desired—a happy moment, for that was the certain prelude to an outing. There was the coat on a peg, easily leaped for and caught off, and another peg held the fur cap, and in another corner was the fishing tackle—to be gingerly mouthed, but willingly, because of the promise of fresh fish attached with delightful memories.

Moreover, even the heavy javelins might be required by a glance, and these should be borne carefully by the wooden hafts, otherwise the iron would grate horribly upon sensitive teeth. And then, too, a glance at the wood bin meant one thing—a fixed look, when the wood bin was empty. This was not a difficult task. One went to the door, pulled down the leather latch thong with the teeth, and then bumped the door open with the shoulder. Outside were masses of wood piled against the wall of the cabin, but most of these were sizable logs, possible, but very heavy to carry. What was wanted, and what was easiest to handle, were the bits of chopped-up wood, with more of the smell of the steel axe blade upon them, and it was a simple matter to scamper back and forth and bring them in and drop them into the wood bin. It was soon filled.

In all of these things, there was no question of reward or payment of bits of food. Those came, also, but they were tokens of affection and friendship, not payments for tasks done. The man was busy; the wolf was busy, also. They talked much to one another, but the voice was rarely used. Usually it was a movement of head, foot, eye, that made the communication, so that, before that long, cold winter ended, they spent most of their time together in keenly regarding one another's face.

For if the wolf could learn much from the man in this fashion, the man also could learn much from the wolf. By the very manner of Gray Cloud's scamper, his swift and furtive stalking, or his creeping forward on his belly, the hunter could tell quite well the nature of the game that Gray Cloud had discovered, from rabbit to elk, from wildcat to mountain lion. Also, as a weather prophet, Gray Cloud was valuable. He was by no means certain, but when he sniffed the distance and eyed the sky with his head doubtfully canted to one side and then was reluctant to leave warm quarters, his companion discovered that it was a very good idea to give up all plans for hunting for that day.

For another thing, there was no danger in pressing forward on the trail of wounded game, with Gray Cloud to lead the way; that hair-trigger bundle of senses was certain to discover danger wherever it was, before them or behind.

So that when young Dave was out on the trail, armed like a Robinson Crusoe with a huge axe whose blade was balanced at the back of a mighty spike, and with a pair of his heavy javelins at his back, and snowshoes on his feet, he gave only half of his attention to the scene around him, and the other half to the movements of the hunting wolf. Gray Cloud knew it very well, and that it was better to keep himself constantly in view of the man, so that a running fire of trail language, as it were, could be maintained between them. Every raising or lowering of the head of Gray Cloud had a meaning, every arching of his back, and his manner of coming to a pause with ears pricked or lowered.

Many other things Dave Reagan learned; many other things he taught. The nature of the man was fully as simple as the nature of the dumb beast. A distance of language separated them, but they rapidly invented a medium to take the place of the spoken word.

In his wanderings, Dave hit upon a better place for a house, and planned to construct one at a point where a rivulet came into the creek, drilling its way among the hills. There was more open ground. The trees were loftier. And better hunting grounds were closer at hand. He came back with the wolf from his final excursion to the spot, after leaving a blaze on the trees that would be felled to make the house, and others that would be cut down to increase the clearing.

For the end of winter was clearly at hand. In the day the sun had power that filled the mind with drowsiness; the creek was beginning to roar with added waters; the snow was melting everywhere, and patches of black earth began to appear. Gray Cloud panted in his runs. Plainly only a few days of warm wind were needed to strip away the white of winter.

So after visiting his traps and taking the pelts—three of the wolf's wild brothers of the mountains had died that day to say nothing of a fine fox and an unusually rash wolverine—Reagan loaded the pelts, his spare axe, and two traps for repair onto the light sled, harnessed Gray Cloud to the traces, and, having visited the site for the new house, came slowly back up the valley to his cabin.

He stood in front of the door, and he was to remember all the days of his life the scene over which his eyes lingered in this moment, for the sun was still blazing above the icy tops of the western peaks, and snows were still streaked among the dark forests of pine that covered the upper slopes, and it seemed to Reagan that the whole world could not give him another such scene of grandeur and mighty solitude.

Solitude for others, perhaps, but for him every tree spoke with a voice, and the gray wolf beside him was companion enough. He turned from the scene and entered the cabin. Never again was he to look upon the valley with a quiet mind.

He cooked supper for himself, fed the wolf, and, having finished a knee patch on a pair of his deerskin leggings, he was about to turn in for the night when the wolf rose with a muttering whine, and faced the door, hair bristling.

He had barely sufficient time to snatch up a javelin, when the door was thrust open and a man stood in the entrance with a rifle at the ready, the muzzle pointed at his breast—a big man, as tall and heavy as Reagan himself, but size made no difference now—in the crook of his forefinger he held sufficient power to rule the cabin and the life of Dave Reagan.

CHAPTER SIXTEEN

"Hello, partner," said the big stranger. "Sorry I threw open the door like that on a white man. There are some 'breeds holed up here in the mountains that wouldn't let a man come in for the night without trouble."

"No trouble here about that," said Reagan. "Come in. You can put up here, and welcome."

"Thanks," said the stranger. "My sister's with me."

He cast one swift and comprehensive glance around the cabin, taking in the crudeness of the handmade furniture, and the strangeness of the broad-bladed javelin that was in the ample grasp of Dave Reagan. Then he stepped back into the gloom of the night.

"All right, Mary," he said. "Come on in."

She stepped into the doorway, tall and straight and light of movement. The thick collar of her Mackinaw was turned up about her face, and yet the keen glance of Reagan could make her out clearly enough. She, also, had a Winchester and the look of one who can use it. As she came into the light, he saw that she was almost as brown as a Mexican from continual life in the open, and walking or riding through the sharp air of the night had made her color high. Reagan was ill at ease. He always was, in the presence of women, particularly of young ones. Their smiling was a mystery that he could not penetrate; they seemed to be filled with mirth and mockery directed at him.

"That dog looks like a patch of trouble to me," she said. "Is he all right?"

"He's a wolf, not a dog," said Reagan. "But he's all right. He'll stay in a corner, but I wouldn't crowd him."

As he spoke, he found the eye of Gray Cloud, and sent him into the farthest corner with a glance. There the great fellow crouched, and waited, his green-burning eyes traveling with suspicion and hate and fear from one stranger to the other.

The others came in. The big man was closing the door behind him as he said: "I've heard of wolves tamed before, but they're a treacherous lot, I suppose?"

"He's good-natured with me," Reagan said, putting down the javelin. "You're hungry, I suppose?"

They were starved, they said, so he built up a fire and went into the half of his cabin that he used as a store shed to cut meat. He brought out an ample supply of venison and oatmeal, put the meat on the skillet he had made, and began to mix up the meal with water to make the thin, hard cakes that were all he could manage with such flour as he had made, without any seasoning but salt. He was busy at that mixing, when suddenly there was a snarl of rage from the wolf, and a clatter of iron on the hard-beaten earthen floor of the cabin.

The big stranger leaped halfway to the door. "That confounded wolf means murder!" he exclaimed. He was far from his rifle, but a revolver was winking in his hand.

"Don't shoot!" shouted Reagan. "He saw you handle that spear of mine. That was all."

"He's a half-trigger devil . . . that's plain," the stranger gasped out. "What you keep such a four-footed murderer for? By the way, my name's Jack, and my sister's name is Mary."

To Reagan, it did not appear exactly natural that the last name should be left out. Nevertheless, he answered: "Glad to know you." He paused an instant. There was some value in not telling a last name, if one wished to remain unmolested by the world at large, but, after all, he himself would be sufficiently identified as soon as the great silver wolf was mentioned.

"I'm Dave Reagan," he said.

The girl smiled and nodded in acknowledgment of the introduction. She was sitting on one of the clumsy chairs rather near the stove. She had hardly uttered a word, but her dark eyes were constantly roving.

"About that wolf . . . what good is it to you?" Jack asked half angrily. "I'd brain the beast before he was around me a day."

"You see," said Reagan, "I couldn't get on very well without him. He's a great hunter, and I need a hunter to help me. I haven't a gun."

"Hold on," said Jack. "How long you been without a gun?" He frowned as he spoke, and thrust his head forward in a keen, inquisitive way. There was a resemblance to his comely sister, but only a resemblance. All the features of his face were roughened out with a sort of strange carelessness. An expression of grim and impatient resolution was the one that appeared in him most frequently.

It was there now. He looked for all the world like a savage Indian peering at an enemy.

"I've been without a gun all winter . . . all autumn . . . ever since I came here last summer, early," Dave said.

"Great Scott!" exclaimed Jack. He half rose and turned to the girl. "What do you think of that, Mary?" he asked. She said nothing, and Jack, shaking his head as though in doubt, rose and went to the stove. The oven was opened, steaming, and Reagan pulled out the thin iron tray on which he baked his bread. Jack regarded the thin cakes critically, his head cantered to one side. "Run out of baking powder?" he demanded.

"I never had any," Dave explained. "This is just oatmeal that I rubbed out of some wild oats. It's pretty rough stuff, I'm afraid."

"Never had any coffee . . . or tea, maybe?" snapped Jack, staring critically at his host as he noticed the lack of the most essential elements in the feast.

"No," said Reagan. "I didn't have anything like that."

"Look here," pursued Jack, "what did you have, anyway?"

In his aggressive way, he took a half step forward. A gray bolt flashed at them from the corner—the whole mass of Gray Cloud, his bared fangs gleaming.

Reagan desperately caught him in mid-air, staggered with the mighty shock, and then waved to the corner. Gray Cloud reluctantly backed up into it.

Jack began to mop his forehead with a handkerchief, and slowly put up the revolver that he had produced with wonderful speed. "That devil wants to cut my throat," he said. "Can't you send him outside?"

"Yes, I could," said Reagan. He hesitated. "Gray Cloud would be pretty unhappy away from me," he suggested. "And he won't bother you unless he thinks that you're bothering me."

The other muttered, shrugged his shoulders, and stretched his hands over the stove, warming them. "Look here, Reagan," he said. "What *did* you bring in with you, when you came into the valley?"

"Why, I brought the clothes I stood up in, and a fire stick. You know . . . a sort of bow and string and rubbing boards for making fire by friction."

"Fire by friction . . . great thunder," breathed the other. "And how did you make all this?" He waved rather wildly about him.

"Why, with my hands," Dave answered.

There was a pause. Then the girl said: "I thought it was something like that."

CHAPTER SEVENTEEN

There was a certain assurance to be gained from the girl's quiet remark, and Reagan ventured a glance at her as he served out venison steak, oatmeal cakes, and cold water to his guests.

They sat down at the table, Jack with a wry face as he considered the thin sparkle of the water in the wooden tumbler before him. "Well, that's all right," he said. "Anything's all right . . . when you're hungry enough."

"Don't be ungrateful, Jack," said his sister.

He shrugged his mighty shoulders and made an impatient gesture all about him. The wolf growled softly again. "You mean that you made all of this . . . with your bare hands . . . and the clothes you stood up in?" he demanded.

"I found the wreck of two big wagons in the valley not far from here," said Reagan. "So I built a forge, made charcoal, melted some iron, and made myself a hammer. A good hard rock was the first anvil that I had . . . afterward, I made a good one in a mold. I got plenty of iron out of the big tires and the frame of those two wagons, and with a hammer . . . well, I've done a good deal of blacksmithing."

"Humph!" said Jack. Disbelief was dark in his face. "But that doesn't explain how you cut the logs that made this cabin so snug."

"Why," said the girl, "if he had a forge and knew blacksmithing, he could make himself an axe, of course."

"Oh, maybe, maybe," Jack said.

Dave Reagan picked up one of his broad-bladed axes, and offered it. "Here's one of them. I had to make several," he said.

Jack took the heavy tool, weighted it in his hand, and then looked up with surprise at the face and next at the thick shoulders of Dave. His own were wider, but perhaps he lacked some of the depth of that rounded chest. He gave those shoulders of his a shrug, and handed back the axe—a gesture that the wolf watched with angry eyes. "So you made everything with your own hands?" he muttered.

"It took time, that was all," said Dave. "I'll do better when I start making things over. I have some wood seasoning, for one thing. I had to use green wood, of course, except for the chairs . . . I found enough hard wood in dead stumps, here and there, for that purpose."

Jack continued eating for a time, but the shadow was still on his brow.

"Cheer up," whispered the girl to him.

"Oh, it's a sell," he answered gloomily. "Nobody could do all this."

He had lowered his voice, but he had not lowered it enough. The girl glanced askance at Reagan, and saw by the set expression of his face that he had heard. She flushed, and Reagan saw that flush. It eased the anger in his heart.

"Those lanterns, then . . . you made them, did you?" Jack pursued, pointing toward the walls against which they were bracketed.

Dave Reagan picked one from its place and set it on the table. "It's made of horn, you see?" he explained. "You take just a shell of the horn and you can eventually rub it down with oil, and it's like a dull glass. The next cabin I build, I'll put in two windows to get the sun, and fill the panes with this."

"So," said Jack, "you started with your bare hands, and started a home, and got a wolf out of the forest for a friend . . .

well, that's a cheap way to set up housekeeping."

"Yes, if you have the brains to do it, and the patience, and the courage," the girl said.

Reagan was loading the stove with wood, and he paused as he heard this. He dared not turn, lest he should see on her face an expression of scorn and mockery. He blushed, and made a pause before he turned to them again.

"Brains, and all that . . . that's all right," said Jack. He seemed more and more irritated by what he had heard. "You say the wolf's useful, eh?" he asked.

"Yes," answered Reagan.

Jack flushed with anger. He pointed toward the wall, where the rifles were leaning, side-by-side. "There's a pair of Winchesters," he said. "I'll give you one of 'em and ammunition to keep you going a while, if you'll tell me how that wolf is really useful. Hunting, you said?"

"Well, he pulls a sled for me, and that's one thing," answered Reagan.

"How long did you beat him to teach him to pull a sled?" asked Jack.

"Beat him? I never struck him," Reagan said, opening his eyes.

"You're kidding me along, eh?" Jack mocked, his lip curling to an expression very much like that which Gray Cloud wore, from time to time. "You taught that wolf without beating him?"

"Yes."

"That's a good one." The laugh of Jack was short and hard.

"Drop it, Jack," the girl said quietly, with an anxious look.

He waved a hand to silence her. "I'm going to get down to the bottom of this thing," he said. "I don't mind a joke, but. . . ." He turned on Reagan. "How *did* you train him, then?"

"I found him in a trap. There was a grass fire coming. He was too crippled to walk. So I carried him through the fire. He was grateful for that. That started to make us friends."

Jack stared. His anger seemed to be increasing. "Why did you waste that on a wolf?" he demanded.

"Why? I don't know," said Dave. "There was no fear in him. That was the chief thing, I suppose. It seemed a pity to let him die like that . . . in a grass fire. He looked me in the eye like a man."

"If a grizzly looked you in the eye like a man, you'd go up and shake hands with him, eh?" Jack said, sneering.

"Jack, Jack!" the girl protested softly.

"Leave me alone, Mary!" he commanded. "You can see when a thing's reduced to an absurdity, can't you? What does he do for you on the trail . . . this wolf pet of yours?"

"He trails game, and tells me what's ahead."

"Tells you what's ahead?" exclaimed Jack.

Reagan flushed. He answered, his voice low: "I can tell by his actions, more or less."

Jack turned with a grin of sarcastic triumph to his sister. "You see?" he said.

She looked down at the table. She, also, had flushed a little, and when he saw that, a fire of misery passed through the body of Reagan.

"Handy around the house, too, I suppose?" Jack said as he finished his steak, and helped himself to another great portion.

"Yes, he's useful here. He does odd jobs and errands that save time for me."

The sneer darkened on the face of Jack. "Let's see one," he suggested.

"Well," murmured Dave. "All right, I'll show you one." He sat down, pulled off the loose, furred slippers that he wore, and with a nod of his head brought Gray Cloud to him. A sidelong glance and snarl the wolf gave to the visitors in passing the table. Then, obedient to the glance of Reagan, he slipped to the bunk and brought from beneath it a pair of strong moccasins. Reagan pulled them on and drew up the laces. Then he looked up and saw on the face of the girl a pleased bewilderment, on the face of her brother—angry disbelief.

"Fool trick," Jack said. "Any pup can be taught to fetch things."

"But without a word, Jack!" exclaimed the girl.

"I dunno about that," Jack said. "I'm not so sure. I wasn't listening. He whispered to him. You wouldn't claim that he'll fetch and carry without a command, would you?"

"Yes," said Reagan.

"Well, show me," Jack declared bluntly.

Reagan found the eye of the attentive wolf, then looked into the corner. Gray Cloud was gone in a moment and brought back a snowshoe, then another.

Jack sat stunned with amazement. His sister clapped her hands together with delight.

"Wonderful!" she cried out.

And Jack muttered: "He wins a rifle for his boss, on that fool trick. That's your gun, Reagan. The one on the left."

"I can't take your gun," said Reagan.

"No? Can't take it?" demanded Jack.

"I only take presents from friends," Dave Reagan said.

CHAPTER EIGHTEEN

The nature of Jack was such inflammable tinder that he leaped to his feet, at this, and stared at the flushed face of Reagan.

His sister was already out of her chair, and, running around the table, she caught the arm of her brother. "Jack, watch yourself. We're his guests," she said.

He held himself in with an effort that convulsed his face. "I'm trying," he muttered. "All right. I'll wait. There's a morning coming."

Dave Reagan, greatly troubled, now murmured: "I didn't mean to insult you. I only meant. . . ."

"That's all right," said the other. He raised his hand with a bow of ironical politeness. "What you said doesn't matter. We'll have a talk in the morning."

So Reagan, mutely miserable, began making up beds for the two. He stripped from the bunk the robes he had been using and threw them into his storeroom. He could sleep there with Gray Cloud. For the girl, he took out two big blankets made after a fashion he had heard of from a friend of Bush Reagan who had been to the Arctic—ropes of soft rabbit fur being woven together to make a robe of incomparable softness, lightness, and warmth.

She stood protesting against turning him out of the only bunk in the place, all the while admiring the texture of those blankets; her brother, his arms folded, his dark sullen eyes bent on the floor, spoke not a word while Reagan left the cabin and returned with a great armful of the softest pine boughs, which he built skillfully into a bed and laid over it a sufficiency of robes.

At the door of the storeroom, Reagan paused. "You'll blow out the lanterns before you turn in, please?" he requested. "I'm sorry," he added, "that I made any trouble. I only meant. . . ."

"We'll do the explaining in the morning," Jack said, without lifting his dark head from his contemplation of the floor.

Big Dave Reagan went into the storeroom, rolled in his furs, and strove to sleep, but across his closed eyes the vision of the two faces returned again and again—the savage air of Jack, and the kinder look of the girl. There had been a sort of pity in her face as she looked at her brother that Dave was familiar with—a pity with which more than one woman had looked at him.

Hours passed, it seemed to him, yet he knew that it could be no more than wretched minutes, before he heard the voice of Jack raised in the next room, exclaiming: "I'm going to teach him a lesson!"

And the girl responded: "The poor, big, simple lad . . . you wouldn't lose your temper about such a hermit, Jack, would you?"

Shame burned up the very soul of Dave Reagan, and so he lay stretched on a rack through nearly the entire night, while his mind threshed the problem out as well as he could.

It was simply clear that he could not exist with happiness around other human beings. The wilderness was better for him. In a single hour, these two had given him more suffering than all the months of hard labor. No, those months seemed delightful, in contrast. He could hardly recall a single disagreeable instant. No, unhappiness came with men, and with them only.

At last he slept, and vaguely dreamed of what the morning might bring—a scathing denunciation from big Jack, who would call him a fool and a half-wit in the tones of Bush Reagan.

Then he wakened and found that the morning had come.

He tapped on the door of the next room, and found them both up, and a fire burning in the stove, so he put on water to heat for them, and for himself went down and shaved in the icy water of the creek, and washed as well as he could with the soft soap.

Then he came back, wondering how they would make out with the clean, dry moss, in lieu of towels. Truly, he was living like a hermit, as the girl had said. And, ah, the contempt that had been in her tone.

He struggled with yawns as he cooked the breakfast for them. It was a wretched meal, Jack glaring gloomily at the table, the girl anxiously watching him and trying to make some sort of conversation, which neither of the men supported with any spirit.

Very glad was Reagan when the breakfast ended. But then as the girl went with her brother to the door of the shack, Jack turned back, and pointed to the Winchester that still leaned against the wall.

"You won the bet, and you get the gun," he said. "And for the hardtack and meat that you fed us, here's five dollars."

He held out the gold piece, while Dave colored hotly.

"I'm not a hotelkeeper, Jack," he said mildly. "I can't take money for what little I gave you."

Jack flung down the coin on the ground. "You only can take things from friends, eh?" he said.

Gray Cloud lifted his voice in a snarl. His mane bristled. Reagan stepped through the door and dropped the outer latch to keep the wolf from making more trouble. He had brought with him the gold piece and the rifle. These he now held out.

"I can't take all this," he persisted. He wanted to explain the reasons that were in the back of his mind. He wanted to say that every taint of civilization was a misery to him, and that the sight of man was a trouble, and that every man-made thing was not of his desire. But he could find no words easily.

"Now," Jack said, "we're out in the open, and not in your house, and I want to know what you meant . . . you only take gifts from friends, is what you said."

"Jack!" called his sister. She came hurrying, stretching out a hand, her face white with alarm. "Don't hurt him, Jack! *Don't* hurt him!" she cried.

But it seemed that the big fellow rushed on with the quarrel to forestall her coming. "If you don't take gifts except from friends, take this," he said under his breath, and did very much what Doc Weaver had done in the saloon—he struck Dave Reagan with the flat of his hand across the face.

Again Dave could have avoided the blow, and again he stood fast and allowed it to land. He hardly felt it, but a red sheet of flame rushed up across his mind. Yet he did not offer to strike back. He simply threw down the $5 gold piece and the rifle on the ground before the stranger. "These things go with you," he said shortly.

"You yellow cur," Jack said through his teeth, and struck again, not so heavily as before, but a mere flick of his fingers across the cheek of Reagan, as though to dismiss him from the ranks of men, and class him with beasts beneath contempt.

But even that Reagan could have endured. It was the expression of horror and disgust in the face of the girl that started him into action. For she had halted with a cry as the first blow was struck, and now she remained there, calling: "Jack, Jack, in the name of decency . . . !"

With a groan, Reagan drove blindly at the form before him. His blow was parried easily. His fist glanced from the heavy arm of the other as though from a beam. He heard a deep grunt of pleasure and surprise, and then a thunderbolt struck him on the point of the chin and flung him back against the wall of the cabin. He almost fell, but not quite. In the distance, through blurred eyes, he saw that the girl had covered her face. She would not see him beaten so cruelly? Was that it? The thought washed his brain clear as crystal, and as cold.

Jack stood easily on guard, magnificent in his strength and surety. "That's to teach you manners, Reagan," he said. "You may not have coffee in your cabin, but you ought to have manners."

Reagan drew down a great breath. "I've tried to keep away from you," he said slowly. "I haven't wanted to fight you. But now I'm going to beat you till you get down on your knees . . . and beg."

"Are you?" taunted Jack. "That's good, too. That's as good as the story of the trick wolf. Come on, brother."

He laughed with a savage pleasure, and Reagan went in to wipe the laughter from that dark face.

It was long since he had boxed with Jud Lawler of the clever, broken hands, but a life in the wilderness does not dull the eye or slow the nerves. He went straight in, weaving his head. Two rapid drives he slipped, and feinted for the head with the left, and then drove the same hand to the body. Aye, there was magic in it, as Jud Lawler had declared. It twisted the other man around, and, stunned as Jack was by the blow, there was more astonishment than pain in his face, it seemed to Reagan. There was the faint shadow of the sneer left, also. Therefore, he crossed with the right and felt the click and thud of a perfectly timed punch as it landed on the chin and whipped back the heavy head of Jack.

He fell forward on his face, his arms cast out around the feet of Reagan.

Dave Reagan, panting as he looked down, saw the girl kneel by the body of her brother, saw her amazement as she looked up to him.

"Go back into the house. I'll manage to get him away, all right," she said.

"I'd like to go back," said Reagan, "but I told him I'd keep on till he asked me to stop. I've got to do it."

"I tell you," cried the girl, "he'll be a raging madman, when he gets up! He'll. . . ."

Something quite outside of Dave and his volition made him act, then. He took her by the arm, and opened the door of the shack. One gesture sent the wolf to a corner. "Sit still, and don't move," he told the girl, "and Gray Cloud won't harm you." Then he thrust her inside with irresistible power and again latched the door from the outside.

He heard her outcry. The snarl of the wolf cut it short, and, as he turned, he saw big Jack lifting himself from the ground, to hands and knees.

It was a true warning that the girl had given him. For all human sense had gone out of the face of Jack, and, like an animal about to spring, he crouched on hands and knees, looking up with such a grin on his face as Reagan never had seen before, and hoped never to see again.

Then the leap came.

With all his strength, Reagan lashed his fist into the face of the other. It was like striking against iron, and instantly Jack had closed with him.

CHAPTER NINETEEN

Fear of the unknown was what unnerved Dave Reagan. The blow that he had delivered to the charging enemy had been more than enough, he was certain, to fell an ordinary man, even one of Jack's proportions.

But he had heard a thousand times that a man in a frenzy, a man whose nerves are gathered to an ecstasy of outburst, is capable of tenfold effort. His powers are focused, as it were, upon a single burning point. That is why a frail invalid, in the passion of madness, fully employs three or four powerful men, throwing them easily about.

And perhaps that was why he could do nothing with Jack— why he was borne headlong before the charge of the big fellow.

A horrible, unearthly clamor broke out. It was the voice of Gray Cloud, in the cabin, eager to get at the fray where his friend was engaged for a fight for life. But it seemed to Reagan, as he stared into the bulging eyes and the convulsed face of the other, that it was a proper voice to issue from Jack's swelling throat.

He knew from Jud Lawler the proper way to oppose the efforts of another man—in close. He knew how to drop his elbows inside the driving arms and block them. He knew how to give his weight as a stony burden for the enemy to handle, and, at the same time, how to concentrate his force in short, jarring punches to head or body.

But what would be the use of hammering with the fists at a

two-hundred-and-thirty-pound mountain lion? And like a great cat was Jack, as he leaped in, and smashed or tore with his hands.

In the insane height of his passion, his head was pulled over to the side, and his mouth drawn awry. His eyes glared and rolled. Yet his madness was sufficiently controlled to enable him to hit out with terrible, straight blows that bruised the arms of Reagan as he blocked them, or swayed to make them glance. If once he was knocked down or wrestled down, he dreaded to think what might happen to him from the maniacal rage of the other.

The voice of the girl was crying out from the cabin again, now. Through the hideous clamor of the wolf, or in its pauses, she was appealing to her brother to remember that the other was their host—that he had more strength in his hands than was safe for him to use.

Just as Reagan understood this appeal, the thing that he had been dreading happened—a full-arm punch clipped the point of his chin, and he fell into shadowy senselessness, on his face.

The shock of meeting the earth half roused him. And then the noise of a beastly snarl that could hardly have issued from a human throat went like a needlepoint through his brain.

It was Jack, hurling himself with raging satisfaction on his prostrate enemy. There was no more sense of a sporting spirit, no more feeling for fair play, than there would have been in a beast of prey.

Reagan, fully withdrawn from his senselessness by that sound, twitched his body over with a swift rolling motion. Jack dived past him, missed a full grip, whirled, and found Reagan already staggering to his feet. He came in with his guard down, his hands reaching, horrible murder in his face. And into that face Reagan struck. Not with the right, for a blow with the right brought him too close to the man, but with that left that had

117

seemed magic to Lawler. He planted that long left twice in the face of Jack. The big man rushed on, but wildly, and a side-step let him go by. Jack turned again. The same fist, like a bronze-headed walking beam, was instantly battering at him. He could not get on balance to resume his charge. He was teetering this way and that. It seemed to Reagan like trying to keep a vast weight propped up on a hillside with a shower of blows—once the weight began to roll, its immediate headway would crush all to ruin in its path. He danced back from the lunges of Jack, then hit with both fists. One miss would let him into a clinch—that might be the fatal end.

But there was a change in Jack's face. His eyes were no longer glaring with such fanatical frenzy. A dim gleam of bewildered reason appeared in them. As he saw it, a savage triumph poured through the brain of Reagan. He used that same crashing left to clear the way, and, when it put Jack back on his heels, he hammered the long right over to the very button. And the tower fell.

The knees buckled, the mouth sagged, the eyes turned dull. Upon one knee and one hand fell Jack. With the free hand, he tugged out the long-barreled Colt and fired.

Murder was his intent, clearly enough. The bullet whistled through the long, shaggy hair of Reagan. Then his swinging moccasin reached the gun and kicked it, spinning, far away.

The girl screamed wildly from the cabin.

Reagan stood back from the other. He said, turning his head so that his voice would reach the girl: "It's all right. He didn't hit me, that time, and his gun is gone now. But . . . he gets his lesson, starting now." He added: "Stand up."

Jack came instantly to his feet. He swayed a little. His head was lowered. In his face there was a baffled look of bewilderment, like one waking from a dream, the very face of a sleepwalker.

"We're only starting," said Reagan. "Come on, Jack."

The latter made a half pace backward. "What's happened?" he muttered.

"You tried to beat me because I wouldn't take your money and your gun," said Reagan. "Then, when you knocked me flat, you tried to throttle me while I was lying on the ground. When I put you down, just now, you tried to send a bullet through me. So the fight goes on, until you get down on your knees and beg me to quit. You understand, Jack? I know the sort of a devil you are. It's win or die, for you, and you don't care much how you win. But I'm going to try to teach you the other side of it."

"I'll break you in two," said the bleeding lips of Jack, and he charged.

He was no maniac now, however. A quick jab stopped him and shook him like jelly. Right in stepped Reagan, fearless of a clinch now, and picked an uppercut from the very ground, and slammed it like a heavy stone under the chin of Jack. And he dropped to hands and knees once more.

"Have you had enough?" asked Reagan.

Jack staggered to his feet. Where the blood had not painted his face, it was terribly white. "I'll get my hands on you and strangle you for this," he said.

"Here," said Reagan. "Take first grip." He was himself half blinded by the blood that ran down his bruised and cut face, where the glancing knuckles of Jack had torn the flesh to the bone. But still he offered the first grip, as a teacher to a pupil.

He had the mighty arms of Jack around him in an instant, and knew that he was struggling with a trained wrestler, and a desperate one. He was so taken by surprise, having felt himself the undoubted master at this sort of a struggle, that he was instantly on the ground, and a strangling full nelson clamped on his throat.

That hold had not settled when he broke it in the only possible way—bridging back on his head and neck, and flinging his body over backward like a great steel spring let loose from a weight. He would either break his neck or the hold, in this way. Fortune and the speed of the maneuver gave him luck, and he was free. He staggered away, uncertain of his footing. A band of fire was still burning into his throat where the grip had lain.

"This time I'll take you!" Jack snarled, coming dodging in, his head cleared by that near taste of victory.

He was met. He was lifted, whirled, and crashed to the ground. And when his eyes opened, he lay on his face, his arms twisted behind him in the small of his back. The pain that roused him was the agony as his wrists were forced higher and higher up his back. Something warm splashed on his neck—the blood that was running down from Reagan's face.

And the voice of Reagan, iron-hard, was saying: "You've tried every way of murder that you could. Now I've got you. You can beg for your life now. You can whine for it. Tell me you've had enough, and I let you go. If you won't beg, I'll smash your arms for you."

The pressure increased. Jack drew in a tearing, gasping breath. He tried to struggle. But every effort he made seemed to bring more weight against his shoulders.

"Quit it!" he gasped instinctively. "I give in . . . I've had enough."

Reagan stood up. He took the other under the armpits and lifted him to his feet, but the legs of Jack failed, and he slumped to the ground. He tried to support his body on his arms, but had not strength even for that, and slid sidelong to the earth.

Reagan looked down at him, shaking his head, which was only gradually clearing from the battle. He went back to the cabin, and jerked open the door. The wolf was by him like a flash. On the dirt floor lay the girl, in a faint.

Aye, for she would be able to look through a crack at the progress of all that fight.

Reagan turned.

Gray Cloud was not at the enemy with his teeth. He seemed to realize that the war was ended, and, with his forepaws planted on the breast of the fallen man, he pointed his nose at the sky and howled loud and long, the cry for the kill at the end of the trail.

Reagan picked up the girl, put her on the bunk, and poured a bit of water over her throat. She stirred and moaned, so he went back and lifted in his arms the loose bulk of Jack, and bore it back into the shack.

CHAPTER TWENTY

In an hour they would be leaving the cabin forever, Dave had thought. Jack was the one problem, as soon as breath came back to the girl. But as the young man struggled through the door of the cabin with the loose bulk of Jack in his arms, he heard a wild, low-pitched, muttering voice, and, glancing to the side, he saw the girl plucking at her throat with both hands, her head tossing from side to side, her eyes closed. He dropped Jack hastily on the bed of pine boughs, and hurried to her.

Her face was crimson, and burning to the touch. And her body was convulsively shaking from head to foot.

Terror came over Dave worse than that which he had felt when he saw Jack turned into a maniacal man-killer before his very eyes.

A faint groan sounded at his ear. It was Jack, wavering where he stood and with a face that was a shapeless crimson blur, while he stammered through thickened lips: "What have I done? What have I done?"

"You've killed her," muttered Reagan savagely.

"I've killed her?" cried Jack. "She always said that I'd kill somebody. And she's the one! She never could stand seeing a fight. And this one. . . . Reagan, if you can help her, I'll be a slave to you. I'm rich. My money is yours if you can help me get her back on her feet."

"I'm not a doctor," Dave Reagan said. "I'll do what I can . . .

but, if you mention your money to me again . . . or what you want . . . I'll tear your throat out."

The first week he dared not close his eyes, except when the exquisite agony of fatigue unnerved the eyelids and let them fall against his will.

Then the fever broke.

The second week she lay still for three days. On the fourth day she could sit up again. After that, she grew better rapidly. Strength returned to her on that perfectly plain but nourishing diet that Reagan could offer to her. The purity of the mountain air helped. And it seemed as though some of the strength of the awakening year began to come to her, for spring was at work as she lay bedridden, and when she could sit outside the door in the invalid's easy chair that Dave Reagan had built for her, the thaw was in full progress.

The frozen banked and heaped snows of the upper mountain slopes were melting. Every day the ice cap on the summits shrank, and the creek was a thundering torrent that sent misty arms of yellow and white forever flying high above its banks.

The noise it made rendered easier the rôle that Reagan had adopted, which was that of a man incapable of speech. For he told himself that only with the coming of the two had misery rushed in upon him like a flood, and all contact with them must be avoided, if possible. Their physical presence he could not avoid. They were inescapably there with him. But at least he could avoid the more vital contact of the mind.

Therefore, after the few savage words he had spoken to Jack as he stood at the side of the bunk, looking down at the girl in her delirium, he never parted his lips for utterance so long as they were in the cabin.

It was doubly hard because, until the delirium left her, the mere presence of her brother sent her fever up, and the sound of his voice started her raving. All the burden of the care fell upon Reagan, and silently he performed it.

Afterward, when her mind cleared, she had tried to talk with him, but the thundering of the flooded creek made it a simpler matter for him to answer with signs until, gradually, she understood that language was not to be had from him.

Words were not needed with Gray Cloud. He, through all of this time, stalked like a ghost about the cabin, and then took to sleeping out in the woods at night. He rarely came inside. If he did so, he no longer snarled at either the girl or her brother, but he slinked rapidly out of their way and kept his eyes fixed faster than ever to the face of Reagan, as though he wished to read the innermost depths of the mind of the man, and thereby learn the heart of this mystery.

After the first week, there had to be hunting for fresh meat, and those hours of freedom on the trail Reagan looked forward to, every day. But every day he found them a hollow mockery of the old content. Something had been subtracted from his life; something was gone from the glory of the old solitude. The presence of the two in the camp had done this.

If he were clever like other men, he felt that he might have been able to understand, but, as it was, he only knew that all beauty, all content, was gone from the cabin and its surroundings. They had poisoned the very ground on which he had built.

And day by day he yearned for their departure. Only their departure—that was all he wanted. Afterward, he would remove from this tainted place and go far back among the higher mountains, far, far back, where men would not come. He would have to take a wilder situation, one where the trees were small, where timberline was close above him, and where the mountain peaks arose about him like a raging sea, frozen at the highest leap of the waves. Life would be a sterner matter there—game would be farther and harder to hunt—labor in every way would be increased. But, at least, the curse of man would be removed from the tainted air.

So he thought, looking grimly forward to the future.

Strangest of all, he was far less troubled by the man than by the girl.

Jack came to him before many days, and said: "Reagan, the things that I want to tell you, I can't say. I had to have a lesson. I had to be beaten like a dog before I could learn it. I've had the beating from you, but I don't bear malice. If there's any worth in my life, after this, it's due to you. If I tell you that every drop of blood in my body belongs to you, you have a right to laugh in my face. I want a chance to prove that I'm no longer the mad dog that I was before. Not mad, either . . . that's too dignified a word. But half crazy with selfish interest in myself, and confidence in my hands, so to speak. I have a story that you may not want to hear. It begins with the fact that I'm Jack Clinton, the son of John Harvey Clinton. And I'll very gladly tell you the rest whenever you ask me for it."

Reagan had listened to that statement, looking calmly into the eyes of the other, and, when the words finished, he had made an apologetic gesture of refusal and excuse, and gone off up the trail with the wolf.

But after that moment Jack Clinton dropped back to a mere lay figure. What was important was the girl.

Dave had heard—or had he read it in a book?—that women are the root of all evil. And certainly there was evil in her that struck root in him, and grew and prospered. He could not understand the thing.

There were times when to be near her, to meet her eyes, to hear her voice, was to find an odd thrill of joy leaping through him as it sometimes had leaped before when he saw the gold of sunset rolling on a wave through the purples of a ravine, a beauty that would endure only a moment and then be lost forever. Or the lifting of the moon when it blew up along the forested side of an eastern mountain could have loveliness in the same sense, with a haunting melancholy that remained after the moment had gone and that same broad, yellow sphere of mystery had passed on into the black sea of the night and become merely a disk of burnished steel.

There was this difference, that from the girl came a melancholy that invaded every moment of his day, and followed him through his dreams at night. And he could not be freed from this, no matter how he struggled against the feeling.

He told himself that it was a folly, but, nevertheless, it clung to him, as a fever stays close to the vitals, consuming him. He could hardly have defined the emotion. It was a discontent with everything. It was a sense of emptiness that could not be filled. Even Gray Cloud on the trail was nothing. The joy was stolen from the world.

So Dave endured this pain continually, and sought to keep from the eyes of the girl as much as possible. For, though she never attempted to speak to him, and had not since she first understood his desire of silence, when he was near her, he felt her eyes upon him, following him here and there with a melancholy look.

Yet when he was away from her he was not eased of his trouble. If anything, it was even worse. Nothing could free him, he was sure, except the moment when the valley was delivered from the presence of these people. And now that moment came.

The third week she had taken a walk each day, a short one at first, and then a longer and a longer. The first four days had exhausted her, but on the fifth she returned with her brother from the longest tramp of all and seemed to have rediscovered the fountain of lost energy. There was a sheen in her eyes, a glow in her face, a lightness in her step.

That evening, Jack Clinton said: "We'll be able to go right

away, Reagan. Let's have tomorrow to make sure that Mary's really on the upgrade and able to take the trail. We'll go on the day after."

Reagan, as usual, simply nodded, and looked across at the wolf—then sitting in the doorway—seeking quiet comfort in the thought that they would soon be there alone together.

So the next day passed, and on the following morning the two prepared for the trek. There was no further offering of the rifle. They would not venture on that or on any other payment, at the least, and this was something gained.

They slung the guns over their shoulders and stepped out into the open. Flowers covered the meadow beside the creek so thickly that the green of the grass hardly showed through. And the warmth of the spring was working in the trees, and the brush was beginning to shoot buds everywhere.

The girl came to him and took his hand. She had always seemed a tall, a stately figure, no matter how much he had tended her in illness, but now suddenly she appeared slender, very small, and a helpless creature to venture out among the shaggy heights of the mountains.

So, looking up at him, he saw that her eyes were brown, like her brother's. It was odd that he had only noticed their darkness, and not their color, before.

"We don't want this to be good bye, Dave," she said, "but I know you're glad the day has come. Thanking is a foolish thing, so far as words go. But someday . . . and for your own sake I hope the day won't come, but for our sakes I hope it will . . . you may want friends. Try the ones who you'll find in Granite Creek."

She went off, after that, not making such a pause that he would be embarrassed by maintaining his silence.

Jack Clinton came and wrung the big hand of Dave. There was one scar remaining on his face, a jagged red line over the right cheek bone, where one of those piston-like lefts had landed on the day of days. Somehow, Dave Reagan could not take his glance from that mark of the battle.

"I've gone to school again, up here, Dave," Clinton said. "And you've been the master. God bless you."

It was a very strange thing—the honest straightforwardness with which he looked into the eyes of silent Dave Reagan.

Then he was gone with the girl.

At the edge of the woods, they both turned and waved their hands to him. He could see the smile of the girl, coming like sunshine through the shadows, and then her back was turned, and he remained alone, at last, in the familiar ravine, with the thundering of the creek seeming to take on words for which one could strain the ear, but never quite follow the utterance.

"Thank heaven," said Dave Reagan. But his voice was swallowed by the noise of the creek.

Suddenly he found himself wondering if ever again he would speak human words to a human being?

He turned back toward the cabin. It looked small, a wretched hovel. The door was the dark entrance to an animal's cave. He turned hastily away, and strode off on a trail with the wolf before him, bounding like a puppy.

Chapter Twenty-One

Now that the two Clintons were gone, Dave Reagan observed this mystery: that the thought of them haunted him even more than when they had actually been with him in the cabin. The thought of them was ever walking up to the cabin, or departing from it, and a hundred times he heard the sound of their voices, lost somewhere in the background of his mind.

There was a curse left by them—he had half expected it—on the ravine in which the cabin stood. Therefore, he cast far afield among the mountains to discover for himself a better post. He found places here and there, encamped in one of them for three days to try out the surroundings, but the same emptiness continued in his mind. He simply could not fight successfully against it.

He thought of removing to an entirely different part of the country, to the middle of some desert, or to some more barren, some more mighty range of mountains.

One day he sat above timberline, in one of those bee meadows where the ground is covered with myriads and myriads of tiny flowers on which the honey makers hardly settle an instant before they had gathered all the pollen, so that their flight is interrupted by uncounted pauses. The humming had always been a particularly pleasant music in his ears, but now it was a monotonous dirge.

The view was nothing to him. He was on one of the crests of the waves of mountains, and he could see the other summits wonderfully near at hand—until the eye dropped into the shadows of the great gorges between. Such a position, before this day, had always given him a sense of great accomplishment, and of greater possibilities. But today the peaks meant no more to him than wave markings on a beach.

He was staring blankly before him when a head and shoulders grew up from the rim of the mountain, and a man came toward him, walking with a light and easy step, as though the rigors of the climb had taken not a whit of strength from him. He was dressed like any mountaineer, and his rifle was slung in his hand, swinging freely with each step. From his carriage, from his slender erectness, and from an expression of happiness that was visible by its own shining even from a distance, it seemed to Dave Reagan that he was being approached by a mere youth in his teens. But when the man came nearer, there was something older than years in his face.

He was an Indian, and age usually does not show itself in the face of an Indian as it does in the face of a white man. Only the extremity of many decades finally will wither and pucker the features. This man showed hardly a line, but in the very smoothness of his face there was a hard texture that indicated the passage of years.

He waved his hand in salute as he drew near. Dave Reagan stood up to greet him. He was not glad to have another human with him, but he was very glad that it was an Indian, and not a white man.

"I came to shoot a wolf," said the Indian in a gentle voice, "and I find that it is a man's dog."

"It's a wolf, but a tame one," said Dave Reagan.

Gray Cloud sat down before him; it was the habit of the big fellow to put himself between Reagan and any stranger.

"Well," said the other, "if it's a wolf, you paid a high price for it."

"Not a penny," Reagan said.

"I don't mean money," said the Indian. "I mean . . . you paid his own price, and a big one."

Reagan frowned. It seemed hard that even a poor red man should be able to talk over his head in this manner. In another moment, perhaps, the fellow would be smiling with that half-contemptuous and half-pitying air that Reagan had seen so often in the faces of white men. Even the boys in Rusty Creek looked at him with such an air.

"I do not understand that," he said.

The other made a gesture that seemed to have an apology in it. "I've lived alone here in the mountains for so long," he said, "that when I meet people, I find myself speaking my thoughts aloud. And, of course, naked thoughts need to be dressed up before they make conversation."

Reagan stared again. Vaguely he got at a meaning behind these words, but the meaning was not clear or entire. He answered: "I don't quite understand even that. I could understand words like those better if they were written."

The other nodded. "That's from living so much alone, also," he said. "I went to the Carlisle school, you see. Not that I learned a great deal. But I suppose I picked up a stilted habit of speech. Being an Indian, for a good many years I took a pride in using the largest words and the most sounding phrases possible." He smiled as he said it.

"You've lived a lot alone in the mountains, have you?" said Reagan.

"Thirty years," said the Indian.

"I want to do that," said Reagan. "I want to spend the rest of my life in 'em."

"You can't do that until you've paid the price to them," said the other.

"You're talking of prices . . . the price of the wolf . . . the price of the mountains . . . what does that mean?" asked Dave.

"Well," the Indian answered, "I suppose that I mean this . . . you only get out of the world what you pay for. Some people never get anything out of life because they're never able to pay the right price. No one gets something for nothing. There's the wolf, now, that you've tamed. It loves you, trusts you. Very well, you paid a price for that. A wolf lives by fighting, danger, starvation . . . it's armed with suspicion. Before you took the suspicion away from that wolf, you paid down something as close to your heart as blood. You went through a good deal. You can't beat a wolf into being your friend."

Reagan stared. "That's very true," he said. "I never struck Gray Cloud. And I did go through fire for him."

The Indian nodded.

"You know a lot," said Reagan with his usual bluntness.

"No. I don't know a lot. But, for everything that I know, I paid the right price. I know about what a man of my age ought to know."

"What ought a man of your age to know?" asked Dave. "And what's your name? Will you tell me that?"

"I have a good many names. Some of my tribe call me Walking Thunder. Others call me other things. The Cheyennes used to call me Thief-By-Night. No name ever gave me so much pleasure as that, in the wearing. It also cost me a good many scars. But at college I was called Howard Lee, and I'm in the government books as Howard Lee."

"My name is Dave Reagan," said the young man. "I'm glad to know you. And, now, what is it that people ought to know at your age?"

"My sort of a man," said the other, "ought to know that the end of life is the best part, and that days are pleasanter when there are fewer of them left. I know that it is foolish to be bored, because even to live is a privilege."

"But you stay out here in the mountains?"

"I bought the right to do that."

"How did you buy it? I want to live alone in the mountains, too. I don't quite understand everything that you're saying, but I try to understand."

Walking Thunder, for a moment, drew himself up to his full height and stared at the white man with a penetration that was almost offensive. Then he said: "In order to earn the right to live alone, one has first to live exactly as other people live. If they are on ranches, you must live on ranches . . . but if your kind of man lives in town, then you must go to cities. And in the cities you must do as the others do. For my part, I lived in a small town, and I taught school in it. I had a small house and a truck garden. I married a woman who I loved for several years, until she lost her front teeth and her temper." He paused, and smiled rather faintly at Dave Reagan. Then he went on: "I had three children by her. They were growing big. The oldest was seven. Then, one night while I was away, a grass fire came suddenly, and caught the house. The house burned, and two of the children in it. My wife had picked up the baby and started to run, but the fire caught her, and killed her and the baby, also. I was just thirty at that time. It seemed to me that I had bought the right to live alone, so I gave away all my possessions and came up into the mountains, and I have been here ever since. My home now has a back yard a hundred miles long, and my front yard is bigger still. But I think that I have paid for my solitary life. Now do you understand what I mean?"

CHAPTER TWENTY-TWO

So much was implied in this speech that Reagan looked into the face of the other, and then past him at the immeasurably deep, thin line of the horizon. He stared back again at Walking Thunder.

"I'm trying to understand," Dave Reagan said, his eyes rather blank. It was the same thing that he had said in school, while his irate teachers came closer to fury and despair: *I'm trying to understand.*

The Indian, however, had a great store of patience. One would have said that he had spent all his days among children, teaching. "You know," he said, "everyone has to lead a life like other people. He's never excused, unless there's a reason. You think that you want to live alone in the mountains. But you're too young for that. I suppose that there's a girl behind it, eh?"

Reagan started. "Girl?" he said. He shook his head. Then he repeated: "A girl? It's not because of her. I've never got on with people. That's the reason I want to be alone."

The Indian nodded. "Nobody knows what he wants until he's tasted everything," he said. "May I ask you why you can't get on with people?"

"I'm too slow in the mind," Dave answered. He found it amazingly easy to talk to Walking Thunder. "Some people," he added calmly, "think that I'm only half-witted."

The Indian offered no polite and sympathetic denial. Neither did he frown with disgust. He merely said: "That gives you a motive for leaving the world . . . but no right to do so."

"Why not?" asked Dave. "Everybody's free, in this country, I suppose."

"Not at all," said the other. "Freedom is only a term. It doesn't mean a great deal. Free to do what? To live if you work for your food . . . or steal it. To be happy . . . if you can beg or borrow the means to it. Free to pay taxes, free to die. But not free to do as you please. No man is. Now that you've run off into the mountains, you're not free, either. You might enjoy it for a time, but you haven't earned the right to be alone. You'll be pulled back into the world, before very long."

This was all spoken so simply that Dave Reagan followed it perfectly, and what made it exciting was the truth that he felt in his own experience.

"You're a wise man . . . you know a great deal," said Dave.

"No, I don't know a great deal," said the Indian. "But I've done a little thinking about the things that have happened to me. That's all. I'm not wise, though. But I could guess that you'd be happier among men than you would be among the mountains."

"What makes you guess that?" Dave asked.

"Well," said Walking Thunder, "people have called you slow-witted. What they felt about you has driven you out, not what you felt about them."

"That may be true. I begin to think that may be true," Dave said. "I never thought of it that way before. No, if they had liked me, if people had. . . ." He paused.

"If they'd praised you, if you'd been a hero to them, if they had looked up to you . . . you never would have thought of sneaking off to the mountains, I dare say?" suggested Walking Thunder.

Dave flushed hotly. Then he admitted, with a good deal of honesty: "No, I don't suppose that I would."

"However," said the other, "it won't last long. Women are strong enough to pull back older men than you."

Again Reagan started. "What made you speak of women to me?" he asked.

Walking Thunder could not keep back a smile. "You are young, brother," he said gently. "And a woman will be in a young man's mind, even before he has seen her."

"I hope never to see her again," Reagan said, frowning.

But, now that he framed and uttered the words, he began to wonder if they were true. He looked up with a troubled face at the Indian, and found that the latter was still smiling, but that there was no derision in his face. Suddenly the sense of youth and helplessness rushed overpoweringly upon Reagan, and he exclaimed: "Tell me, then, what you would do, if you were I?"

"I'd go back to the house of my father," the other said unhesitatingly. "You can find happiness there. If you cannot find it, you can make it."

Reagan shook his head. "My father and mother are dead," he said. "My other relations call me fool and half-wit to my face."

"Then follow the woman," the Indian said with instant surety.

Dave sighed. "I hardly spoke to her," he said truthfully.

"But she is much in your mind?"

"Yes, but never happily."

"Women do not draw men with happiness," said the Indian. "Nothing that is happy cleaves close to the bone. A fever of the body, a fever of the mind . . . they are what move us. To love is to desire. And what we desire is what we cannot possess. A great man said that long ago. Love is not a good, but it is a force. But I think it is also true that only foolish people fight against it."

"Love," Reagan said, using the word hesitantly, "cannot be what troubles me. When . . . she . . . was near me every day, I only wished her to be away."

"Why?" said the Indian.

"Because she made me unhappy."

"And when she left?"

"I was more unhappy than ever."

"Then go to her," Walking Thunder said.

"What should I do when I see her?" asked Dave.

"Tell her that you were more unhappy, after she left."

Reagan blushed. "They are great people . . . I am nothing," he said.

"They are no more than men and women," said the Indian. He raised his hand as he said this. There seemed about him the surety of inspiration.

Dave Reagan could only stare. At last he said: "You know a great deal out of books and out of your own thinking, but it's different with me."

"I am a man with a red skin, and I live in a nation of white people," the Indian stated simply. "What is your curse compared with mine?"

Reagan was silenced. He had forgotten, as the talk proceeded, the color of that dark, coppery complexion. He made a gesture as though banishing this last suggestion far away, but he knew at once that it was not banished. He merely said: "I could not go to her."

"Is she far away?" asked Walking Thunder.

"She lives in a place called Granite Creek," Dave answered.

"I know where it is. In two marches you can be there . . . in less, perhaps, because you have long legs." Then he added, his voice pitched lower, his eyes searching the face of the white man: "I'll go with you, if you like, and show you the trail."

"Would you do that?" Dave asked excitedly.

"Yes, gladly. Because I see how much you wish to go."

"I must go back to my cabin first," said Reagan.

"Have you a horse there?"

"No. I have nothing but the wolf."

"Guns, then?"

"No. I've lived without guns."

"Ah?" said the other. For the first time he showed genuine surprise. He made a distinct pause. Then he said: "Leave your cabin and come with me. If there is nothing to rust and nothing to die while you are away, let us start now for Granite Creek."

Reagan felt his heart jump. "I'll go with you!" he exclaimed. "We can stop at your cabin on the march, if you need to."

"There is nothing in my place to die or to rust, either," said the Indian. "But I'm not so good a man as you, brother. I could not live with a wolf alone. I had to keep a gun with me."

CHAPTER TWENTY-THREE

Toward the end of an afternoon, they came up through a narrow defile, with the trail slanting up before them.

"Gray Cloud sees something. We'd better go slowly, and you might unlimber that rifle," big Dave Reagan said.

The Indian did as he suggested, but he murmured: "I think I know what he sees."

Then they came up with the great wolf, and Reagan looked down into the immense gorge of Granite Creek, which here described a lordly bend. Below them, the ravine extended straight on into blue distance. To the left, it split into two parts, and the mountains thrust up higher and higher. And almost immediately under their eyes a vast dam was rising.

Through the glare of the afternoon sun and the rising of smoke and dust, Reagan had to squint his eyes, for it was like looking into a fire to see what is happening behind the flames. Then he could make out a forest of derricks from which great cables hung—no larger at this distance, than spider threads, visible only when they were touched with light. And these threads were lifting or dragging heavy masses, and the voice that came up from the dam was between a moan and a scream, that never ended.

Reagan listened to it, with his eyes half closed, as were the eyes of the wolf, and he made out in the clamoring the shouting of human voices, piping far and thin, and the clank of iron on iron unceasingly, and the panting of engines, and the long roar of chains suddenly released and running over pulleys. Dave Reagan shuddered. Suddenly it seemed that this was his first true sight of men—and it was like a glimpse into hell.

"There to the left is the town," the Indian said, touching Dave's shoulder. "You go down there and find your woman. I'll wait here till you bring her back."

The simplicity with which he spoke made Reagan stare.

"Do you think, Walking Thunder," he said," that I can manage it all in a moment?"

"No. It may take you a day, or a week, or even longer. But I'll be waiting here."

"But there's no place here for you to live," Dave said, looking around him into the woods.

The Indian smiled. "The sky is an excellent roof. It never keeps in the smoke of a fire. There is plenty of wood for heat. There are pine branches for a bed. And, although the big game is gone, of course, I know where to find trout in that stream, and rabbits in that brush. I'll live very well while I wait for you."

Reagan took his hand. "I'll come back to you when I can," he said. "To have you even as near as this is a great comfort. You are my friend, Walking Thunder."

"Brother," said the Indian, "I am your friend, indeed. Now go quickly. It is a bad thing to stop to think after the battle has once begun."

Reagan, therefore, went rapidly down the farther slope with the wolf scouting before him, as usual, until he was close to the outskirts of the town. Then he spoke, and instantly Gray Cloud dropped behind him and slinked there in a soft, stealthy trot as a dog runs behind the heels of a horse, constantly pulsing ahead and slowing as it seems about to run into the swinging, driving legs.

It was well to have Gray Cloud under control in this fashion.

And when he was in this position—which they used sometimes on the trail when the man wished to employ his own unaided wits on a problem—Gray Cloud was held more strongly than with steel chains. But now, in a moment, they were attracting a great deal of attention.

The dark, coppery hair of Dave Reagan had been uncut for many a month and flowed down onto his wide shoulders. He kept it out of his face and eyes by the simple expedient of a band tied around his forehead, but this gave him an increasingly wild look, for there was no hat on his head. He looked far more Indian than white man, with his sun-bronzed face and his straight-glancing eyes. There was about him an Indian's dignity, too, for when men have learned to trust themselves to the dangers of the wilderness, they loom more importantly in their own eyes. It is not vanity that they feel, but the pride of Nature. Where does one see a humble beast except one that has been tamed by man? Where does one see a humble man except when he has been thoroughly tamed by other men?

Dave Reagan was very ill at ease. He felt that he would not have had courage to go forward, except that the Indian had told him in that exact and simple way exactly what he was to do. And the weight of authority was behind the words of Walking Thunder.

Children began to gather at the heels of the swiftly striding giant. He tried to use them to some purpose, by halting and asking a keen-eyed boy: "Can you tell me where John Harvey Clinton lives in this town?"

A wild whoop of joy burst from the lips of the boy. "Hey!" he yelled, dancing as he told the news to his companions. "He wants to know does J.H. Clinton live here. That's what he wants to know. Oh, what a guy!"

A chorus of shrill laughter went up. The first thing children learn to do is to mock. It is a savage instinct, and therefore near the heart. So they mocked and yelled at the heels of the big man with the flowing hair and the clumsily made deerskin clothes, and the bare head, and the wolfish creature at his heels.

Dave Reagan was utterly dismayed by the noise. He would rather have endured anything—even the pointing of guns. He was being cried out to the entire town.

He came to the yawning double doors of a blacksmith shop where a dozen horses and mules were tied outside, waiting to be shod, and half a dozen more were already being worked upon inside. It was a big place. Billows of blue-brown smoke kept rolling out the doors and boiling up among the rafters inside, and, as usual, there was a considerable group of lookers-on. Dave Reagan paused at the door.

It was a huge establishment, compared with Jud Lawler's, but it was, nevertheless, a sort of blacksmith shop, and therefore he felt some familiarity and surety in it.

A dispute was waging, at the moment when he arrived. Someone had brought in a jagged rock, a foot long, dark as iron, and a powerful blacksmith had laid on it with a fourteen-pound sledge. He was now stepping back and wiping his forehead with a hand that left a great dark smudge behind it.

"That ain't a rock at all. That's metal . . . some kind or other. Look at the sound of it." He tapped it with his hammer, and it gave out a dull, clinking sound.

"You're listenin' to the hammer, not to the rock," said the fellow who had brought in the stone. "It's a rock, all right. But it'd take a man to crack it."

"You try, stranger," the blacksmith said angrily, offering his hammer as he spoke.

But the other was little, and shifty of eye, and rather narrow of shoulder.

"I ain't got beam enough. But a *real* man could crack it, all right."

He began to look around him. There was more laughter. It extended to the fringe of youngsters who had gathered at the door of the blacksmith shop and grown quiet, sharing their interest in the big, wild-looking stranger and in the eternal mysteries of craftsmanship that went on around the forge.

Someone tapped Reagan on the shoulder. "That a real wolf?" he asked.

"I don't know," Reagan answered shortly.

After all, who could tell, unless he knew the pedigree? And talk on this point was apt to direct attention to the fact that there was a $2,500 reward for the scalp of this beef-eater.

"Well, he's enough wolf-lookin' to do me," said the other. "There you are, Alf. There's one that would do in your dog for you. There ain't any dog that can stand up to the jaws of a wolf. Say, stranger, would you try that wolf of yours on a fightin' dog, for a little hard cash?"

"No," Reagan said as shortly as before. He disliked this attention to Gray Cloud more and more. He turned away.

Vaguely only he heard the other saying: "Go on, Alf. Once it starts, what's *he* goin' to do? I'll bet you a hundred."

"Mike'll swaller that bit of fur," Alf said, laughing.

The two disappeared in haste.

The little man who had brought in the black rock was still talking. "I've seen men that could swing a hammer and crack a stone like that. Yeah, I've seen 'em, but not lately. Not the kind of men that I've seen lately." He laughed again, and then picked out Reagan, partly for his size—though there were other men in the place as large—and partly for his strange appearance. "You, now, brother, might you take a hand at crackin' that rock for us?"

And the big man answered, in his usual gentle manner: "Why, I could try."

"There you are . . . there's somebody that wants to prove

143

that he's a real man!" exclaimed the little man.

The crowd was instantly murmuring with pleasant excitement. They pressed around. The head blacksmith, his hair showing gray where it was not smudged black with coal smoke, made a clearing.

"I'm losin' money on all this fool business," he said. "But lemme have a look at the wild man, here . . . no offense, stranger. And lemme see him swing a hammer harder than Bill can swing it."

"Here you are, son," Bill said, looking at the long-haired man with a professional contempt, and then offering him the fourteen-pound sledge.

Dave Reagan seized it, weighted it, swung it in a light circle. "How many tries have I?" he asked.

"Why, make it three tries," said the little man. "You wouldn't want to take enough whacks to whittle it away to nothin', would you?"

Reagan shook his head. "Have you got a heavier hammer?" he inquired of the head blacksmith.

"Ain't that got enough pounds in it?" asked the other. "Here," he went on in mockery, his eyes snapping. "Here's another fourteen-pounder. Take 'em both."

He laughed as he spoke. Everyone else laughed, and Dave Reagan looked around him in a sad bewilderment. It was always like this. Whatever he did among men, there was laughter to greet him. Even Walking Thunder had been forced to smile, now and then, during the last two days of traveling through the mountains, but his smiling was nothing compared with this roar of mirth.

"I'll take the second hammer, too," Dave said. "And a length of baling wire, if you've got some handy."

It was brought. A silence of anticipation and doubt spread through the onlookers.

"Goin' to do some jugglin' for us, is he?" asked the head blacksmith.

And everyone laughed at this, also. They would laugh at anything. And the sorrow and the darkness increased in the mind of Dave Reagan. If simple people like these were already mocking him, how would it be among the Clinton family that was rich? He sighed.

In the meantime, his strong fingers had actively been employed in lashing and double lashing the second hammer so that its head fitted nicely above the head of the first. When it seemed secure, he stood up, and stripped off his outer jacket. Beneath it was a shirt of the thinnest doeskin. In fair weather, he generally was clad with nothing above the waist, but he had donned this winter shirt for the trek among the high mountains. It fitted him closely; it was far paler than his own sun-blackened skin, where it showed on arms and shoulders and neck.

Now, as he stood forward and weighted the clumsy double hammer, a gasp and a hushing sound went through the watchers. Many of them had seen professional strong men and wrestlers with heavier bodies and far more bulging muscles, but not a man there could believe that he had ever beheld more power and speed combined. Like snakes the muscles were slipping under a polished skin, and even through the thin leather shirt they could see the quicksilver ripples of power moving.

"Give him room," said the head smith. "Got the look of a man about him. But many a gent that looks big in the street looks dog-gone' small in a blacksmith shop."

Dave Reagan felt a good deal of doubt as to the propriety of this adventure that he had undertaken. He had not wanted to call down on himself so much attention. It was his least wise course, he was sure, and yet, when the question had been asked of him, he could hardly refuse to accept.

Now he said: "I'm a blacksmith myself, so I ought to know a

little about swinging a hammer."

"Are you a blacksmith, brother?" the head smith asked, running his eye lightly over the shoulders and the flowing hair of the stranger. "You looked a lot more to me like a medicine man."

People began to laugh in their ready way at this remark, and suddenly someone shouted: "He's Chief What-Not, of the Washout tribe!"

At this, a hearty roar followed, and when Dave Reagan looked around with big, grave, solemn eyes of protest, there was another roar.

"I'm not a chief. I'm not an Indian at all," he protested gravely, when he could be heard.

Another vast roar of delight thundered in his ears. They were all laughing now. And many of them had tears of pleasure in their eyes. They stood on tiptoe and danced a little up and down, assisting one another in laughter.

Dave Reagan, after surveying them with a gloom that heightened their enjoyment, swung the hammer back and forth and prepared for the stroke.

They were serious enough instantly.

"Bet you a hundred bucks that the chief don't crack it," said one man.

"I'll take that bet, even if he's a Washout," said another audibly.

But there was only a subdued chuckle in answer to this sally.

Dave Reagan hardly heard it. No matter how this affair turned out, he wanted to be done with it and out of the place. So he swayed the hammer far forward, then brought it back, retreating half a step with it. And as the great sledge shot up to the height of the swing, he stepped forward again, his hair flying out, so that he looked like a charging giant, and he put all his anger, his bewilderment, his sorrow, into the might of the downward stroke.

Fair and full it smote the rock. The stone flew into two pieces. The hammer lodged in the ground, and remained there, its handles standing up and quivering.

Dave Reagan stepped back and pulled on his shirt. But he was hardly allowed to do so. For people wanted to pat his back, and they kept shouting and swarming about him. It was not fear that he felt for them suddenly, but a great disgust. Whatever he was, he would not be as one of these.

With his jacket on, the head smith came suddenly before him, and wrung his hand.

"I thought that old Bill was the best hand with a sledge that I ever seen," he said. "But you beat him. You've got the shoulders, and you've got the head, too. It takes a head to handle a hammer like that."

"It takes a chief of the great Washout tribe," said someone.

Then a wild yell split that crowd wide open.

"Look out! Mike's loose!"

Chapter Twenty-Four

There was a shouting, and, as the people scattered, Dave saw a brindled monster of a dog coming straight for him—or perhaps it was not for him so much as for Gray Cloud—and suddenly he remembered the men who had asked him if he would match the wolf against a dog. There they were, now, the two of them.

A wolf against a dog?

Aye, but what a dog. It looked like a cross between a mastiff and a mountain lion. There must have been two hundred pounds of it, even in its perfect condition, and it came like a charge of cavalry to overwhelm all opposition.

One wave of the hand freed Gray Cloud to meet the enemy, and at the same time an odd thing happened.

The smallest of the youngsters who had gathered at the heels of big Dave Reagan—a red-faced little five-year-old—in running to get out of the path of disaster fell sprawling in the dust of the roadway, and straight across the boy leaped Gray Cloud to meet the foe. It seemed, for the moment, that the work of civilization was being reversed, and that wolf was fighting for man against man's companion, the dog.

More than one gun had jumped from holsters when the child was seen to fall, but no one fired. There was not time, for Gray Cloud was instantly at the other.

He swerved at the instant before impact, more neatly than a side-stepping prize fighter, and laid open the brawny shoulder of the dog, then leaped away, ready for the next stroke of mischief.

"Take off that dog!" shouted Reagan. "He'll be killed . . . he'll have his throat cut in another second. You . . . take off that dog!" He pointed a hand at the burly, unshaven fellow who had been addressed earlier as Alf by the first mischief-maker.

"Nobody can take him off. And he won't have his throat cut, neither. He'll eat that wolf. He'll swaller him whole!"

It hardly looked like it.

Mike charged valiantly a second time, his jaws widening for a hold, but he struck a whirl of dust out of which came Gray Cloud and drew a red slash down the flank of the monster dog.

It might have seemed like a fight to the other watchers, but Dave Reagan knew that it was only a massacre. Gray Cloud was not battling. He was enjoying himself with an idle, silly game. Mike had no more chance of catching him than he had of tagging a thunderbolt, and when he chose, Gray Cloud would slide under the chin of the big fellow and open his throat from ear to ear. To prevent that, Reagan whistled. Instantly Gray Cloud bounded to him and took position behind his legs.

Mike, with a roar like a bull, charged in pursuit. There was a man between him and his enemy. The way to remove a man is to leap for the throat. So, in hearty earnest, Mike jumped for the throat, and was gripped by two mighty hands that shut off his wind and slammed him on his back.

He strove right and left to set his capable fangs in the arms of the man, but he failed. He was collared by a terrific grip as if with burning, rigid steel. His tongue lolled out. His eyes popped.

"You're killin' him!" Alf shouted suddenly, producing muzzle, collar, and chain. "You're killin' him, you fool! Leave go that dog!"

Poor Mike was surrendered to the hands of his master and collared and muzzled in a moment. Once on his feet, he began to make straight again at the sedate form of Gray Cloud, who sat with one eye on his master's face and one on the distance of the blue and kindly mountains.

"Why not let 'em fight it out?" Alf was demanding angrily. "Mike would've swallered that wolf. Who are you, anyway?"

"Break him open and see, Alf?" said someone.

"I wouldn't mind openin' him up," Alf said, still blind with rage because of the foiling of his great dog. "There ain't a man in this town that I'm scared of. If they're too big for my hands, they ain't too big for my gun."

"You're not fit to own a dog," Dave Reagan said, thoroughly angered for one of the very few times in his life. "You . . . you're a worse brute than you've made of that dog, Mike."

"I'm a dog, am I?" yelled Alf. "Now, I'll show you, you half-breed, what comes of callin' your betters names!" He had the gun out as he spoke.

Half a dozen voices shouted, but damage would have been done in spite of them except for the length of Reagan's arm. He caught the gun wrist of Alf, and under his grip the Colt was squeezed from the fingers like a seed from orange pulp.

Reagan kicked it to a distance. He took the fellow by the nape of the neck. His hands were iron, and Alf yelled with pain.

"You're a rat," Dave Reagan told him. "I'm ashamed to see you walk on two feet like a man. Get out of my sight."

He flung the fellow from him, and Alf stumbled, cursing, down the road. He paused to scoop up his revolver, but he made no attempt to use it. Instead, with his free hand, he was rubbing the back of his neck, where the terrible hand of Reagan had crushed it. And at his heels moved a shouting, whooping, mocking throng of children.

A little bowlegged man, with a narrow white beard on his chin, and eyes as young and blue as those of a boy, stepped out to Reagan. "I thought the old days was dead, son," he said.

"The West has been turned into a camping ground for crooks and thugs and mean pickpockets and roaring bullies. But today I've had a chance to see a man, once more, like the old breed, and l want to shake your hand."

So he shook the mighty hand of Dave Reagan, and the young man looked down at him with wonder and embarrassment.

"Will you come with me and have a drink?" said the other. "I'm Tom Hagger."

"I'll go with you, but not for a drink," Reagan said.

Tom Hagger hooked an arm through Dave's, and they walked down the street together.

"I'll come back later for my horse," Hagger said over his shoulder.

"Right, Colonel," said the head blacksmith.

"It was a fine thing, and a clean thing," said Hagger. "Not the breaking of the rock . . . not the wringing of that blackguard's neck . . . though both of 'em did me a lot of good. But I dunno that I've seen the other man that would risk his throat to save that man-eating dog from its own craziness. And I'm a proud man to walk down the street with you, stranger. If there's anything that I can do, I want to do it for you. You name it."

"I only want to know where I can find the house of John Harvey Clinton," Dave responded.

His companion looked sharply up at him. "You know him?" he asked.

"No. I never heard anything about him but his name."

"He's the engineer that's building the dam," said the colonel. "And it's mostly his money that's building it, too, and it's mostly his land that the water'll flow over. That's who J.H. Clinton is. Now you think you still wanna see him?"

Chapter Twenty-Five

Dave Reagan blinked, very much as he had done when, from the height, he looked down on the turmoil of the labor on the dam. The sun was behind the western mountains. It was not yet setting, but a cold night wind blew from the mountain snows and went through him until his heart shrank.

"I'd heard that he was rich," said Reagan. "That's all that I'd heard."

"What you wanna see him about, son?" asked the colonel.

"I can't tell you that," said Reagan.

"No?"

The colonel was silent for a moment.

"I'd like to tell you, well enough," said Reagan. "But I can't do that. It's a private matter."

"But you never laid eyes on him?"

"No."

"I reckon," said the colonel, with a chuckle, "that you'll think you're handling a fire when you start talking to him. He's a powerful busy man, son. What might your name be?"

"David Reagan."

"That's a good name," said the colonel.

Reagan smiled, but faintly. He liked the colonel. But it was easier, far easier, to talk with the Indian, Walking Thunder.

"Might I ask you one thing?" said the colonel.

"Yes," said Dave.

"You wear your hair that way for warmth, or because you like the style of it, or just because you haven't had a shears handy for a long time?"

Suddenly the smile of Dave Reagan was broad. "You make your guess, Colonel, will you?" he requested.

The colonel started. "Why, by the jumping thunder," he said, "I've known some of the finest men in the world that wore their hair as long as a woman's because they like the dog-gone' looks of it, that way. But I'd say you wore your hair that way because you haven't had a barber handy for a long spell."

"I've been alone for a year," said Dave.

"A year? Alone?"

"Yes."

"Humph!" said the colonel. "I've got an idea that there's some stories in you, Reagan. But I'll let you try your hand on old Black-Powder Jack."

"Who is he?"

"Why, that's the working name of the man that you wanna see that's the name of Mister John Harvey Clinton, the minute his back is turned. I'll tell you what I'll do. I'll take a chance and cart you up the hill and introduce you to him. Maybe he'll blow up. He usually does. But I'll take the chance. Turn here to the right, and come along with me."

They climbed a hill that took them above the level of the dust of the town that blew like a smoke beneath them. That hillside was covered with a gigantic stubble of tree stumps, but they came to a grove with a lofty barbed-wire fence about it and a gate behind which a man was walking up and down.

"Is Black-Powder home?" asked Hagger.

"Not to nobody," said the guard.

"He's home to me," said the colonel.

"Sorry, Colonel. He ain't home to nobody."

"He's home to me. Open that gate, young feller."

"He'll fire me," said the guard.

"How much he give you?"

"Fifty bucks."

"I'll give you forty-five," said the colonel, "if he fires you."

"I'd rather work for you for thirty than for that old volcano for a thousand a minute," the guard said, and unlocked the gate. "Come on in, Colonel."

They went up a winding roadway under the trees, and in the cool shade the colonel said: "He ain't as bad as all that, old Black-Powder Jack. But he's a hard-working man. And when he leaves the dam, he wants to be let alone to rest. He says that he works like a horse for ten hours a day, and the rest of his hours he wants to himself."

They came in front of what was no more than an enlarged log cabin. One could see where a wing had been built onto the original. And down the front of it ran a shambling verandah, whose roof was upheld by sapling poles with the bark still on them.

"He'd as soon live in a wigwam, he would," said the colonel. "Style don't matter to him. Not a bit."

They climbed the verandah steps, and the colonel knocked at the front door. Steps came down the hall inside. A Negress pushed open the screen door and rolled the whites of her eyes.

"Is Black-Powder here, Lindy?" asked Hagger.

Waves of chuckling rolled through the vastness of her. "Yes, sir. He's here. But. . . ."

"Is he pretty bad?"

"He ain't so good as mostly, Colonel," said Lindy.

"You go and tell him that I'm calling with a friend, will you?"

Lindy hesitated. Her eyes rolled toward the tops of the trees again. "You mind goin' and tellin' him that yourself, Colonel?" she asked. And she held open the screen door for him to enter.

And the colonel, with a shrug of his shoulders, muttered: "Wait here a minute, Reagan. You'll hear some skyrocketing, pretty soon." He entered and tapped at a door immediately on the left of the hall.

A loud voice rumbled: "Get out!"

"Hello, John . . . it's the colonel," said Hagger.

"Go hang yourself, Colonel," said the heavy bass voice. "I'm alone, and I'm going to stay alone."

"John, I've got important business to talk to you."

"Then come in, blast it," said the voice.

The door closed. To the shrinking heart of Reagan, it seemed that hope was disappearing down a very rat hole. He wondered at the courage and the kindness of the colonel.

"Sit down," commanded the rumbling voice inside the room. "Sit down and have a drink. I hope it chokes you, too. I don't want to hear your business, you dried-up desert rat."

"Thank you, John," said the colonel. "A drink of water in your house, sir, is sweeter to me than the oldest bourbon. For why? For why, it's the courtesy and the kindness that goes with the glass, John. That's why I love to come up here and waste my time with you."

"Waste your own time as you please," said John Harvey Clinton. "But don't waste mine."

"I can't drink alone, John," said the colonel.

"The devil you can't. Well, give me a drop then. I have office hours. Why don't you come and talk to me in office hours? Why do you come trailing up here and wasting my time? I'll send you a whole keg of that whiskey, if you'll stay away."

"I can't stay away, John," said the colonel. "It ain't so much what you say as the way you say it that draws me to you, John. It's the kind and frank way of you that draws me up here, John. What you reading, there?"

"The best book you ever saw, Colonel," said Clinton. "There's a murder in the first chapter that takes the hair off your head, and I've read thirty more chapters without spotting the man that did the job. Or the woman. That's what I call a book. There's something to it. You can't think about anything else when you're reading a book like that. It's as good as a sound sleep to me to have that sort of reading. Now, what brought you up here? Out with it, and make it short, and then get out, will you?"

"To make a long story short," said the colonel, "I. . . ."

"The shorter the better," Clinton said, "and no story at all would be best of all. But go on."

"I want to introduce you to a friend of mine."

"Wait a minute, Colonel," said Clinton. "Do I follow you? You came all the way up the hill to take my time and introduce me. . . . How did you get by the gate?"

"I dug a hole under the fence and crawled through," said the colonel.

"Then dig another hole and crawl out!" shouted Clinton.

"I'm here, and I'll stay here," said the colonel, "until you meet this man."

"I used to dream that you were a friend of mine," said Clinton.

"This young man . . . ," began the colonel.

"Young?" shouted Clinton. "Did you say that he's young? I don't want to see him. I *won't* see him. I don't want to see any more young men. I have enough of 'em in the house. If I see him, I'll cut his throat."

"You can't cut his throat," said the colonel.

"Why can't I?"

"Because he's made of iron."

"I'll show you how to make junk of iron, then. Get him out of here before I start on him!"

"He's the kind that bullets bounce off," said the colonel. "I've seen him in five minutes swing a thirty-pound sledge like a toy, and squeeze a revolver out of the fingers of a bully, and throttle a two-hundred-pound mad dog."

"Look here, Colonel," said Clinton. "How long have you known this young fellow that you speak of?"

"About one. . . . Oh, I've known him long enough to think he's a friend, John. How many men do I think that about?"

"Too many," said Clinton. "You think I'm a friend, and you're wrong. I'd rather have five minutes' peace than five thousand colonels. Go and take yourself down the hill and your young man with you. I don't want to see him. I don't want to see any more of you, either. Have another drink and get out."

"I'm going to have another drink," said the colonel. "I'm going to have two more, as a matter of fact."

And Clinton groaned: "Well, if you're going to do that, go and bring the brat in here. I might as well waste time on two people as one."

Chapter Twenty-Six

The colonel came out to his young protégé. He winked, but without smiling. "Take everything easy, relax when you fall, and hold your breath while you're under," he advised.

Then he led the way into the house, and pushed open the door to the study of John Harvey Clinton.

Dave Reagan could have recognized him in a crowd as the father of Jack and Mary Clinton. He had the big, bold look of his son, but even more so. Perhaps he was not quite as big, but his gray hair and heavy, coal-black eyebrows gave him a look of greater strength. Even in his moments of greatest relaxation, his jaws seemed to be continually locked with resolution.

He looked up with a scowl, straight at the young man. "Who are you?" he demanded. "What do you want with me?"

"Wait a minute, John," said the colonel. "Don't you go and be rude to my friends. I'm introducing you by privilege to David Reagan."

"Well?" said Clinton. "Well? What is it you want?" Suddenly he stood up and pointed. "Where did you get that wolf?" he asked.

"I got him from a trap," said Dave.

"Oh, you got him from a trap, did you?"

"Yes."

"Got him out of a trap, he says," Clinton remarked to the colonel. "Look here . . . you know that wolves kill chickens?"

"I suppose that they will," said Dave.

"You suppose? Supposing isn't worth anything in this world. Knowledge is the thing that counts. You hear me?"

"Yes," Dave Reagan said.

He hoped that the colonel would intercede for him against this tirade. He was growing more and more frightened, and, backing a little away, and with each retiring movement that he made, the voice of Clinton grew louder and more threatening.

"Something more for you to know, and not for you to suppose is that we have a lot of chickens in our yard, here," went on Clinton. "How did you train that wolf?"

"With time and a good deal of trouble. We learned to work together."

"Together? What, like partners?"

"Yes. He taught me more than I taught him."

"Well now!" exclaimed Clinton. "What are you . . . a Nature faker?"

"I don't know what that means," Dave said.

"That's what he is. He's a Nature faker," Clinton said to the colonel. "Now, what d'you want with me?"

The young man looked at the colonel. "May I talk to him alone for a minute?" he asked.

"Certainly," said the latter, and started to leave the room.

"You stay here, Colonel," said Clinton. "You're finishing your whiskey, and you finish it in here where I can watch you. For all I know, you may pour that drink into a flask."

"I wouldn't pour whiskey like this into a flask, John," said the colonel. "I wouldn't be spoiling a good flask with whiskey like this. I wouldn't even pour it into an Indian. I've got too much sympathy to do a trick like that."

"Bah!" said Clinton. "Now, young man, what d'you want to talk to me about? Stop backing up and come here where I can see you."

CHAPTER TWENTY-SEVEN

The wolf had been watching this proceeding for a considerable time, and now as Clinton threw out his arm with a vigorous gesture to beckon the youth nearer, Gray Cloud decided that there might be a missile in that hand and he leaped forward with a snarl.

A quick gesture from his master checked him, but such was the violence of his rush that he skidded a considerable distance on the floor, his nails making a loud metallic scraping sound. Now, at another gesture, he retreated to the heel of big Dave Reagan once more.

Clinton stared. "Hold on," he said. "I've heard about a man and a wolf, somewhere. I. . . . What d'you want to say to me? Out with it. I'm a busy man."

Dave Reagan pulled himself together. It was very hard to speak to this insulting man, but he managed to say: "I wanted to get your permission to speak to your daughter."

"The devil you did," Clinton said, staring.

And the colonel suddenly jumped up from the chair he was sitting in, and spilled some of the whiskey from his glass.

Dave Reagan retreated a little more toward the door.

"Stand still!" shouted Clinton. Reagan stood. "You want my permission?" Clinton queried. "Why should you have my permission? My daughter can speak for herself. What d'you want to say to her . . . good evening? Why do you ask permission?"

Dave Reagan flushed. "She belongs to you, I suppose," he said.

The colonel suddenly laughed. "That's a good one," he said.

"Don't laugh like a braying donkey, Colonel," said Clinton. "This boy has something on his mind. I don't know what it is. I don't know what sort of a mind he has, if he thinks that fathers have any control over their daughters, in these days. I own her, do I? You know something, young man?"

"Yes, sir?" Dave said respectfully.

"I own more acres of blue sky than I own moments of my daughter's time and attention. But she can speak for herself. I'm going to get at the bottom of this. Mary!" He raised his voice to a thunder that made the entire house shake. "Mary!" he roared again. "Never here!" exclaimed Clinton. "Never where I want her. Out hunting some deer, or something like that. Hunting a deer or climbing a mountain, or swimming a cataract, or some such thing. Mary!"

As the thunder of the last call died out, the door of the room was pushed open, and she entered the room.

"Yes, Father?" she answered. Then she saw Reagan and came hastily to him and took his hand and looked up into his face with amazement and pleasure. "How glad and how amazed I am, Dave," she said. "I thought that you'd never waste time to come to Granite Creek!"

"Who the devil is this fellow?" broke in Clinton. "Tell me!"

"Jack and I have been telling you about nothing else since we came back," said the girl. "Why, are you blind, Father? There's Gray Cloud, every inch of him, I suppose, but he looks smaller than my memory of him. D'you think I dare to touch him, Dave?"

"I wouldn't," said the young man. He was watching her with his head held rigidly high, and it seemed to him that in the shadow of the room behind her he could see the face of Walking

Thunder. For the Indian had been right in telling him to come. He could feel the rightness of that counsel as he looked at the girl.

Clinton had come hastily from behind his table, his carpet slippers slapping on the floor. "Why didn't you tell me that you're Dave Reagan?" he demanded.

"I did," said the young man.

"You did not," Clinton insisted. "There might be ten thousand David Reagans in the world. Yes, and with wolves. Confound you, Colonel, why didn't you tell me that this is Dave? Where's Jack? Hello! Jack! Jack! Come here! Oh, Jack!"

Jack came and shouted at the sight of Dave Reagan. His somber, rugged face brightened as he gripped the hand of the man from the wilderness.

"Is this the fellow that licked you?" asked Clinton.

"He's the man that made me say I had enough," said Clinton.

Dave Reagan, in pain, lifted a protesting hand.

"How about it?" asked Clinton. "Did you lick my boy?"

"I've trained at boxing for years," said Dave. "I had a lot of advantages. I don't want to remember that day."

"The devil you don't!" exclaimed Clinton. "I wish I could thrash him myself. I could have eaten him alive, when I was his age, but not now. I'm getting old. You let this fellow in deerskin thump you, did you, Jack? I'm ashamed of you."

Jack said nothing. He merely smiled and nodded at Dave Reagan.

"Don't mind Father," said the girl, keeping the eyes of Reagan carefully on her own. "He's always roaring and thundering, but the lightning never strikes. It's just noise and bluff, the lot of it."

"That's a confused misrepresentation, Mary," said Clinton. "I could call it by a shorter word. But Dave, here, has something to say."

The colonel slipped through the door, unheeded.

"What is it, Dave?" asked Jack.

"It's something about Mary," said Clinton. "Fire away, Dave?"

The girl frowned with wonder.

Reagan found his voice. "I was glad when you two left the cabin," he said. "I thought that I'd be happy again as I had been before. But I was wrong. Every day, since then, I've been thinking about you. I came down to Granite Creek to tell you that, Mary."

"Are you blushing, Mary?" her father inserted.

"No, I don't think so," she said.

"Wait till I light the lamp. I think you're blushing. Where are the matches? Never anything that I want in this house. Here, now." He lit the lamp and held it up.

"That's not fair, Father," said the girl.

Her face was rosy, and there was a gleaming moisture in her eyes.

"Bad, bad, very bad," Clinton said, scowling. "A couple of fever patients on my hands . . . and a thousand miles from any good doctors. But I can prescribe one thing, and that's a change of climate for you, young lady! Look at her, Jack. Look at Dave, too. Blushing like a pair of fools. I never saw anything so disgusting in my life. Young man," he roared, turning on Dave, "d'you dare to say that you're in love with my daughter?"

"I don't know," said Dave Reagan.

"What do you mean by not knowing?" shouted Clinton.

"I never was in love before," said the young man.

"Jack, you'd better go away," Mary Clinton said.

Jack, with a look of trouble and a shake of the head, started for the door.

"Come back here!" cried his father. "You can't desert me like this if you call yourself a man."

"I'm no good here," Jack said. "I guess you're no good, either. You'd better leave everything to Mary." He passed on into the hall.

"Leave everything to Mary? Everything to a baby like Mary?" protested Clinton. "I can't do that. Sit down. Mary, sit down!"

"I'll have to stand," she said. "I can't sit down now."

"Nonsense," her father said, but he went on. "Now you, Dave Reagan, if you're not in love with my girl, what are you?"

"I don't know, really," Dave answered.

"He doesn't know," groaned Clinton. "Doesn't know anything! What are the symptoms? What made you come to Granite Creek without being invited?"

"He was invited," the girl said hastily.

"Be still," commanded her father abruptly. "Let me handle this. Go on and answer me, young man. Don't stand there like a dummy."

"I came because I was lonely," said Dave Reagan. "It wasn't that way before. For a year I got along very well alone. But after Jack and Mary left it was different."

"How was it different?"

"Well, the mountains were sort of empty."

"They were, were they?"

"Yes."

"Weren't there just as many trees and creeks and deer and wolves and what-not around you?"

"Yes, there were just as many."

"Then what rot are you talking about the mountains being empty?"

"They seemed empty to me. There was nothing about them that filled up my mind any longer. I'm not very clever with words, and I can't very well say what I felt."

"Not clever with words, eh?" Clinton said. "That's what every politician tells the crowd. He's giving 'em plain facts, not oratory. I begin to be suspicious about you, young man. You go right on and tell us how you felt."

"Empty," Dave repeated. "And it was like homesickness, too."

The girl laughed. She seemed to feel a personal triumph in this explanation.

Her father glared at her. "Go on!" he commanded Dave Reagan. "You felt empty, did you? You felt homesick, did you? What else did you feel?"

The young man shook his head. He looked straight before him and strained to recover the mental sight of the thing. "You know," he said, "how mountains go back from green to brown, and then turn blue?"

"Yes, I know, and what of it?"

"Well, I used to like to walk out there, now and then, and climb through the passes and get into the blue . . . I mean, of course, it wasn't blue when I got there, but it was sport to walk into undiscovered country with Gray Cloud, here. I thought that was the happiest thing in the world, very nearly. But after Mary and Jack left there was no longer any pleasure in going through the mountains. Every creek that was talking in the valleys seemed to be growling at me that I was a fool, and that I'd never be happy again."

"He says that he can't express himself," Clinton grumbled, staring at Dave. "He's probably a reporter, or poet, or something like that. Probably lives on the words he writes. Well, young man. . . . By the way, what college did you go to?"

"I never went to college, or to high school, even," said Dave.

"The devil you didn't! Where did you learn to talk about walking into the blue, then?"

Dave Reagan was silent, shaking his head.

"Now," Clinton said, "since you had to come here, as you say, and since you've arrived, what about it? What are you going to do about it?"

"I don't know," said Dave.

Clinton threw up his hands with a roar.

"There you are," he complained to his daughter. "That's the way with him. When I get him cornered, he doesn't know. Can't you tell me what you want, now that you're here?"

"Yes, I can tell you what I want."

"Tell me, then, confound it!"

Dave Reagan turned to the girl. "I want you," he said.

Her lips parted.

"Mary!" shouted her father. "Don't say a word. You . . . Reagan . . . get out of here! Get out . . . you hear me?"

"Of course I hear you," Reagan said. "But I can't leave this instant."

"You can't? You can't? You can. . . ."

Reagan raised his hand, and, strangely enough, the older man was instantly silent. "Shall I go, Mary?" asked the young man.

"Will you join the colonel for a few moments?" asked the girl.

"Yes, I'll join the colonel," said Reagan.

And he turned to Clinton and bowed his head a little, and then left the room.

Clinton rushed to the girl, caught her by the arms, and thrust her into a chair where the flood of the lamplight struck full upon her face. He kneeled before her in order to study her more closely.

"Mary," he whispered, "what's this nonsense? What does he mean by saying that he wants you?"

"I only know what he says," said the girl.

"I don't believe him," Clinton said.

"Not believe him?" she asked, lifting her eyebrows.

"Why should I?" asked Clinton.

"Why," said the girl, "he couldn't tell a lie . . . it would kill him to tell a lie, Father. Can't you see that?"

"He says he wants you, then, and he means it. Grant him that," argued Clinton. "But that's nothing, Mary. A thousand men have wanted you before. A thousand finer men than that long-haired piece of deerskin and fake. You know that. You know that he's no good. If he were any good, he'd not be wearing that stuff. He's trying to pose as another Buffalo Bill, or something like that. Don't be a fool, Mary. Open your eyes and look at the facts about him."

"I'm seeing every fact about him as clearly as though he were standing here in the sun," said the girl. "As though there were the same sunshine on every minute of the time we spent with him."

"Listen to me, Mary," said the father. "You've been away from your own kind of people, and this fellow may appeal to you because he's a freak. He'd be a laughingstock, a disgrace to the family. You can see that. He wants you, but, of course, you're only sorry for him."

"Sorry for him?"

"Yes, of course you are. You see the distance between you. Dreadful thing, that distance . . . that social ostracism. To be laughed at by your fellows. . . ."

"Father, did you ever see a man who could afford to laugh at Dave Reagan?" she asked him suddenly. The mighty form dawned on the mind of her father. As he hesitated, she went on quietly: "No, you never met a man who could afford to laugh at Dave . . . and I can answer for the women."

"You mean, Mary, that you like him?"

"I like him a lot," she averred.

"Naturally, naturally," Clinton commented, moisture glistening on his forehead as he spoke. "You like him a lot. So do I. A brave, powerful young fellow . . . I understand all that. I like him, too. Grateful to him for knocking the nonsense out of Jack and bringing him back to his sound senses. Very grateful to him, and I intend to reward him for it, too."

"How would you reward him, Father?"

"A good, fat, easy job," he said, "with plenty of money."

"Money means nothing to him," Mary advised. She seemed rather amused, probing her father's ideas of Dave.

"The whole point is, Mary," said Clinton, "that he wants you. He's had his fancy turned by your pretty face, my dear. But though you like him, admire him, respect him, are grateful to him, feel that he's amazingly gentle . . . as his care of you showed . . . and a natural gentleman . . . which I might admit, also, under some pressure . . . still, Mary, of course . . . it's only to be laughed at . . . you don't want him, do you?"

"Will it hurt you much if I say that I do?"

"Hurt me? It'll tear the heart out of me, Mary."

"Then I'll wait."

"Do you mean that you really want him?"

"I've been sick for him all these days," said the girl.

Her father rose from his knees, started to speak, changed his mind, and went with short steps back to his table. He slumped into his chair, picked up a paper, let it fall again.

The girl followed and leaned beside him. "In another week or so I would have gone back to look for him," she said.

Her father raised his hand. "Get out of here and leave me alone, Mary," he said. "I have to think. Go on . . . scatter!"

She went obediently to the door, paused, looked back at him, and, seeing his head drop slowly into his two big hands, she stepped hastily into the hallway and closed the door soundlessly behind her.

On the verandah she found the colonel and big Dave Reagan waiting in silence.

CHAPTER TWENTY-EIGHT

When, five minutes later, John Harvey Clinton walked out onto the verandah, there was no sign in his face of the storm and the trouble through which he had passed.

"All of you people listen to me," he said. Then, as he gathered their attention, he went on: "This is all going to turn out to everybody's content and happiness. Mary, I want to talk to you. Dave, come and see me in my office tomorrow morning at nine. Good evening, my boy. Be sharp at nine!"

He took Mary's arm and went back into the house with her, and she called good night to Reagan over her shoulder.

"Look, Mary," said her father in the darkness of the hall. "You think you love that fellow, do you?"

"That's just what I think," she said.

"I'm going to find out something about him," said her father. "Maybe I'll have news for you in the morning. You be up for a seven-thirty breakfast, will you?"

He left her, and, going to the back of the house, he threw open the door of a room. Two young fellows were playing cards in their shirt sleeves.

"Write this down, but not on paper," said Clinton. "I want to find out about a man named David Reagan, six feet three, two hundred and what-not pounds, twenty-one or so years old, now wearing homemade deerskins and long red hair. Buzz through the town. Get on the trail of news about him. Get on that trail and stay there. He's tamed a wild wolf for a running mate. If you pick up a clue, then burn up the telegraph wires and follow the lead. I don't care what you spend, but lay a picture of Dave Reagan on my breakfast table tomorrow morning."

He left them and went back to his own room to walk up and down restlessly, unhappily. His hands kept opening and shutting of their own accord.

Down the hill, in the meantime, walked Dave Reagan with Jack and the colonel. Jack was pressing the young man to stay the night in the house. His father had simply forgot to ask him.

"I can't stay," said Dave. "I have a friend waiting for me on the other side of town."

Jack left him at the gate. The colonel went on down the hill to the town, with Dave striding beside him.

"John Harvey Clinton is a rough man," said the colonel. "And when he gets smooth, he's a lot more dangerous than when he shouts and roars. The noise is nothing. When he's quiet, he's thinking. And he has a brain . . . don't doubt that. He was pretty smooth just now when he came out on the verandah. And that's why I tell you to be careful, mighty careful. There's trouble in the air for you. A lot of trouble, you mark my words."

"I'll try to be careful," Reagan said vaguely. "But what could he do?"

"What could he do?" exploded the colonel. "He can build that dam that a hundred engineers said would never be built. He can blast open the dog-gone' mountains and build that dam, for one thing. And he's done other things, too, harder than building dams. The men that have stood up against him have all gone down, and they've dropped so hard that they've stayed down. You understand?"

"Yes," said Dave.

The colonel went on: "You want his girl, Mary. She means

more to him than his money. More than his name and his fame. If he doesn't think that you ought to have her, there's trouble ahead for you. Understand me?"

"I understand," Dave said. "But I still don't understand just what he'd do."

"Anything but murder, I'd say," snapped the colonel. "You better come home with me. I can tell you some things that will be useful."

"I can't," said Reagan. "I have a friend waiting for me on the other side of the town." He shook hands with the colonel and thanked him.

"All I did was get you in touch with the enemy," warned the colonel. "All I did was get you in touch with trouble. Understand? Watch yourself, son, watch yourself."

They parted, and through the dusk Dave Reagan crossed the small town and climbed up the steep slope to the place where he had left the Indian.

A voice spoke from the deep shadows beneath a tree. "Follow me, brother," it said.

It was Walking Thunder, who stood up from the darkness and led the way back into the covert to a small clearing in which there was a single shining eye of red that glared at them from the ground.

Walking Thunder raked off the top ashes from the fire, and by the gleam of it Dave saw the inclined wooden spits on which were portions of roasted meat warming.

"Eat," said the Indian.

Reagan sat down, cross-legged, and in silence he ate a great portion.

When he had finished eating, he followed the noise of running water, drank from the spring he found, and came back to Walking Thunder.

"Will she come?" asked the Indian.

"She would come," said Dave, "but I must talk again to her father."

"That means that he will ask you to pay a price for her," said the Indian.

"I don't think so," Dave said. "He's very rich. I'm very poor."

"Money is only one form of wealth," said the other. "This great, rich man ought to know something that the Indians learned long ago, that what a man loves ought to be given away, but never sold. And he may learn it, too, but it may cost you a terrible price to pay, and he may have blood for the payment . . . blood for the payment." He stopped talking abruptly. "It has been a long day, and I think that your trail may begin to grow harder tomorrow, brother," he finished. Then he wrapped himself in his blankets and lay down.

But Dave remained awake for a long time, sitting on the edge of the woods and looking down into the great gorge of the ravine, out of which the noise of labor constantly ascended, for work on the dam never ended, day or night.

He felt that he was on the middle of a great, perilous bridge that might link his old life with a strange future. The bridge was narrow, the height was great, and one wrong step would dash him out of existence. But on the other side of it was Mary Clinton.

Quietly he set his teeth and clenched them. He said nothing, but he must have looked up, for suddenly Gray Cloud leaped to his feet and stood before his master, staring through the starlight into the young man's face. There was something uncanny about it all that made the heart of Dave jump.

Trouble was ahead. The colonel foresaw it. The Indian guessed at it. Dave's own nerves began to hum with electric messages of danger.

CHAPTER TWENTY-NINE

Mary sat alone with her father the next morning at breakfast. Jack had risen before dawn to take the trail toward newly reported sign of grizzly bear.

John Harvey Clinton fingered some slips of paper that lay beside his plate. "Now, Mary," he said, "what d'you know about this fellow, Reagan?"

"Six feet two or three," she said. "Weight, two hundred and twenty or thirty, blue eyes, red hair worn long, homemade moccasins. . . ."

"Stop it," he commanded.

She was silent, smiling at her father's scowling face.

"I mean, what d'you know about who he is?"

"He's a man," said the girl. "That's all I want to know about him."

"Well, well, well," said her father. "I suppose that he's a man, well enough. He might be able to tackle a grizzly bear with his bare hands, for all I know. But this isn't a world where strong hands count. They're a hindrance. I'd have done twice as much as I've managed if I'd been a skinny little freak of a man. Twice as much. The more pounds you weigh, the bigger the load that you have to carry around."

She watched him carefully, and said nothing.

"I mean," he continued, "what d'you know about his past, and his family, and all of that?"

"Nothing," she said. "And I care less."

"You'll care more when you hear what I've found."

"Have you been spying on his past, Father?" asked the girl.

"Don't use that word to me," he snapped in anger.

She was silent, but her head was up, and she was equally angered, it was plain.

"You're my daughter," he said. "A fellow walks out of the woods and tells you to follow him. You get ready to pack your grip and go. I'd be a fool if I didn't make a few inquiries, wouldn't I?"

She shrugged her shoulders.

"Now listen to a few facts," he began. "He comes from a small town called Rusty Creek. Had the reputation of being the town half-wit and fool . . . lived with a down-at-the-heel tribe of cousins, who'd taken him in when his parents threw him out onto the world. The last seen of him in Rusty Creek, he got into a saloon brawl . . . then he ran to keep away from the bad consequences that might follow on the heels of it. Ran away, mind you.

"The wolf that follows him around was a cattle killer with a twenty-five-hundred-dollar reward on its scalp. He sneaked away with it when he bolted. Wanted to do as much harm as he could to his cousins, I suppose. Used to work in a blacksmith shop. Did odd jobs around the ranch of his cousin. That's the pretty picture that I've uncovered for you to look at, Mary."

"Well," she said, "according to that report, he's a fool, a sneak, and a coward. Isn't that right?"

"Nobody is known, except in his own home town," said her father with energy.

"What's the only place where a prophet is without honor?" she countered.

"I give you facts, and you answer me with talk and tommyrot," said Clinton.

"I'll give you facts, too," she said. "He's the town half-wit,

says your report. Well, that half-wit was able to tame a wild wolf
. . . able to go into the wilderness with his bare hands and build
a home and make himself comfortable in it. I've told you about
the things that he'd made."

"Any cheap Yankee mechanic could make such things," he
said.

She went on, paying little attention to his answer: "The report
calls him a sneak. A sneak doesn't come down out of the hills
and face you the way he faced you, and ask your permission to
speak to me. A sneak would try to come to me on the sly."

"Just a clever little stroke, that's all," said her father.

"They call him a coward, but I saw him stand up to Jack
when Jack was half crazy with his wild temper . . . that Dave
took out of him. Father, if there's gratitude in you, and I know
there is, you have to be grateful for what he did for Jack."

He merely replied: "Facts don't count with you. Right here in
Granite Creek he walks into town and gets into a brawl. At
once . . . gets into a dog fight. A dog fight! Not a man fight.
Think of that!"

"I heard that yarn. Lindy told me. The whole place is wondering and shuddering over it, and admiring Dave for what he did.
Rather than let his wolf kill the dog, he caught the great beast
by the throat . . . with his bare hands. A hundred people saw
him do it. That's what made the colonel his friend. And Colonel
Hagger is not a fool, Father."

"There's no use arguing with a woman," Clinton said gloomily. "There's always a torrent of words poured on the head of
the unlucky devil who tries to argue with a woman for her own
good. Mary, what will you say if I put down my foot and forbid
you to have anything more to do with this fellow?"

"I'll walk out of the house and find him and marry him and
go away with him."

Clinton stood up from the table, thrusting himself out of his chair with a movement of his powerful arms. "I'm ashamed to hear you talk like this, Mary," he said, the black of his eyebrows gathering. "I'll have some more to say to you at noon."

He stamped out of the house and down the hill. And when he reached his office—built on the verge of the ravine, so that from the windows he could scan every operation of importance—he found a tall, impassive figure standing at the entrance, with the gray wolf lying at his feet.

"Good morning, Mister Clinton," Dave said.

" 'Morning, 'morning," said the other. "Come in, Dave. I'm glad to see you." He took Reagan into the office and sat him on one side of the table, while he took a place opposite. "I've been thinking everything over, Dave," he said. "I was surprised yesterday when you appeared and spoke about Mary. But what I feel is not a matter of importance. What *is* important is that you want Mary, and Mary wants you. And that's that." He slapped the flat of his hand on the table and smiled at Dave Reagan.

The young man waited. He could not believe his ears.

"However, we have to be practical men," said the engineer. "The fact is that my girl has been raised one way, and you've been raised in another. Your backgrounds are different. And that makes for unhappiness, eh? Now, then, I have a plan that will put you on the same level with Mary. This is the plan. You go abroad and pick up the sort of an education that you need . . . the sort of an education that Mary and her friends have had. You travel. You pick up some languages. You broaden your mind. Say you spend two years doing that. I foot the bills with pleasure. Ten thousand a year, say. Glad . . . happy and willing to do it. The two years go by like a song. You're young. So is Mary. Too young for marriage, as a matter of fact. At the end of two years you come back, and the wedding takes place, and you'll be happy ever after, and I'll look after your business future. Now, how does that picture appeal to you?"

Dave stared. Then slowly he shook his head. "I can't do it," he said. "I can't take your money, Mister Clinton."

"Hold on!" exclaimed the other. "You can't do what? Look here, young man. Suppose you were married to Mary today, what would you do for money? How would you live?"

Dave lifted his two big hands and looked down at them vaguely. "I'd work for her," he said.

Clinton flung up his massive arms high above his head. "Go into the woods and live like an Indian? Is that what you mean?" he asked.

The young man was silent for a moment again. Then he shook his head once more. "I'd talk to her. I would want to do the thing that would make her happy. But I could never use your money."

Clinton was so overwhelmed by this remark that he rose from the table, went to the window, stared out at a world that was spinning before his eyes, and groaned with bewilderment. He was rich. He had millions. He would have still other millions before long. And the thought that the flow of them would be cut off between him and the eventual husband of his girl was a thing that baffled him. It would mean the snapping of all the wires of control. It would mean reducing him to a nonentity in the life of Mary.

He turned abruptly. "Well, lad," he said, "I thought that I could make some pleasant suggestions to you before I asked for a favor. But the suggestions haven't worked. Suppose that I put the shoe on the other foot. You won't let me do anything for you, but will you do something for me?"

The young man stood up and smiled. "I'll be glad to do that," he said.

Gray Cloud sat down before him and stared into the face of the master, canting his head to one side in the profound concentration of his study.

"As a matter of fact Dave," said the older man gravely and gently, "this is a delicate business. I thought of trusting it to Jack, but Jack isn't yet a keen enough mountaineer, and he'd be apt to go astray. You're just the fellow for the job, if you'll undertake it."

"Let me try," Dave Reagan said eagerly. "Let me try my hand. What is it?"

His eagerness merely appeared to sadden and darken the face of the other. But Clinton went on: "I want to get some money to a man who used to work for me . . . a clever fellow . . . a good brain . . . a man who gave me ideas that I'm still using in the building of the dam. But, Dave, he's a rascal. You understand? He's a rascal pure and simple. And a wave out of his past overtook him and nearly swamped him right here in Granite Creek. He ran out, escaped by the fringe of his back hair, and jumped off into the mountains, where he began herding with a gang of outlaws fed by Melvaney Jones. Ever hear of him?"

Melvaney Jones? But who had not heard of him—cunning and dangerous rascal that he was.

The face of the young man grew very grave. "Yes, yes," he said. "I've heard of him, of course. Everybody's heard of Melvaney Jones." He shook his head as he said this.

The eyes of the older man narrowed, watching him carefully. "This fellow that I'm speaking about," he said, "is called Ray Martin. Young fellow. Thirty or so. Amusing devil. Full of fun. Full of deviltry. Blue eyes. Red hair like yours . . . but a brighter red. Understand?"

"Yes," Dave said.

"I want," said the other, "to get ten thousand dollars in cash into the hands of Red Martin. Red is his nickname, d'you see?"

"Yes." Dave Reagan nodded.

"But you see my predicament?" said the other. "I want to get ten thousand dollars . . . a pretty considerable sum . . . into the hands of a man wanted by the law. Well, I could be jailed for that trick, my lad. I could be thrown into jail and given a good, stiff sentence for upholding and protecting an outlawed man. Furthermore, it's no easy job to find that crowd of thugs. I'd need a brave man and an absolutely trustworthy man. That's why I thought of giving the job to Jack. But, as a matter of fact, you're practically in the family, my lad. And in thinking the problem over, I told myself that I might win your good nature by making these other proffers to you . . . and then I'd ask you to hunt up Red Martin for me. But I don't suppose that you'll want to undertake a job like that, will you?"

"I'll start now . . . in five minutes I'll be started," said the young man.

"Will you?" asked the other critically. "You'll be wanting to say good bye to Mary first, I suppose?"

"No," Dave Reagan said. "I want to do this thing first. You've not been happy . . . thinking about me and Mary. If this will make you happier, I'll start now. I'll not think of anything else. I'll not dream of anything else. I'll say good bye and go." He held out his hand.

"Wait," said the other. "You haven't the money yet. By the eternal thunder, Dave, there's something about you that warms my heart for me, let me tell you that."

Chapter Thirty

Twenty $500 bills were wrapped in oiled silk, and the thin sheaf was handed to Dave Reagan. He took it with a smile of happiness.

"I ought to be there in two or three days, and back again in a week, at the most. Do you want me to say anything special to Red Martin for you? Shall I take a letter?"

A faint frown puckered the brow of big John Harvey Clinton. "Suppose that letter dropped out of your pocket, Dave," he said, "and a sheriff picked it up? How long would it take them to put me in jail?"

The young man nodded. "Ah, I understand," he said. He held out his great hand; the equally large and almost equally brawny paw of John Harvey Clinton met it and gripped it.

"Good bye, and good luck," said Clinton. "I'll be glad when you're safely back, Dave." Then he added in a changed voice: "You understand, Dave? It's dangerous business? You understand that ten thousand dollars is a lot of money to be carrying around? Not to you . . . no, ten thousand or ten thousand million, I suppose," he went on almost bitterly, "would not mean very much to you. But you're different from the others. There are backwoodsmen who would take your scalp for ten hundred, to say nothing of ten thousand."

"Do you think so?" the young man said naïvely. "Well, then, I'll have to be careful every moment that I'm away."

"You will," said the other. "You decidedly will. Another thing,

Dave . . . how does it happen that you speak such good English? So few slips in grammar, though you've been raised on the range?"

"My father and mother spoke carefully, and I've read a good deal in the evenings . . . and I could remember the way they talked at home. That's all."

"You're a remarkable fellow, Dave," said the engineer. "You're one of those who are not easily marked. The stains slip away from a naturally clean surface. Good bye, my lad."

"Good bye, sir."

He went out through the doorway, with the wolf running eagerly a little before him, a single step, and turning continually to watch the face of the master.

That was the picture that big John Clinton saw from the window of his office. Suddenly he stamped. "Red!" he called.

Through a door came a slender man with a quick, active, noiseless step, and flaming red hair and wildly blue eyes. "Yeah, chief?" he demanded. The other turned slowly around. "You saw him, Martin?" he asked.

"Yeah. I saw him."

"You heard what I said to him?"

"Yeah, every word."

"Do you think that you can get that money from him?"

"Why, all I have to do is to walk up and ask for it, the way you staged the play," said Red Martin.

"That's exactly it. Now listen to me . . . the point is that he's not to find you. If you can keep away from him for six weeks, say, then you can step up to him and ask for the money . . . or let him give it to you. And if you manage to keep him away that long, you can check in here again and get another ten thousand. Is that clear?"

Red Martin checked off the points. "If the big boy don't turn up here for six weeks, I'm good for the coin that's on him and another ten grand at the office."

"That's it. But, better than that, I'd like to have the money taken away from him."

"What's the general idea, chief?" asked Red Martin.

"The general idea," the big man explained, "is that if he happens to appear like a fool, and perhaps like a crooked fool, it will be satisfactory to me. Understand?"

"Suppose that I tell Melvaney Jones that there's a lone *hombre* with ten grand walking around loose in the woods . . . how long would the Reagan be carrying the hard cash?"

"You might tell Melvaney Jones," agreed the other, but he frowned as he said it.

"Let's get this straight," said Red Martin. "D'you want this fellow tapped over the head or not? That's the easiest way . . . just to roll him under the sod."

"This morning," said the other, "I would have been better pleased to have him planted underground, I think. Now I've changed my mind. There's something to him. No, no matter what happens, I don't want him harmed."

"Look," said Martin, "Melvaney Jones is a rough bird, you know. He won't be wearing gloves when he starts after ten thousand bucks."

"Tell Melvaney Jones that the point of the game is to get the money away from the young man without hurting him. Melvaney has a name for cleverness."

"Sure, he has, and he could pick the gold fillings out of that kid's teeth . . . if he's got any. Pick 'em out while he talks, and he wouldn't know they were gone till he began to eat candy the next time. Sure, he'll take the ten grand, all right . . . only, I just wondered, in case anything happened. He's hard and mean . . . is Melvaney."

"Well," the engineer said grimly, "this is not a world arranged for weaklings and fools. If the boy can't protect himself . . . let him go under. But, under the circumstances, I should say that if you play fair with me, Red, young Mister Dave Reagan will never have a chance to deliver his money, and will simply have it taken away from him on the road. I warned him of that, didn't I?"

"You warned him, fair and square. I'd like to know the lay of the land behind this game, chief."

"I've told you enough. Let it go at that."

"All right. I can't help wondering, though, how any gent like him can be worth this much trouble and cash to you. For my part, all I can do is thank you again."

"Never mind the thanks," said the other. "Do the job as I tell you to do it and we'll all be square. Are you sure you can get out of town without being recognized?"

"Sure," said Red Martin. "The gents in this town, they don't think of nothin' except the dam, and the work, and the noise, and all of that. They ain't got any eyes. All I need is a sombrero on my head to put a shadow on my face, and the mustang'll take me through the main street, and nobody'll ever look twice at me."

"Then get out there on the heels of the kid," Clinton said sharply.

"I'm gone," Martin announced, turning to the door. "Melvaney Jones will laugh his head off when he hears what an easy job this is he's got before him."

"Let him laugh, then. I've no objection to his laughing. Only, I don't want any bloodshed. You hear me? I'll double the cash all around if you turn the trick without harming that young fellow. Because he's brave, and he's honest, I think. And no matter what a fool he may be, courage and honesty are worth something to the world in these days. Now get out of here, Red. I'm playing a dirty trick, and I'm depending on you to play it straight for me. If you do it wrong, I'll manage so that nothing can hold you away from me. I'll get you and I'll do you brown. Believe that?"

"I believe you," the other said, grinning broadly.

He waved his hand and was instantly gone through the side door.

He had hardly disappeared when a man came rushing in heatedly, hardly pausing to rap at the front door, and then stood, panting, in front of the table of the engineer.

"Mister Clinton," he breathed, "I got an idea that I saw Red Martin, that's wanted by the cops, just comin' out of the side office door a minute ago."

"Red Martin? No, no . . . that's another fellow," said Clinton. "Poor Red wouldn't dare to risk his neck by riding into town."

"All right," said the other, "only I was just thinkin'. . . ."

"Don't think too much," said Clinton. "Thinking too much is what put Red Martin in jail."

"It's what brought him out again, too." The other grinned.

"Friends are what brought him out again," Clinton said sternly. "Now get on about your business."

The other, with a sober face, disappeared, but Clinton remained gloomily staring out through his window at Dave, who had not yet disappeared down the street of the town. He was going with a fine, long stride. His head was high. He could be picked out by his size and bearing, and moreover the silver wolf was close to him, like a spotlight.

It was even easy to see how people in the crowd made way for him. And he was continually raising his hand in salutation right and left.

Yes, the rough men of Granite Creek knew the youth already. It might be that he, John Clinton, would wish to know him better before the end. And he wondered darkly if he had taken the right course.

CHAPTER THIRTY-ONE

Up the slope above the dam, above the chief roar of it, above the sooty smoke and the dust clouds, where only a subdued noise pursued him constantly, Dave found Walking Thunder at the appointed place. The wolf, slipping ahead, stopped at the rock behind which the Indian was sitting, and finally Walking Thunder stood up from behind it. Gray Cloud looked back to his master for orders.

He received the sign that brought him again to heel as Reagan quickly told what had happened in the office of John Clinton.

"Let me see the money," said the Indian.

It was willingly shown at once, the oiled silk being unwrapped and the twenty $500 bills counted over, one by one.

Walking Thunder rewrapped them and shook his head. He looked less youthful than usual, more hardened and withered by time as he handed back the sum to the young man.

"So much money means so much trouble. I am too old for it. I must leave you, brother, to go on your own way," he said.

"I don't see how there can be much trouble," said Dave. "It's true that people will commit all sorts of crimes for the sake of cash. But then, on the other hand, who will know about it? Nobody would suspect me of carrying such a fortune." He looked down at his rudely made clothes and smiled.

"Tell me, brother," said the Indian, "can you know where the dead cattle are falling on the range?"

"Why, no," said the young man.

"Can the buzzards tell, though?"

"Yes," said Dave.

"How are they able to tell? Do you know?"

"Well, they have a special sense. One of 'em sees the death coming, and as that buzzard drops out of the sky, his cousin down the wind sees him go, and sails up to inquire. I suppose that's the way of it. They have a special sense. What of it, Walking Thunder?"

"I see you walk along through the woods, with your head up, taking your ease, when you're walking upwind and Gray Cloud is running ahead. Why is that?"

"Of course, that's because Gray Cloud can scent trouble of any sort a long time before I could ever see it."

"And it's the same way with money," said the Indian. "There are people in the world, brother, who can see it and scent it a thousand miles away, and they come like the buzzards and like the wolves. You will not be long on the trail before trouble begins to stalk you."

He said it with much solemnity, and the young man stared.

"Mister Clinton said the same thing," he replied. "I don't understand it, but I'll take your word for it. I don't want you to go where there's danger in the way, Walking Thunder. But perhaps you can tell me where I should look for Red Martin?"

"I never heard of his name," said the Indian. "But if he's one of the men of Melvaney Jones . . . well, I can take you to a man who'll know where to find Melvaney Jones, if he cares to talk about it. Three hours on the trail will bring us to him. Come!"

He turned at once and struck out across the hills.

A trail was what he had spoken of, but there was no sign of a trail for a single step of the way until, near the end, they came upon a winding cattle path that brought them to a wreck of a

Mexican village—one of those that once were spotted through the Southwest, but which have melted away with lack of use and care, the rains washing them, and the winds whittling them away little by little.

In the whole tangle of that little town, one adobe shack remained occupied. Two children were playing about it, and an old woman came to the shadowy doorway in answer to the voice of the Indian. She raised her hand, and from under the shelter of her hand she peered silently at them.

"Where is Miguel?" asked Walking Thunder.

She was silent still, and staring.

"I am Walking Thunder," said the Indian. "That is a name that Miguel knows."

The crone turned from the door, passed back into the shack, and presently a trailing step approached, and in the doorway stood a middle-aged man with one arm in a sling and a bandage about his head. It was a fresh wound, and poorly bandaged, for the ugly red of blood was soaking through the cloth.

There was a certain untidy gaiety about the clothes of this fellow, and a certain sneering insolence in the expression of his face that Dave Reagan disliked.

The first long, keen critical look fell upon Dave's face; the second was a mere glance at Walking Thunder.

"You want what?" asked Miguel.

"I want a favor for my friend. His name is David Reagan. He wants to find Melvaney Jones. Can you tell him where to look for him?"

"I know nothing of Melvaney Jones," the other said, lapsing into his native tongue.

"Whatever you know, brother, let me use, if you can," the Indian said in the same language. "This is an honest man, and a kind man. I understand him very well. He comes to make no trouble. He has good news for one of the companions of Melvaney Jones. Very good news."

"So?" said the Mexican. He stared critically, cynically at young Dave Reagan again. Then he answered: "Go across the range to the Winnimaw Valley. And find the ranch of *Señor* Todd. Tell him that you have come to find Melvaney Jones. And then stay near the ranch. They will try to drive you away, but stay in spite of that. After a time, if you can stay there, Melvaney Jones will come." He paused and laughed, and his laugh had a snarl in it that sent electric tinglings up the spine of the young man.

"Stay there, and Melvaney Jones will come," repeated the Mexican. Then he turned on his heel and disappeared into the shadows of the house.

"Are you going on to find the ranch of Todd?" Walking Thunder asked.

"Why, yes," said Dave. "Of course I'll go."

"You've seen the first blood on the trail," said Walking Thunder, "but it is not the last. Sometimes, my son, old men see with the marrow of their bones, and in that way I see red danger ahead for you. Take my good advice. Turn and go back to John Clinton. Give him the money and tell him that you have given up the trail."

"I can't do that," Dave said.

"Well, then," said the Indian, "it's clear that I've come to the end of the way. I can't go on where you're bound to be stepping. Good bye, brother. I'm sorry to leave you, but now you begin to lengthen your stride and step over mountains and moon and all, so that I must go."

He took the hand of the young man in a grip that lasted a long moment, while he searched the eyes of Dave Reagan. Then he turned and went rapidly back over the cattle path by which they had come to the broken little Mexican town.

Reagan turned back with a sigh. The children were no longer playing. They stood in the shadow by the house with a furtive look, as though they were ready to flee the instant that they were noticed. Under shocks of black hair, wild, active eyes glittered at him as he went past them. And so he took the trail to the Winnimaw Valley.

He climbed with that long and rapid stride that devoured miles so rapidly, up the twisting ravine, to the watershed above, and found a cañon of blue ice, far above timberline, that split through the mountain crest and gave him, from the farther side, a sight of Winnimaw Valley.

It was a wildly beautiful place, with big timber scattered everywhere, and a stream dropping down the center of it from one small lake to another.

A hard wind blew flurries of snow into the face of Dave Reagan. It was as though an invisible hand had been raised, warning him back from this place. He thought of Walking Thunder's solemn warning, and for a moment he stood without taking a step, merely leaning his body into the wind.

Gray Cloud looked back at him, the wind ruffling his hair and parting it down to the fine underwool. It seemed clear to Reagan that he had come to a distinct crossing of the ways, and that all the laws of common sense directed him to go back over the road by which he had advanced.

But something put his feet in motion, and he walked straight on down the upper slope of the valley. The instant he left the height the wind fell away to a mere breeze, and he took that as a portent. He had perhaps crossed the worst trial, and would advance into better fortune.

Up and down the valley he could see five ranch houses; he chose the second one from the top and went to it. It stood close to the creek, which swept in a half circle around it. All the ground was beaten to bare earth by the feet of men and animals; there was a tangle of corrals and sheds behind the house. The place looked like any one of ten thousand similar establishments in the West, and he felt more at home as he regarded it closely.

He went up to the door and rapped.

A voice bawled out: "Come in!"

He pushed the door open and saw a long room with bunks built against the wall on either side of it. About a rickety table in the center, three men were playing cards. Another, a monstrous figure of a man, lay sprawled on one of the bunks. He was so huge that although his knees were bent and his head was bowed down, still he filled the bunk from one end to the other.

"Is this the Todd Ranch?" Dave Reagan asked.

The three men turned their heads and looked at him. Then they looked back at one another.

He thought that he heard a quiet voice say: "It's him." But he was not at all sure that he really had made out the remark.

Then the youngest of the three asked: "What about the Todd Ranch?"

Another said: "Tie your dog outside, partner, and come on in."

With a gesture, Reagan obediently caused Gray Cloud to crouch beside the door, which he now closed, and then stood on the threshold, with his cap in his hand.

"If this was the Todd Ranch," said the youth at the center table in an insolent and careless manner, "what would that mean to you?"

"I want to reach Ray Martin," Reagan answered. "Red Martin he's called, I believe. I have a message for him, and I understand that I can find him here, perhaps."

"Perhaps you can," said the youth at the table. He held out his hand. "Gimme your message for Red Martin, will you?" he asked, yawning. "I'll get it to him."

"I have to give it to him myself," Dave said.

The youth turned with a shrug of the shoulders. The other two men glanced aside at Reagan with sinister grins. They were not a pretty lot, this trio, and it was an odd thing to find three cowpunchers on a ranch idling through a weekday when there must be a thousand things waiting to be done on the range.

"Hey, Lumber," said the young fellow. "Lumber . . . wake up!"

The giant on the bunk uncurled himself, stirred, sat up. He put his great boots on the floor and stretched his hands above his head. They seemed almost to reach the low ceiling. If he were so vast seated, what would he be when he stood up?

"Ain't this the kid that you're lookin' for, Lumber?" asked the young fellow at the table.

"Where?" asked the giant. His voice came thick and hoarse. He turned his vast head from side to side. The face was strangely misshapen, for all the upper part of it was small enough to have gone with the features of a child, but the lower part, in vast slopes, projected downward and forward. The nose was inhumanly large, the chin was still more enormous, and the mouth was an endless, crooked ravine that split the face into two halves. But the eyes of this monster were as small as the eyes of a child, and they were a pale, indeterminate color. The flesh of Dave Reagan crawled as he stared at the huge creature.

"Ain't that the fellow you want, Jack Lumber?"

The giant arose. It seemed that he would never be done lifting himself toward the ceiling of the room. "Why, I dunno," he said, "but maybe that's him. I guess maybe it is him." He took a few strides that carried him in front of Reagan, and stood there with his hands on his hips, teetering a little backward and forward on his immense feet, and grinning crookedly down at the young man.

He could not have been many inches short of seven feet, and, except for a bit of fat about the waist, he seemed in perfect condition. He was no freak, except in the face. The rest of him was nobly proportioned.

"I don't think that I've seen you before," said Reagan.

"Ain't you, brother?" The giant grinned. "But I've seen you, all right. Or, leastwise, I've heard about you. Turn around so's I can look you over." His incredible hand fairly swallowed the shoulder of Dave Reagan and turned him with a jerk toward the light of the window. "Yeah," said the giant, "you got the fool look that they said you'd have. You got the red hair, wore long. And you got the ten thousand bucks in your jeans. So just shell 'em out, brother."

Reagan, utterly amazed, stared helplessly up into the big fellow's face. But a loud and brutal laughter from the three at the center table assured him that this was not a mere nightmare, but a fact. The Indian and John Clinton had both been right—$10,000, it appeared, announced its coming from a distance, and he was made a prize in a den of thieves.

CHAPTER THIRTY-TWO

Jud Lawler was not the man to be without certain devices that were more necessary to a man in trouble than they were legal in the ring. One of them was a simple affair, but most effective when well executed. It consisted in stamping on the instep of an assailant and at the same time driving an elbow into the pit of the stomach.

Dave Reagan would have hesitated to use such means, but he saw that the three at the table had turned about in their chairs and were looking on with wide grins of appreciation at this little performance. He knew, therefore, that he could expect nothing from them in the way of fair play.

So suddenly he used the device of Jud Lawler. It was sufficient to make the giant jump away with an outcry. But, reaching full striking distance with that leap, Jack Lumber drove a fist as large as a bucket at the head of Reagan, and howled with rage and pain at the same instant with a voice that made the room tremble and overwhelmed the very mind of Reagan.

Dave sprang away, struck a chair behind him, and tumbled head over heels. A tremendous shout of laughter poured into his ears as he rolled, half stunned, to his feet, and saw the giant closing on him with arms outstretched, so sure of his prey that he was not striking, but aiming to set his talons on the smaller man. And the beastly face of him turned Reagan sick.

He ducked under those great arms, and, as he side-stepped, he drove the long left upward into the face of the huge fellow. A human face should be bony and hard to a full-weight punch, but this man's seemed loose and fleshy.

The three spectators whooped. The youngest of the crew jumped on top of the table and began to yell encouragement to both of them.

"Go it, Davie Reagan! Whop him, Lumber! Dodge him, Davie! Sock him, Jack!"

Jack Lumber was doing his best to tear the smaller man to pieces, but he was having bad luck. The room was not wide, but it was long, and it was cluttered with a chair here, a table there, and Dave Reagan seemed to have eyes in the back of his head as he fled before the hurricane of murderous anger.

He kept not at a distance, but just so that the trip-hammer blows and the clutching fingers of the other were brushing him, without effectively touching his body. For when they even touched, it was as though a great beam were driving past him.

Reagan, in turn, fought with his mind cold. That was what Jud Lawler was always telling him—the harder the fight, the more time should be taken. One solid blow is worth ten light ones. And he hit solidly, nearly always with that magic left that went in and out and let him keep still at a distance. He would have to use the right more often before the end.

Under the blows that fell on Lumber, the giant yelled with rage and with pain.

The three spectators were in an ecstasy of laughter and excitement. The young fellow who had mounted the table was yelling an offer of $100 to $50 that Dave Reagan would last out a full five minutes, and, as he shouted his bet, it was taken by one of the others greedily.

"Lumber'll get his teeth in and swaller him whole in a second or so!" he cried.

Now at that moment Jack Lumber had missed a rush and received a long left with such jarring force in it that the hair on

his head flew upward. He howled like a wild beast, and, checking his rush eagerly, he swung about, a shade off balance, to
charge again.

It was what Reagan had been waiting for. Now, as the giant
tottered, he ran straight in and smashed the craggy end of that
ponderous jaw of Lumber. He shifted and whipped the same
good right hand to the same point. He would have struck a
third time, but now he saw that the arms of the giant had fallen.
His bleeding mouth was open. He stared with small, dull eyes
at the enemy, and his huge knees began to shudder and bend.

"He's going down!" yelled the young fellow who was on the
table, and he leaped to the floor at the same time that Jack
Lumber dropped on hands and knees and so supported himself,
so brain-shocked that he wavered from side to side, his
shoulders thrusting up from the weight that was leaning on his
arms.

"We've gotta finish this job, boys!" called one of the others.
"Take him on that side, Harry. Bud, cut in behind."

Not until that instant did the slow mind of Dave Reagan
remember that there was an invaluable ally crouched outside
the house. He whistled, and into the window sprang the wolf,
and balanced there on the sill, bright silver in the shaft of the
sunlight.

Reagan himself had caught up a heavy stool and poised it,
ready to hurl. It was a small weapon, though, against three guns
that were glistening in expert hands. Panting, he said: "Back up
or I'll send the wolf in at you. He'll cut one throat before he's
finished. D'you hear?"

He had waved his hand, and Gray Cloud dipped from the
window sill and skulked in the shadows in the corner of the
room, crouched, ready to spring. A snap shot might stop him—
but, again, it might not. And though the three with their guns
were a hardy lot, none of them cared to take a chance at such

close quarters.

They hesitated, and while they paused, Reagan acted. He sprang back, threw open the door, and, as he jumped outside, his whistle brought the wolf flashing through the window to rejoin him.

Damage might have been done even in that second of time. For one marksman tried a shot at the wolf; another with a bullet split the door from top to bottom as it slammed shut. But both shots failed to reach flesh, and, running straight around the back of the house, Reagan was in another moment among the trees.

There he paused, panting, to take stock of what might happen in the pursuit. But there were no signs of pursuit for the moment. A deep, dead silence covered the house. The smoke rose with a slow, leisurely twist above the chimney. Nothing could have been more peaceful than this picture that was offered to his eyes.

Then, with a rush, came action. A door slammed open. Voices thundered in the open. And as Reagan withdrew softly through the brush, he heard the whinny of a horse, then the beating of hoofs, and finally the long, deep baying of dogs.

It was that sound that sent a dripping chill through his spinal marrow, but he turned with Gray Cloud laughing up into his face beside him, and began to run at full speed through the woods. It would take them a little while to give the scent to the dogs. In the meantime, he might be able to construct for them a small trail problem or two.

He got to a little tributary of the main creek, leaped from the bank to a stone in the center of the water, then bounded forward from rock to rock, and at the end of thirty yards jumped again to the same bank from which he had taken to the rocks.

The wolf followed, dripping, for Gray Cloud slipped from one of the stones into the swift stream. But it was a joyous moment for him. Days had been dull for him recently, but he could understand the game of flight as well as he could understand the more familiar game of a hunt. They were being pursued, and with every line of his body as he slinked forward, Gray Cloud declared his eagerness to play this game well.

Up the bank of the stream Reagan ran on for a half mile, and heard the roar of the pursuit reach the creek, pause there, and remain at the one place, the voices dwindling a little as he ran on.

Then, finding a convenient place, he went through exactly the same maneuver that he had executed before, returning to the left bank of the stream once more. They would not be quick to suspect him of trying the same trick twice in succession, perhaps, and he, in the meantime, heard the noise of the hunt rushing up the creek behind him. They had caught the true trail. He cut back through the woods and doubled straight back toward the ranch house, where he had roused this pack of cruel devils.

One thing he had not yet found out, and that was the name of the place. He had not yet learned whether he had indeed come to the Todd Ranch.

So with a calm singleness of mind, he ran on over the pine needles, and, as he doubled past the course of the hunters going upstream, he heard the men cursing the dogs and urging them forward. Loud were the threats that they uttered, these angry hunters. But Dave Reagan laughed as he ran, and the wolf sprang up and down before him, rejoicing in the game that they played, rejoicing in the wisdom of this perfect partner, whether for the hunt or for the flight.

When he came to the trees near the house, he paused for a moment to survey the lay of the land and the possibilities before him. And he saw a half-breed woman come out from the back door of the house with a bucket of dirty dishwater in her hand.

She flung the contents into the dust in two or three long, dark splashes, and a few chickens came squawking and scampering to pick in the mud for scraps of food.

The half-breed paid no heed to them, but, with her face raised and an evil grin on it, she listened to the receding clamor of the hunt of men and dogs.

Big Dave Reagan left the wolf to skulk in the shadow and walked out into the open. He saw the woman start as she eyed him, but he smiled on her.

"This the Todd place?" he asked.

She stared at him, amazed, and then shook her head, but not in answer to his question. "You kind of had me thinking that you was that same wolf man that they're huntin' up the creek. But the dogs'll be worryin' his bones for him before long. Yeah, this is the Todd place."

"I want to find Melvaney Jones," he said. It seemed a useless thing to inquire for Red Martin after his first experience.

"Melvaney? Oh, you wanna see Melvaney Jones, do you?" she repeated. She laughed, showing the wide gaps among her yellow teeth. "Maybe if you wait around a while you'll find Melvaney Jones, too," she said. "He might be near and he might be far. *I* ain't one to know."

She began to laugh again, and, still laughing, she went back into the house.

CHAPTER THIRTY-THREE

To be near this house on the Todd Ranch was like being near a leveled gun, and the mind of Dave Reagan was stimulated by that neighborhood. Something in the laughter of the half-breed woman seemed to tell him that Melvaney Jones was near, indeed. If so, he must stay close to the house to find the man.

But how could he remain close to it when the hunt for him was sure, before long, to sweep back to the ranch and circle about it, beating through the woods. He might take shelter in a tree, but the hounds would be sure to bay at the foot of it, and then keen eyes would probe the branches until he was found, and a bullet would bring him crashing to the ground.

No, there was only one safe place to be, and that was in the house itself. He walked straight forward down the side of the house, and when he came to the first window that opened upon the main room, that in which he had fought with the huge Lumber, he slipped through it.

What would happen to the wolf outside? Gray Cloud would simply wait for the return of his master, keeping in the same place. If the hounds roused him and drove him away, he would avoid them. They might as well try to catch a ghost as Gray Cloud in a woodland. When they were tired of chasing, the wolf would return.

Therefore Dave felt himself free to think only of the execution of his mission. And, standing for an instant in the long, gloomy room, he looked at the overturned furniture, and saw a spot of sunlight that made some drops of blood flash where they had fallen to the floor from the bleeding face of the giant. Into a strange and terrible land he had passed from the world of ordinary men.

He could not understand many things—above all, how these people had known that he carried the money with him, or why they were ready with such an instant and savage attack. But that problem, like many another that he had faced with his slow mind, would have to be removed to the future.

He passed out of the room on his noiseless moccasins through a rear door, and found a narrow stairs that led at a sharp angle toward the second story of the house. Up those stairs he went, treading carefully. He could hear a rattling of pans from the kitchen; at any moment the woman might open the door and discover him. Furthermore, he could hear the roar of the hunt now turned and pouring back toward the house.

The upper floor was one long bunkhouse. The walls were hung with saddles, bridles, holsters, coats, Mackinaws, hats. And on the floor beneath all of this apparel were set rows of boots and shoes in various stages of age, with wrinkled uppers leaning this way or that. The smell of old clothes and of stale cigarette smoke hung in the air.

A poor place for a man to attempt to hide, surely.

He stared about him carefully, but with his heart beating more and more wildly, for the cry of the hunt was sounding close to the ranch. Above, cut in the very center of the ceiling, was an opening into an attic. At one side of the room leaned the ladder that was used for mounting to the attic compartment. But if he used that, it would instantly bring the pursuit after him, of course.

He stared closely at the opening, which was in height between nine and ten feet from the floor. He made up his mind at once, and, running lightly forward, bounded high. His fingers brushed the edge of the open hole in the ceiling—that was all. And, in landing, he made his whole body loose, so that he would not crash on the floor with a loud shock.

So did he soften the fall, in fact, that it was only a deep, soft thud that could be heard, though a tremor seemed to run down through the frame of the building, as when an earthquake stirs the earth. He prayed that the half-breed woman in the kitchen would not notice that sound or that tremor, for at that moment the hunt broke from the woods, and the cry of the dogs swept around the house like water rushing around an island when a dam has burst.

Fine cold sweat broke out upon Dave's face. He backed into a corner, set his teeth, and ran forward again. This time he bounded a little higher than before, and, thrusting up one hand only, he was able to reach some vital inches higher than before. The whole of his great weight fell with a wrench upon that shoulder. But his grip held. His left hand now joined the right, and in a moment he had drawn himself up through the opening.

He found himself in the attic, which was a very narrow and cramped space with the rafters crossing only a foot or so from the floor. A low and crowded forest of beams extended the length of the building. He writhed like a snake toward a corner, but as he went, fear made him careful, and he tried the boards cautiously to learn how much they gave and squeaked beneath him. They seemed firmly enough in place, but as for the sounds they might be making, he could not be sure, for the noise outside the house was now very great.

When he had found a secure place, or at least as secure a corner as was there, he lay flat. Before him extended a thick array of the beams. Only through a narrow slit could he see the dark streak that marked the opening in the floor. Just above him, and to the side, there was a second opening, which gave onto the roof. If it had been dark, he would have climbed through it instantly and taken to the roof, for now he heard a well-known sound from the nearby woods—the sharp yelp of a wolf scared into rapid action by a sudden danger.

That was Gray Cloud; the hounds had beaten him out of cover. Now let his swift legs stand him in stead. Now let his cunning brain teach him how to swerve and dodge so that never a bullet might strike him.

Guns exploded with a sudden chattering. The young man held his breath lest the noise of the dogs should die away. But no, the flood of sound streamed swiftly away from the house. Gray Cloud might be hurt, but at least he was not kept from fleeing. Each second the noise diminished. It seemed to drop out of ken into a hollow; it rose more dimly and distantly from a farther rim. And then, louder than the rest, came a single long-drawn, yelling cry. *A death cry,* thought Dave to himself.

Minutes passed. The cry of the hunt had died out entirely, and now came snorting horses and the voices of men back toward the house.

Was that the death cry of Gray Cloud that he had heard? His heart shrank small in him.

Straight up to the house came the cavalcade. There were a surprising number of men, to judge by the voices.

And now, one speaking in a clear, abrupt tone of command was saying: "Look here, Minnie. You see anything come back here near the house?"

"I seen a man comin'," said the voice of the half-breed woman. "He was a big man, with long, copper-colored hair, pretty nigh like an Injun, and his skin was pretty nigh like the skin of an Injun, too, but I reckon that the sun had burned him up a good deal, because his eyes was gray."

"You old fool," said the other. "Where did he go? What did he say to you?"

"Wanted to know if this was the Todd Ranch. That was what he wanted to know. If he was the man you was after, I reckoned that he'd know that this was the Todd Ranch, all right. He said could he find Melvaney Jones around, and I said I didn't know, maybe Melvaney Jones was near, and maybe he was far."

"He's been back here," said the man, his voice rising above the others, a clamor of wonder and of anger. "The dog-gonedest coolest bit of work that I ever heard of. Doubled right back here. Hey, Sam, try to put those dogs on the scent of him again, will you?"

And then a familiar voice said: "I dunno . . . the wolf was hangin' around near the house. You don't think that he could've gone back into the house, do you?"

The heart of Dave grew smaller than ever, and colder. For, unless his memory was a traitor to him, among the party that hunted for his life was his cousin, Pete Reagan!

"You know him better'n I do," said the first speaker. "Would he have the brains to go into the house . . . would he be fool enough to trap himself in there?"

"I dunno, Melvaney," said the voice of Pete Reagan. "Maybe he would, and maybe he wouldn't . . . one of the most foolish things about him is that he dunno when to be rightly afraid."

CHAPTER THIRTY-FOUR

"He'll learn something more about the right time to be afraid before he's through with me," Melvaney Jones declared. "Sam, can you get those fool dogs workin' at all?"

And a voice growled in answer: "They got the heart tore out of 'em. There's Major and Doc all tore up and sick with the hurt of their wounds, and them and the rest are feelin' mean and low because they seen Tiger killed before their eyes. I reckon that they didn't think anything under a grizzly would be able to kill Tiger, but that gray devil, he went and done it, all right."

"Where were you then . . . where were the rest of you?" exclaimed Melvaney Jones. "You were a quarter of a mile ahead of me because my fool of a horse started in pitching. But why couldn't the rest of you be up close enough to shoot that wolf before it came murderin' in among the dogs?"

"It happened mighty quick, and right in the thick of the brush," said Sam. "I was lookin' out sharp, and Tiger, he was givin' tongue and runnin' lickety-split, with the rest of the pack right close in behind him. And then I heard a snarl and a crashin' in the bush like a coupla bears had been started. And then comes the death howl of Tiger. You seen how his body was cut up like knives had been at him?

"And right then, out of the brush and in among the hounds come that jumpin', dodgin' bit of gray lightnin', and gives it to the dogs right and left, and when I out with a gun and tried to put a slug of lead into him, he slides under the belly of my hoss

and into a clump of brush, and I shoot ag'in at the gray streak
of his tail . . . but that was all I could do, and I couldn't get the
dogs to work no more on that trail with any heart. They wanted
to go back and howl a piece around where Tiger was layin'
dead. That was how it was."

"I've got no more men around me," Melvaney Jones said
angrily. "I've got just a pile of lunkheads and fools. You, there
. . . Pete Reagan . . . you dunno whether or not your cousin
would be apt to go back inside the house?"

"I dunno," said Pete Reagan. "There ain't any tellin'. He's
likely to do pretty nigh anything."

"I thought you called him a half-wit around your house?"
Melvaney Jones said. "I reckon that *he* wasn't the half-wit,
though . . . not in *that* house!"

No one laughed at the brutal witticism.

Pete Reagan spoke with a snap. "You can't start in callin' my
family half-wits, Melvaney!" he exclaimed, and his cousin, listening high above, was surprised at the spirit with which Pete dared
to speak to the famous outlaw.

"Aw, shut up," Melvaney Jones said carelessly. "The point is
that the dogs ain't worth anything to foller the trail from now
on. We'll have a look inside the house. If the wolf was hangin'
around that close to it, maybe his boss is inside. He was askin'
for Melvaney Jones, and maybe he's goin' to see him sooner
than he thinks for."

They trailed into the house. The stamping feet were distinctly
audible in the ground floor, and then the narrow stairs began to
groan under the weight of many feet.

Now they mounted into the upper bunk room, and through a
crack in the floor Dave Reagan stared down at them.

He saw his cousin among the rest who were rummaging here
and there, peering under the bunks, aimlessly lifting blankets, as
though the great bulk of Dave Reagan could have been

compressed to a width of an inch. But among all the rest, he did not need help to point out to him the form of the great Melvaney Jones. That gorilla bulk of shoulder and chest and vast, dangling arms set upon the ridiculously short and out-bowed legs was enough to identify him, to say nothing of a face that had been described a thousand times for its brutality of jaw and mouth and brightness of tiny eyes, and shabbiness of brow. He was an animal, not a man, but a clever animal, and one who never yet had been fairly cornered by the law. He stood in the center of the floor, staring around him.

Then the voice of Lumber growled heavily: "I'll have my hands on him . . . somebody else can have the money. That ain't what I want of him, by a long shot."

The face of Jack Lumber was hideously distorted by the blows that had fallen on it. On the left side there was nothing except a great red bruise on the side of the chin, but the right side was cut and puffed out of recognition where the magic long left had landed with terrible force again and again.

"If we get him, maybe we'll throw him to you, Lumber," said Melvaney Jones. "But I dunno. Unless we tie one of his hands behind him, maybe that wildcat'll claw the life out of you."

"Leave me have a fair grip on him, is all I ask for," said the giant. "That's all I want, is a fair grip on him."

"He ain't here," said one of the men. "There ain't a place where a hulk like that could be stowed. Besides, he ain't likely to've come back here. Not even a half-wit would come back to wait for you in your own house, Melvaney."

Melvaney Jones chuckled. "Yeah, and maybe not," he said. "But what about him being up there in the attic?"

"How would he get there?" Pete Reagan asked, canting his head to one side. "There's the ladder over in the corner, where it always is. How would he climb up through the thin air?"

"He could jump, maybe," Melvaney Jones suggested. "He's

such a wildcat that maybe he could jump."

"Let Lumber try," suggested Pete Reagan.

"Here, Jack," commanded Melvaney Jones. "You take a jump and try to catch the edge of the floor up there. Don't pull the roof down on us, though, if you can help it."

Jack Lumber measured the distance, nodded, and then, running forward with steps that made the house quake, he stamped down on one foot and sprang for the ceiling. His fingers brushed the edge of the opening, and he came down with a crash of breaking boards.

"Look out . . . you'll dive clean through to the next floor," Melvaney Jones said, laughing. "I reckon that he couldn't get up that high in the air, eh? What about it, Pete? You know what he can do."

"There ain't hardly anybody that knows just what he can do," said Pete. "He could beat Jack up with his hands, and maybe he could jump higher, too."

"It won't cost much to take a look," said another.

The ladder was brought and put in place. And big Dave Reagan gathered himself—then he relaxed once more. He was helpless against their guns if they found him. He would simply have to surrender and come down among them—to be given to the vast hands of terrible Jack Lumber.

Melvaney himself mounted the ladder.

As his head came up through the opening, Pete Reagan said: "He could always climb like a cat. He liked walkin' through trees better than walkin' on the ground. I bet that he's perched up in the trees somewhere like a cat. That's where he is."

Melvaney Jones rolled his bright, small eyes around the attic, but he looked down to the others again at once. "He ain't up here," he said. "I might've known that he wasn't up here. Boys, we'll scatter and have a look through the trees. But he's had plenty of time to get out before this." He climbed back down the ladder.

It seemed to young Dave Reagan that the eyes of the bandit had looked fairly and squarely into his own, during one electric moment of agony—but there he was, visibly returning to the men below.

"Scatter out around the house, boys," he said. "I'm goin' to get him if I have to spend a year lookin'. He's cost me the best dog that I ever had the first day that he come to call. And I'm goin' to have enough blood out of him to make up for Tiger. The gent that brings him down out of a tree, or up out of a hole in the ground, or wherever he is, is a friend of mine . . . and you boys all know what that means to me."

They went down the stairs, all except Pete Reagan, who sat down on a bunk, and began to pull off his boots.

"You, too, Pete. You'd recognize him quicker than the rest," Melvaney Jones said.

"I've gotta get out of these new boots," Pete Reagan said. "They're killin' me. I'll be down in a minute." And as their heads disappeared below the level of the floor, he sang out after them: "Look for somebody a dog-gone' sight bigger than what he looks to be. He don't seem no six foot three till he starts movin' close to you!"

The others went downstairs and out into the open, from where their voices seemed strangely far away.

Dave Reagan drew a great breath, but he drew it carefully, for even a sigh might be heard. Now he saw his cousin, in stocking feet, pick up a coiled lariat and run up the ladder. As his head and shoulders rose above the level of the attic floor, he whispered: "Dave . . . Dave. Where are you?"

Then, as Dave Reagan lay still, amazed and half frightened by the whispered summons, his cousin saw him and pointed.

"Dave," he muttered, "I knew you'd be up here. I knew that

you'd play the game the wild way. But you're wrong. These gents don't aim to play square with you. Murder is their middle name, every one of 'em."

Dave Reagan, amazed at any show of concern for him in the voice of the other, lifted to his knees. "Then what are you doing among 'em, Pete?" he asked.

"I'm a fool," Pete said. "I had a scrap with pa and Hank after you left. I've been on the drift ever since. Kid, you gotta get out of here. You wanna find out where Red Martin is, ain't that the game?"

"Yes. Where is he?"

"I dunno. They don't talk much to me about this, because they're afraid that I'll remember we got some of the same blood in us . . . though I ain't been actin' as if we had. Will you listen to me?"

"Yes, I'll listen."

"Then keep clear of Melvaney Jones. Wait till it's dark, climb onto the roof, and let yourself down with this here rope. Then start going, and go fast and go far. Because Melvaney Jones is a worse devil than any you ever saw. I tell you, and I know. I thought I was mean enough to fit in any crew, but these here are fiends . . . they've scared me into wantin' to go straight again. Dave, good luck. Heaven help you if Melvaney puts his hands on you."

He ducked down the ladder again and hurried to pull on an old pair of boots.

CHAPTER THIRTY-FIVE

To lie in wait with anxious thoughts meant nothing but pain and effort to no avail. Nothing could be done, it seemed, until the darkness fell. Therefore, Dave Reagan pillowed his head on one mighty arm and fell asleep, suddenly, as by a special command.

When he wakened, he was buried in thick blackness, and so far forgot where he was that he lifted his head suddenly, for he thought that he heard the roar of an engulfing stream that was rushing down upon him in a cañon.

The lifting of his head bumped it solidly against a beam, and when the shower of stars had ceased whirling before his eyes, he remembered thoroughly where he was, and the murmur of noise had sunk into the sound of talking voices.

Someone laughed, a loud, bawling laughter.

Dave got up, using the sense of feeling in his hands in the place of a light. The rope he knotted around one of the rafters. He pushed open the skylight, climbed onto the roof, and looked out on the night.

All was placid. There was only a whisper of wind, now and then, about his ears, and a vague and faraway rushing noise as of waters, through the forest. Beneath him, the vibrant human voices continued to sound. They were sitting around the supper table, probably, chattering and drinking their coffee. As for him, he was so hungry that before he made another move, he drew up his belt two notches. He yawned, stretched, and then gave his thoughts to the wolf. *Where was Gray Cloud now? Driven away from the house into a distance, and now resuming his old life with little thought of his human companion?*

It was not that Dave Reagan felt a sense of loss of possession, but, rather, it was a sense of the loss of a great and understanding companion. They had known hunger, weariness, cold, and heat together, and that association was worth more than words to them.

He tested the strength of the rope now, found that it would endure his weight easily, threw the loose end of the coil over the edge of the roof, and heard it slap the ground beneath. Then he swung over the edge, and lowered himself until his feet were upon the ground.

An instant later, something sniffed at his leg, and he dropped his hand upon the great head of the wolf. Gray Cloud flung himself into a transport of joy, like a colt in a pasture, except that in this case, as he hurled himself again and again at his human friend, there was not a sound made except the soft beating of the pads against the dusty ground.

At length a hiss from the man made him quiet. Dave Reagan caught him by the scruff of the neck, knitting his fingers well into the loose fur and hide, and shook him violently. It was the only caress that had any meaning to Gray Cloud; it would have broken the neck of an ordinary dog.

Dave stepped around the side of the house with the wolf close at his heels, and, at the window that gave upon the long room, he looked in on the crowd.

The original four had increased to eight men, and there was not a one who was less than a picked champion. Even Pete Reagan looked a man, and a strong man, among the rest of them. And this surprised the youth who watched them through the window.

Yes, Pete might figure well even in a savage crew like this, but it rejoiced the heart of Dave that his cousin had come to loathe them.

At the head of the table sat Melvaney Jones, with four men strung down one side of the long table, and three upon the other. The half-breed was picking up the plates with a great clattering, and the men were filling their coffee cups for a second or a third time, the aromatic fumes of the liquid coming in a sweet agony to the face of Dave Reagan.

Melvaney Jones picked up a ten-gallon stone jug, bent it over one mighty wrist, and so, leaving his left hand unoccupied, poured forth a stream of pale, amber liquid. He passed the jug to Jack Lumber. He splashed out a cupful of the moonshine with consummate ease, with the huge muscles of his forearm bulging until they threatened to burst the flannel shirt that covered them. He passed on the great jug; the next man used both hands to receive it and rose to do his pouring. So did the others. Only in Jack Lumber and in the chief there was power of hand to wield the massive and clumsy weight with a single hand.

Dave wondered, as he watched. He did not envy them the drink, but he wondered if he also could manage it with a single hand. Obviously the tales of the terrible strength of Melvaney Jones were not exaggerated. It seemed clear to the young man at the window that in the squat body of Melvaney Jones there was concentrated as much or more actual power than was spread through all the vaster bulk of Jack Lumber. If they were cornered, man to man, how would he, Dave Reagan, fare with such an enemy?

It was of deeds of might that they were talking now. And that same fellow who had pranced on top of the table and offered $100 that Dave Reagan would last five minutes against the giant, now was declaring loudly: "That bird, he knew how to handle himself. He's been a prize fighter, ain't he, Pete?"

"He could be," Pete said with a family pride. "I'll tell you what he done. . . ."

"He had luck with me," snarled Jack Lumber. "That's all he had . . . luck. He hit me when I was off balance, was all that he did."

"Aw, shut up, Jack," said the first speaker. "He knew how to fight. He had something in his left, like an electric shock. Every time he touched you with that hand, he hurt you. I seen your hair fly up from your head every time he grazed you with that left."

"He had luck, was all," said Jack Lumber.

"Aw, shut up," Melvaney Jones commanded.

Jack Lumber pushed back his chair. "I been told to shut up a couple or three times. I'd like to see the gent that could *make* me shut up!" he exclaimed.

"Which way you wanna look?" snapped the young fellow who had danced on the table top that day.

"You're talkin' of guns. I don't mean murder. I mean hands," Jack Lumber said, thrusting out his battered jaw as he spoke.

"Well, look this way then," the chief of the gang said.

The giant jerked his shoulders around and faced Melvaney Jones. "You been askin' for something for a long while," said Jack Lumber.

Chapter Thirty-Six

"Yeah, and I can take it," Melvaney replied to Lumber. "The part of the world where I was raised . . . well, look at here . . . they'd use a big lump like you for the roustabout. They wouldn't mix him in with the real men. They wouldn't have him sittin' at the table, if you know what I mean."

The jaw of Jack Lumber thrust out farther than ever. "Yeah," he said, "I know what you mean, and I know that you're a bluff. For your size, you're all right, but your size, it ain't much."

"Ain't it?" Melvaney Jones asked pleasantly.

"No, it ain't," insisted Jack Lumber.

"Lemme tell you something, boy," said Melvaney.

"You go on and try to tell me something, then," the giant said.

"I'll put your hand down for you," said Melvaney.

"There ain't anybody in the world that can put my hand down," said the other. "Don't you be a fool, Melvaney!"

The other rested the elbow of his right arm on the edge of the table. "Here's lookin' at you, strong man," he said. He sneered as he spoke.

"Why, I'll break your arm for you," said the giant. And he laughed, putting down his arm opposite.

In fact, disproportionately long as were the arms of Melvaney for his height, yet the hand of the giant was inches above him, a crushing advantage.

"All right," said the chief. "Take your favorite hold."

Their hands locked, and big Jack Lumber threw his whole weight behind the forward thrust with which he strove to break down the resistance of Jones. The arm and the hand of Jones went back. But after receding a little, it steadied. It inclined back from the vertical. A great shuddering took hold of it. Suddenly the head of Jones dropped. His shoulders rose in a great double hump behind his shaggy head. But the arm, instead of giving way, steadied more and more.

There was a ripping sound. The sleeve of Melvaney's shirt split from wrist to elbow and fell back, revealing a great hairy forearm transformed into a mass of small, writhing serpents, as the great muscles worked. The tendons at the wrist stood out in white lumps. A look of bewilderment came over the huge, deformed face of the giant. And as he swore softly, the shorter arm of Melvaney Jones thrust up, and gained a vertical position.

"It ain't possible," said the giant.

But it *was* possible.

And, little by little, the massive forearm of the giant went back and back. It did not seem a matter of mere physical strength, but rather something of the mind, of the unquenchable flames of energy that burned in Melvaney Jones. For, slowly, slowly, down went the arm of the giant. His face was a ghastly thing to watch. He was biting at the air, blinking his eyes. Then, with an audible crunch, his wrist bent sharply back. Was it only the rubbing of bone on bone and the play of tendons? Or was it the actual breakage of something? Jack Lumber groaned aloud, and his hand hit the table with a resounding thump as the burly arm of the other forced it down.

What a yell, then, went up from all of those throats. Every muscle of Dave Reagan was tensed, also, as he saw the thing happen, the incredible marvel, as he would have called it. But there it was, and the huge arm of the giant had been put down by the gorilla arm of the smaller man. There was something inhuman, something disgusting in this act. It was like beast fighting with man.

The giant sat stunned. Melvaney Jones lifted a face that was gray and drawn. His whole body was shaking. "You got something in you, after all, Jack," he said. "That was a trick that I put you down with . . . a trick of the wrist."

The giant looked down sadly at his massive hand that had failed him twice in one day. "I seemed to turn all to putty," he muttered.

"I need a drink," said the other. He snatched up the massive jug, which had been returned to his side, and poured the drink, sloshing as much on the table as he got into the cup. Then, putting the jug down, he grasped the cup. The shuddering of his hand spilled another portion. He grasped the right hand at the wrist with the left, and, so steadied, bore the cup to his mouth, tilted back his head, so that the great, swarthy throat was exposed, and drank. After that, he dropped his head once more, as though he had felt a bullet crash through the brain. His head fell again into the hollow of his arm. He sat motionlessly, while the others looked on a moment in a silent awe.

Then Pete Reagan said: "Lemme tell you gents something. When the day comes that the chief and Dave ever meet up with one another . . . that'll be a fight, and a grand fight. They got the same stuff in 'em."

"Them two?" said another man. "Why, the chief'll eat him. He's got the speed . . . and he can put down the hand of the big boy."

Jack Lumber, disconsolate, continued to stare at the hand that had failed him. Now he muttered: "I wouldn't mind much, cutting that hand off. It ain't no good."

Pete Reagan was saying: "Dave's got the same thing. He's able to save himself up, and then explode everything in a second, is what he's able to do. I never seen anything like it, except the chief. If ever they meet up, that's goin' to be a fight."

The chief jerked up his head. "Yeah," he said, "maybe you're right. Maybe that'd be a fight worth havin'." He leaped to his feet. There was fire in his eye. "I tell you what's the matter with this here life that a gent leads . . . there ain't anything to it. There ain't any sort of real work to do. Gents . . . they're made of putty. There ain't any real work to do."

He extended both of his vast arms, and muttered: "I tell you what . . . one of these days, I'd give my soul to fight it out, hand to hand, tooth to tooth . . . if you know what I mean . . . for the life . . . bare hands to bare hands. But the whole lot of you . . . you couldn't make a match with me. You're all putty. There ain't the makings of one real man in the whole lot of you." He made a gesture. "I'm goin' to go out and get a whiff of air, and forget the tribe of you."

In silence they watched him striding for the door. Their eyes did not seek one another in shame, or in anger, or in revolt. There was simply acceptance, and wonder, and admiration, and fear in every face of that brutal lot as they watched their master stride to the door, fling it open, and hurl it shut with a report like a pistol shot.

He stepped down into the darkness, blinded by the dark of the night, and as he stepped, big Dave Reagan, waiting half crouched, straightened, lunged in, and with all his might, with all the speed of his hand, with all the twisting strength of his body, smashed home the blow, and found the very button.

He stepped back, and waited for the man to fall a disintegrating wreck to the ground. Instead, the clumsy gorilla-like figure merely staggered several paces, and stooped over, as though to steady himself by touching one hand against the ground.

Reagan leaped in again, with a wild panic throttling him. If he lost that early advantage that he had gained, what would happen in a fight with this beast of a man? So he leaped in, cat-like, and smote again, and again found the very end of the chin.

This time, the second shock, with all that the man had been through immediately before, told the story, and the clumsy bulk of Melvaney Jones slumped to the ground.

For an instant, big Dave Reagan waited. It seemed to him that the sound of the two blows he had delivered, like the clapping of hands together, must bring out a flood of men from within the house. If not that, then the sound of the falling body. But no, not a footfall came toward them. Inside the house, the blanket of awful silence still covered them all, and kept them hushed.

So Reagan gathered up the body in his arms, and carried him out toward the nearest barn, where he had seen horses taken. There was not a stir in the weight he bore as they reached the barn. He thrust the door back, careful not to allow the rollers to make a loud noise upon the running rail on which the weight of the door rested. Then he reached inside and found what he wanted—a bridle hanging close to the door. He took it from the peg, tore the reins away, and then burst the leather of the strong reins with a powerful twist of his hands. With the two ends, he lashed the hands of his captive, separately and together.

The man began to stir a bit and groan. Dave reached, next, into the clothes of Melvaney Jones and found two revolvers in armpit holsters, and a long, heavy Bowie knife. He appropriated all three. Later, when he had a chance to search more thoroughly, he might be able to find still other weapons, more carefully hidden. But in the meantime, this was enough to fill his hands. There was a groan, and a deep sigh from the prisoner, and then silence. With a loose end of the reins, Dave Reagan tied his captive to the nearest manger. Melvaney Jones found his feet and stood swaying in the darkness.

The young man stepped back to the side of the door, found a lantern with the first reach of his hand, opened and lit it.

"Pick out the best two horses here, Melvaney," he said. "Because you and I are going to ride together."

He was amazed, in spite of his order, when a perfectly clear and calm voice answered him: "Take the roan and the big bay gelding. They're the best. And when you and I ride together, Reagan, we gotta ride on the best, or on nothin' at all."

His senses must have completely returned to him only the second before, and yet he spoke as though all of this had happened in the full sunshine of perfect self-possession, and not through the mist of a stunned brain.

Dave Reagan found the roan, built long and low, with a lump of a head but with quarters and shoulders worthy of the bearing of a king, and the tall bay gelding, as beautiful as the other was ugly, and filled with a stately strength. He saddled and bridled the pair. He picked off two quirts. Then he led the horses out of the barn, tied the lead rope of the roan to the pommel of the saddle of the bay, and returned to bring out his prisoner. He helped him to mount, and when he was seated on the roan, he took his own place on the back of the bay.

"Well, kid, you wanna know the way to Red Martin, don't you?" Melvaney Jones asked.

"That's the way that I want to ride," said Dave.

"Well," Melvaney Jones went on, "you come to headquarters to find out, all right. But suppose that Red Martin, he don't want see you, kid?"

"That doesn't matter, very much, I suppose," said Dave. "My job is to find him. That's really all I know."

"The big boy sent you, eh?" Melvaney Jones asked.

Dave Reagan looked far into the night, toward the brightness of the stars. Nothing, it seemed to him, could have been stranger since the beginning of time than the calm, steady voice of the brute who sat on the roan horse beside him.

"Who do you mean?" he asked.

"I mean . . . you know . . . J.H. Clinton. He sent you, kid, didn't he?"

"Well . . . that doesn't matter, either," young Reagan said, amazed again by this information that the whole world seemed to have.

"You been sold," said the bandit. "But you want me to take you to Red, anyway, eh?"

"That's where I want to go," Dave said.

"Suppose," said the other, "that I forget all about the couple pokes that you took at my jaw, and everything like that. Suppose that I just figger it out that you and me could work together. Because you got brains, and a pair of hands . . . and I got brains and a pair of hands, too, though you mightn't believe all of that."

"I believe it," Dave said.

"Why, then," Melvaney Jones said brightly, "you and me could do something together, couldn't we? Why would you wanna waste your time on Red Martin, when Red Martin's boss would work with you and do something for you?"

"I've got to find Martin," Dave said, more startled than ever by this amiable talk.

"I never thought that nobody could do it to me," murmured the other. "I never thought that nobody could put me out, even when my head was turned. Not even with a chunk of lead pipe. I didn't think that anybody could put me out. But you done it. It wasn't with a club that you socked me, was it, kid?" There was only gentle and pleasant inquiry in his voice.

"No, not with a club," Dave assured him slowly.

"Well, well, well," murmured the other. "Don't that beat everything, though? Come along, and we'll look up Red for you."

Chapter Thirty-Seven

Under the guidance of Melvaney Jones, they rode up to the cañon of the Winnimaw, where the waters were closed in by high rocky walls, and hardly more than a vibration of sound came from the running waters, the roar of them being confined and flung straight up against the sky.

They were a scant half hour, at a walking pace, before they came to a cabin with a dull light shining through the open doorway.

"There's your man. There's Red, where that light is," Melvaney Jones announced. Then he laughed, adding: "You go in and give him your present, and see how glad he is." He chuckled again as he ended.

But Dave could make nothing of this mirth. "I'd like to turn you loose, Melvaney. But I'm afraid to."

"Why?" asked Jones. "The minute that I'm freed, I ride back to the Todd place and pull the saddle and the bridle off this nag, and go into the house and get to bed. You think that I'm goin' to let anybody guess that I been kidnaped?"

"You might do as you say," Dave reasoned aloud, "or again, you might come in behind me when I'm there in the cabin with Martin . . . that seems more likely to me. I'm afraid that I've got to try to tie you up and keep you here, Melvaney. I don't want to, but it seems to me that I have to do it."

"Anything you say, brother," Melvaney Jones said with great good nature.

So it was that they dismounted, and, with the rope that hung at his saddle horn, big Dave Reagan tied his prisoner to a tree, hand and foot. He apologized as he drew the ropes tight, and added: "The minute that I'm through with Martin, I'll come back and set you free, Melvaney. I don't want to take you in with me. They say that you're wanted and that there's a price on your head, but I don't want blood money."

"You don't, eh?" Melvaney Jones commented. "Now, how does that come, kid?"

Reagan stared upward into the darkness toward the east, and there he saw the pale glow of moonrise commencing. He answered: "There's a price on the head of Gray Cloud, too. And how would I feel if he were shot for the sake of that price, Melvaney?"

"Me and a wolf, eh? Kind of the same?" Melvaney chuckled.

"I don't know," Dave said. "They say some bad things about you, but I'm no judge. They said plenty of bad things about Gray Cloud, too, but he's meant more to me than any man."

He stepped away through the darkness, and went straight toward the door of the cabin. He was only careful to make his step noiseless. As for the stalking, Gray Cloud attended to that, for he crawled ahead, and, flattening on his belly at the open door of the shack, his body grew rigid, and his head pointed a little to the side.

To the right of the doorway, then, inside the cabin, there was something worth attention. And what could that be except Red Martin?

So Dave stepped quietly into the doorway, and, glancing inside, he saw a half-ruined hut with a fire burning in a rickety stove at one end of the room, and an odor of food clinging in the air. To the right of the doorway, the light was given by a lantern that sat on an apple box, and on a stool beside it was a slender fellow with a rim of flaming red hair showing under the edge of his hat. He was reading a much worn and rumpled magazine. A veritable river of pleasure ran through the heart of the young man, as he saw the end of his quest so close before him.

"Hello, partner," he said, and stepped forward into the room with the snaky head of the wolf advancing beside his knee, lowered, as Gray Cloud made himself ready for a spring.

The other jumped up from his stool with a muttered exclamation, and his startled eyes had a look of horror in them, it seemed to Reagan, as he noted the wolf and then the size of the man.

"Dave Reagan," he muttered.

"And you're Red Martin?" said Reagan.

"Yeah, and what else would I be?" Martin said grimly. His teeth snapped at the close of the last word. "Who steered you to me?" he asked finally.

"Who steered me? Why, it wouldn't be right for me to use any names, I'm afraid," said Dave. "You don't seem glad to see me, and you seem to know who I am, but you can't know that I'm bringing you money . . . a great lot of money, Martin." He smiled as he reached inside his pocket and brought out, at last, the slender sheaf of bills, in their wrapping of oilcloth. These he held out. "If you'll count them, Martin," he said, "you'll find that there's ten thousand dollars there, in five-hundred-dollar bills. John Harvey Clinton asked me to bring the money to you."

"Oh, blast you and the coin and J. Harvey Clinton, too," Red Martin said, grinding his teeth. He snapped his fingers at the proffered cash, and, turning from his visitor, he walked hastily up and down the shack for an instant.

Dave Reagan watched him from under lowered brows. At last he said: "I've brought you the money, Martin."

"I won't take it . . . I won't have it," said Martin.

Reagan scowled more darkly. "I don't know what the trouble is," he said, "but I know that I've been tricked and fooled in a thousand ways. I don't mean to be tricked and fooled now. You'll take the money, Martin . . . if I have to ram it down your throat."

"Will I?" Martin asked. He whirled, his face wrinkled with a thousand lines of anger. And he was drawing his gun as he turned.

Dave Reagan caught his hand just in time. "Don't do that," he said.

Martin groaned under the pressure. "Somebody did me in, or you'd never've found me," he declared.

"Why didn't you want me to find you?" asked Dave.

"You're a fool," Martin snarled. "You wouldn't understand." Then he snapped: "Here, give me the money!" He took the sheaf, flipped one end of it with a grunt, and a shrug of his shoulders, and then snarled: "You want a receipt, eh?"

"I'll have to have a receipt," Dave responded.

"I wouldn't believe it," groaned Red Martin, and he took out an old envelope from his pocket, and a bit of pencil. "I wouldn't believe that anybody would do me dirt, like this." He scratched: *Received from Dave Reagan, $10,000. Ray Martin.*

The envelope he threw to Dave, who caught it out of the air, and placed it carefully in his pocket.

The strange behavior of Red Martin, after all, hardly mattered to him. All that was important was that he had reached the end of the trail, and that he had made the delivery in due course. Now he could return to Granite Creek, and there he would find Mary Clinton. It was as though life had been smoothed for him at a stroke of the hand. The future lay clear and easy before him, with happiness all the way to the end.

"You've done a job, and a good job," said Red Martin. "And you were double-crossed from the start."

"I?" Dave said, amazed.

"Yeah, you." Red Martin sneered. "Look . . . I was in old man Clinton's office two minutes after you left it. I was there listenin', all the time that he was talkin' to you." He trembled with a savage pleasure, as he betrayed the secrets of his benefactor. Animal joy was in his face.

Dave Reagan shook his head. "I don't understand," he said blankly. "If you were there . . . how could you . . . why should Mister Clinton have sent me on the trail to find you? I don't understand at all."

"Sure you don't, because you're a dummy," snapped Ray Martin. "You fool, all he wanted was to get you out of the way. Would he want his girl throwed away on a big half-wit like you? No, he wouldn't, so he figgers to get you out on the trail. Yeah, he's bright. I was to just keep away . . . and then I'd've got twenty thousand, instead of ten. Yeah, and maybe something happened to you, and you don't come back . . . why, I guess that wouldn't make old man Clinton break into tears. Not a bit, it wouldn't. He had you framed. He had you framed good, but you got a break in the luck, that's all."

Gradually the plan dawned clearly upon Dave's mind. So all of that bluff and hearty kindness on the part of Clinton, all of the sympathy was a pretense, and nothing more. He groaned aloud, for Clinton was the father of the girl. There should have been, in the esteem of the youth, a sacred place reserved for such a man.

"Martin, d'you really think that he wanted me to be killed on the trail?"

Martin, savage with disappointment, puckered his face with hate and rage as he answered: "Sure, he did. What else would he want? Didn't he tell you to try to locate me through the gang of Melvaney Jones? Wasn't the Melvaney Jones gang ready to eat you alive the minute that you showed up? Wasn't that orders from Clinton?'

The lies were so fiercely brought forth that it never occurred to Dave to doubt them. He could remember the savagery of the attack upon him as soon as he entered the house of the Todd Ranch. This seemed the final confirmation of everything that Red Martin had spoken.

In the distance, he heard a sudden clattering of the hoofs of a horse, but the noise did not draw near—it departed.

"I begin to see," Dave said. "It makes me a little sick, but I suppose it's the truth. Heaven knows who a man can trust in the world."

"Yeah, who can anybody trust?" Martin agreed. "And what I wanna know is who double-crossed *me* and brought you here?"

"I did," said a voice in the doorway, and, as the two jumped and looked about, they saw the gorilla figure of Melvaney Jones with a leveled gun in his hand.

Chapter Thirty-Eight

The humor of Melvaney Jones was extremely rollicking and pleasant, at that moment. He stepped in another stride, and said: "Don't budge a hand, Reagan. I got you cold, kid, but I dunno that I wanna plaster you all up with lead, just yet. I got some other ideas in my head. You, Red . . . you blockhead . . . why ain't you got a gun on the big boy?"

A long Colt instantly slid into the hand of Martin, while Reagan stood stunned by this catastrophe.

"Send the wolf outside, Reagan," Jones ordered.

It was done. A word—a wave of the hand—and the silver ghost stole away into the blackness of the night. Jones kicked the door shut behind the tail of the wolf.

"Never seen dog or horse or man better trained than that wolf, kid," he said. "And *you're* the one that was called a half-wit, are you? I wouldn't mind havin' your half of a brain, though, to tack onto my half. Here's a gent, Red, that I just been offerin' a fair partnership. Here's a gent that I'd rather have workin' with me than all the rest of you hoboes. Yeah, than all the lot of you. Because he's a man, and because he's young enough to take teachin'. But his heart is soft in him. That's what's wrong with him, and that's what spoils him for me and my uses."

He talked on with great contentment, and now he seated himself on the stool that Martin had occupied when Reagan entered the hut.

"Go through him, Red, and get the guns off of him," he ordered. "Hoist those hands, and keep 'em hoisted, brother," he warned Reagan.

Gloomily Dave Reagan raised his hands to the height of his head, but he kept an impassive face as he watched the squat form of the outlaw, and the steady muzzle of the gun. Something about the strong, careless crooking of the forefinger told him that it would take very little indeed to induce the great Melvaney Jones to crash a bullet through the brain of his captive.

Red Martin, laughing with glee, was taking from Reagan that pair of guns and the knife that he, in his turn, had carefully removed from the keeping of Jones.

"Always keep a third gun handy around me," Jones said in explanation to Dave. "And I have it where it ain't looked for mostly." He continued: "Count that money out. I'll take my half now, brother. Go on, Red, and count it out, and slip me the five grand that comes my way."

Red obediently began to count the money. "I was gettin' down-hearted," he said. "I thought that you'd double-crossed me, chief."

"Sure you did, because you're a fool. I wouldn't double-cross a ten-thousand-buck deal, would I, you dummy? But the kid, here, he played into my hand. You know what he done, Red?"

"You tell me," Red said. "I dunno. He ain't one to talk about what he's done."

"I get sore at the boys, and step out of the house for air, and, as I step, this here mountain falls on my chin a couple times, and I go to sleep. Look at my chin where he slammed me."

"It's swollen up a bit," Red declared. "And the skin's split, too."

"I don't mind that," answered Melvaney Jones. "I don't ever mind gettin' hurt, so long as I can learn something by it. And I learned something tonight. I learned that a gent could put me out with a sock of his bare hand. Yeah, put me right to sleep. What a beautiful whang you got in that mitt of yours, Reagan!"

Dave said nothing. Now that he was disarmed, he ventured on lowering his arms, and Melvaney Jones encouraged this freedom, saying: "That's all right. Make yourself comfortable, now, will you? It ain't likely to be very long. I'll tell you what, kid . . . except for bein' soft-hearted, you would've amounted to something. Yeah, you would've amounted to a lot. But when you pulled up the ropes on my wrists, a minute ago . . . when you was so dog-gone' afraid that you was cuttin' me to the bone . . . why, I pretty near laughed at you, boy. It wasn't nothin' to me. I just kept my muscles hard, and, after you left, there was a lot of play in the rope. It took some workin', but I shook the rope off, and then I got at the bridle rein, and done the same for it. And here I am, shinin' and early!"

He laughed again. Then he went back to his story. "He takes and slams me on the chin, and puts me to sleep, Red, and carries me out to the barn, and ties my hands behind me with a pair of reins. See?"

"I see," Red Martin said, his eyes starting in his head.

"That's all right," went on the other, "but then he takes and throws me onto a horse and asks will I show him the way to Red Martin. Sure, I'll show him the way. The longer the way, the more chances I've got of thinkin' things out. That's how I come to double-cross you, Red. Then, when I got loose, and he'd come in here, I turned loose the big bay geldin' that he'd rode on this far, and I give the bay a slap, and off he went. He's a return horse, you know, and when he gets back to the house, he'll paw at the door till the boys come out and find him. And then they'll pile into the saddle and cut straight for here . . . they'll know that if there's any trouble goin', with me out of the way, it's mighty likely to be centered around this shack."

He leaned his back against the wall, and smiled, with a sigh of contentment.

"You see how everything works, Red?"

"I see," said Red. "If he don't show up inside of another six weeks, then I collect from old man Clinton on the price of his scalp. And I reckon that he don't return inside of six weeks, does he?"

"Not inside of six weeks," the other said, shaking his head. "No, and not inside of six years, neither. He's goin' to go and have a long sleep, pretty soon. But I want the boys to see him before he finishes off. He oughta make a good finish, the kid oughta. He's got the stuff in him. He'll die like a man, eh?"

"I dunno," Red Martin said. "He looks kind of white around the gills, already."

"Are you scared, kid?" Jones asked with an odd, sort of impersonal curiosity.

"Yes," Dave Reagan said honestly.

"Ever so scared before in all your born days?" Melvaney Jones continued.

"Yes," Dave Reagan answered. "It used to be worse than this . . . the first days at the house of Cousin Bush Reagan."

His simplicity made both the other men stare at him.

"All right, kid," Jones said. "Dog-gone me, but I'm sorry that you've gotta be put out of the way. But whatcha think? We get a big pile of coin for this, and after we've cashed in on the six weeks' absence of Mister Dave Reagan, then we're goin' to have a hold on J. Harvey Clinton, and that hold's goin' to be so dog-gone' strong that, if I ain't a fool, I oughta be able to bleed him for a million, before the end. Blackmail, that's goin' to be the job for us to work. And it'll pay so well that we won't have to be ridin' in rough weather, Red." He laughed, as he came to this conclusion, and then added: "Put a pair of ropes on him . . . hands and feet, Red. And draw 'em tight. You got a good rope here? Because an ordinary rope, he'd bust it like pack thread."

"Here's a rope would do," Red Martin said. He picked a lariat from the wall. It was supple rawhide, such as the Mexicans prefer to use, strong as iron and limber as water.

The chief stretched his hand to it, but did not touch it. He nodded his head with satisfied understanding. "Yeah," he said, "that oughta do, all right. Just throw a couple loops. . . . Hi!"

The exclamation left his lips, and a bullet left the muzzle of his gun at the same instant. For Dave Reagan, the instant that he felt attention shifting, even for half of a second, to the rope that was to be used in tying him, had determined to try for his life. At the worst, a bullet would stop him, and end his life. But was it not better to die at once, in that way, than to wait until the rest of the gang had arrived, to enjoy his end as a spectacle?

Little by little, without haste, he had stretched out his hand until it came to the fire-hot top of the lantern on the apple box. And the slowness of the motion had kept it from being noticed. Then, gripping it hard, he had flung the lantern at the head of the seated Jones.

The cry and the bullet had preceded the landing of the blow. Then the lantern crashed on the head of Jones, the light went out, and while Red Martin yelled with terror and amazement, the big man bounded straight for the door, ahead of him.

Dave was bowed, and his shoulder muscles were the cushion that took up the solid shock. That door went down before him like a thing of straw, hardly checking his running stride. The stars whirled before his eyes, like a tangle of fireflies. Two guns spoke together behind him, and something stung his cheek waspishly. He sprang sidewise, and raced around the corner of the shack, with Gray Cloud whining at his side.

Out came the two men from the shack, roaring with rage as they ran.

And from the woods not far away, where the horses had been left and where Melvaney Jones himself had been tied for safekeeping, there broke at this moment a string of riders.

The gang had come, as Melvaney expected, when the return horse had been found at the Todd place.

All retreat was cut off for Dave Reagan in that direction. And as he rounded the farther corner of the shack, he found himself between the wall of the little house, and the rim of the cliff of the ravine, with the roar of the creek far beneath thundering steadily up to him with a grinding sound, as though huge machines were working and throbbing in unison.

He ran at full speed, stooping low. Bullets would be flying, before many moments passed, and, in the meantime, the moon was well up and throwing a powerful white light over the landscape—a light quite good enough to enable such marksmen as these to strike a target as big as Dave Reagan, and at short range.

CHAPTER THIRTY-NINE

Brush grew to the very edge of the river's steep-sided ravine. Through that he fled, dodging this way and that. They had poured around the side of the shack, and were after him.

He heard the terrible voice of Jones ordering a rider out of the saddle that his own bulk would then fill.

Guns roared. Bullets tore the air about Dave. In an instant the charge would sweep up and devour him. And so, as a bullet plucked like thumb and forefingers at his shoulder, clipping through the coat to the skin, he dived forward, rolled with his heels high in the air, and instantly, swerving about, scrambled on all fours into the low scrub, straight back toward the riders.

They would see him, almost certainly. There was a very fair chance that the horses might trample him down, but he had a ghost of a chance to double through the line.

On they swept. They loomed above him, tall as huge, black, moving mountains. They thundered past him.

"He dropped right here!" shouted voices.

Horses were being reined up as he rose to his feet and sprinted toward the trees where he had stopped with Melvaney Jones.

For the roan was still there—the roan that was so clumsily built, so long and low, but which had been selected by no less an authority than Melvaney Jones himself.

Half a dozen racing steps—still they had not seen him.

Then a tingling yell of warning went up to the sky and struck against the face of the shuddering moon, as it seemed to Dave Reagan.

They had spotted him again. They were coming, now, with a thundering of hoofs, but already he was at the outer fringe of the trees. He saw the vague, shadowy form of the horse before him, and leaped at the back of it, sweeping up the reins as he landed in the saddle.

The sharp, eager yip of the wolf sounded close to the head of the horse, as though to urge the mustang to a greater effort. But the roan started as though trying to jump out from beneath the saddle. Nothing in the way of horseflesh can start so fast as a Quarter horse, and this was one of them.

It lengthened; it dug in with hard, short-reaching strides, and presently it was shooting along at full speed, with the branches of the trees reaching like live things at the head of Reagan. This way and that they dodged through the trees. He was flattened on the back of the mustang. The whir of the wind of the gallop was in his ears. He was like part of a projectile.

He heard the wild yelling of the pursuit behind him, and still the mustang swept him forward, and he was gaining, so far as he could tell from the sounds behind, when the horse stepped into a hole and turned a complete somersault, and then lay still.

Dave lay still, also, half stunned by the shock of the fall, and his clothes and flesh torn by the thorns and the twig ends of the brush into which he had dropped. At his side crouched the wolf, and licked his face, as the roar of the pursuit hurtled up— and then swept by!

He got to his feet and ran to the roan. The poor mustang was dead; a broken neck had put an end to its days. But still there might be a chance for Dave, though it was fairly certain that the men of Jones's gang would presently turn about and come scouting back through the woods, as soon as they missed the noise of the fugitive before them. But their own uproar would deafen them to that lack, for a few moments, perhaps.

So big Dave Reagan struck out at a good pace—not full speed, because full speed could not be kept for long. But running well inside his strength, with a wonderfully long and easy stride for a man of his bulk, he headed through the woods. He kept, as well as he could, parallel with the river, the vibration of which was steadily on his right.

Behind him, he heard the hunt turning. Presently a wild outcry seemed to indicate that they had found the dead mustang.

Now which way would they turn—up the river or down it?

They spread in both directions. Bitterly Dave noted that. He could hear the hoof beats receding, and he could hear them advancing. What could he do now, since they were sure to come sweeping through the woods, and presently, in the brightness of the moonlight, they would certainly spot him? Despair choked him.

He turned sharply to the right, since human feet could not carry him out of the reach of the approaching horsemen, and, coming to the edge of the river wall, he looked hungrily over the side. It was a sheer drop of fifty feet to even the first roughness.

Yet as he ran on, he saw a bush projecting from the outer surface of the rocky wall, and below this certain sharp projections, glistening in the moonlight, and yet with a sufficient obscurity about them.

But he was desperate. He felt that already he had had and used more than his normal share of luck, and that the next sight they had of him, the riders would be sure to put their bullets through him. It would not mean a center shot to end the race. Even a graze a little deeper than that which had chipped his face and made the blood run down would be enough, in a few minutes, to drain his strength.

But down the face of the cliff, if he could find his way, perhaps they would not be able to follow. And before they could get to the opposite side of the ravine—well, who could tell what would happen? He was not foreseeing actual safety of a definite and permanent sort—he was merely foreseeing safety for the next few moments.

Dave slid over the edge of the rock, caught the rim of it with his hands, flattened himself as closely as possible against the cliff, and then dropped.

CHAPTER FORTY

As he shot down, his right arm, thrown out, caught over the bush that he had noticed from above, and at which he had aimed. Half the roots of it came out with a loud ripping, tearing sound. But for the rest, it held firmly enough. And just below, he fitted his feet into a good hold on the rock.

Yet though he had provided for himself, for the instant, what about the wolf?

Gray Cloud hovered above, moaning as he ran back and forth above his master's head. In vain Dave made to the wolf the signal to retire. In vain he called, first loudly, and then passionately. Gray Cloud, it appeared, was no longer obeying orders. And there he stood against the skyline, a great and prominent signal to the pursuers. Already the beating of the hoofs of the horses was drawing near through the trees. In a moment they would come into view.

In anger and despair, Dave regarded the betraying figure of the wolf.

But Gray Cloud, now thrusting his head down over the edge of the cliff, bayed loud and long, and dropped on his forelegs, letting his feet hang over the rim of the rock, as though preparing to make the long jump down.

Then, cutting through the thick uproar that the boiling currents of the river maintained below, came the tingling shouts of men above.

They had seen the wolf; they would soon see the master.

Sick with disgust and with fear, Dave Reagan was still more startled when Gray Cloud suddenly launched himself from the ledge and came straight down toward his master. It was like standing beneath a strong avalanche.

But gripping the rock as well as he could with his toes, and securing one strong handhold, with his free hand he tried to catch Gray Cloud as he came down, rushing, scratching vainly at the rocks to diminish his velocity. He was like a great bear falling on the man, and for an instant big Dave Reagan almost flinched to the side to allow the animal to drop. He could not harden his heart to that extent, however. No matter how much Gray Cloud was endangering Reagan, it was love for the man that made the wolf attempt this frantic leap. And so, a moment later, he struck with terrible force and jerked Reagan almost from his hold.

He literally swung out over the abyss, holding the bulk of the wolf by the scruff of the neck. One foothold was lost, and he told himself that he had come to his last instant. But in they swung again.

He could not maintain the weight of Gray Cloud in the descent. Twenty feet below them appeared a narrow ridge, and Dave took the chance of letting the monster fall toward it. He had hardly time to see the big fellow land securely, for above him he heard the yelling of the men, and, looking up, he saw their heads and shoulders as they looked gingerly over the edge of the precipice. He shifted himself downward rapidly.

A number of shots clanged above him, but an irregularity of the surface of the cliff caused the bullets to be shunted off; he could not see the men of Melvaney Jones, for the moment. He stared down. The ledge was close beneath him now, and the wolf was not on the length of it. Had Gray Cloud slipped into the water below? Dave dropped lightly, found the safe, level footing, and then saw what had become of the wolf.

There was an indentation of the rock's face, here, some five or six feet deep, and Gray Cloud was running up and down in the shelter, gamboling and laughing his red, silent laughter of triumph.

Reagan threw himself flat in the shelter and lay panting. He could hardly believe that he was safe again. It might not be for long, but Melvaney Jones and all of his men had been baffled through at least one more stage of the manhunt. Then, as his breath returned to him, Dave set about taking further note of his situation.

Beneath him, the face of the rock descended at a very slight angle for fully fifty feet. And there was one chance of climbing over that surface. It was polished like glass by the hands of the wind and the storm through many centuries. There would be neither foothold nor handhold for him. He might, perhaps, make from his clothes a rope that would support his weight during a part of the descent. And then he could trust himself to dive, for just at the foot of the rock the water was not a rapids, but gathered in what appeared to be a comparatively still pool. If that pool were deep, a diver would be safe; if it were shallow, he would break his neck.

More than that, from the edge of the pool the current began to run again with terrible force, stretching out in long streaks that indicated speed, and quickly sweeping into riffles of white foam. These, gathering in a sort of crescendo to a solid sheet of white, leaped out from the creekbed, and dropped, sheer, some twenty or thirty feet in a waterfall that made up the major part of the voice of thunder that kept echoing and reëchoing through this portion of the gorge.

It was a small, a very small chance of escape that lay before Dave. With set jaw, he considered it. Then he sat down and threw his arm around the neck of Gray Cloud. What lay before them he could not guess, except that there would be danger long drawn out, of one sort or another. It was an incredible comfort to have the great animal beside him.

The moon was now peering straight into the cave, for the cliff faced east, and the moon was a quarter of the way up the sky. Later on, however, its black shadow would fall across the lower part of the cliff, and perhaps at that time he might be able to execute his attempt to get down to the water.

He lay down and looked over the dizzy edge of the rock toward the water below. Just above the point where the water sprang over the fall, there was a little triangular rock that jutted above the surface of the stream. From the edge of it to the base of the cliff was only easy jumping distance and it seemed possible that, in swimming down the whirl of the current, a man might make the rock, instead of being shot over the falls to destruction. It was a narrow chance, indeed, for the strength of the current would play with the power of the strongest swimmer. However, it was something to hope for. Once on the rock, after springing to the shore, there was a narrow apron of detritus at the base of the cliff, and perhaps he could escape along this.

But all would have to wait until the shadow of the moon fell over the cliff and the narrow ravine. Meanwhile, what if marksmen gained the farther bank and opened fire upon him in his open-faced cave? That was a chance that he could only hope against, not alter.

He had reached this conclusion when a rifle bullet fired from above and at a slight angle to his side, hit the rock close to his face and drove several splinters of rock deep into his flesh. He drew back in haste, and began to fumble at the wounds, striving to draw out the stone needles.

Above him, a yell of inhuman triumph rang through the shouting of the currents below. And a cold anger began to grow up in Dave for the first time in his life. Suppose that he could have them in just such a position as this, what would he do? Murder them one by one, he felt, without remorse.

He had reached that conclusion when the wolf sprang to the edge of the shelf, snarling. At the same time, a pendulous shadow struck in from the side. It was the squat bulk of the great Melvaney Jones, swinging on the end of a long rope. Gray Cloud, bristling with rage, waited on the verge of the stone— too near the edge, as it chanced. For as Jones swung, he struck out, and the long-barreled revolver in his hand clipped the great wolf squarely alongside the head.

The weight of the blow wrenched the gun spinning out of the hand of Jones, as he stepped onto the shelf, but also it sent Gray Cloud staggering. For an instant, he clawed at the brink of the cliff—then he fell backward, scratching at the stone, his fangs shown by his grin of earnest effort. He shot out of sight, toward destruction, and as he disappeared, a strange sound of rage and human woe rang in the ears of Dave Reagan. He could hardly realize that it came from his own throat. He could hardly realize that he was springing at Melvaney Jones with the lust for murder in his heart.

Jones flung himself forward on the shelf of rock, and Reagan almost floundered past him and down into the moonlit gulf beneath. He checked himself on the brink of the ledge and, turning, saw the great Jones swinging to his feet, with a second revolver in his grasp. He reached that ever-threatening weapon with a kick that sent it spinning. Jones lunged out and grappled his legs. Together they fell in a tangled knot like two clawing wildcats.

Reagan was uppermost for only a moment. Under him it seemed there was no human shape on which he could lay his grasp, but a writhing mass of muscle and gristle that avoided any solid hold, just like an octopus at sea. Then he was underneath, and two great hands had him firmly by the throat.

"Now I've got you, lad," Jones hissed. "You've led me a chase, but Melvaney Jones always wins in spite of everything."

Through the great corded muscles and tendons in the neck of Reagan those terrible hands were fumbling for the life, and coming close to it. He struck into the distorted face of Jones. It was like striking gristle that yielded but was not hurt. He tore at the hands with his own, but he merely seemed to be giving Melvaney Jones greater force to strangle him. He swung his right arm across his own face. The head of Jones was buried in his shoulder, but the back thrust of his elbow forced the head up a trifle.

Again he jabbed with the elbow, and it tore back across the face of Jones, jerking back his head. Again Dave used the same short resistless blow, and the head of Jones bobbed like a cork in water. His eyes blinked. His hold loosened, and in an instant Dave had twisted out of that death grasp and floundered to his feet.

His throat was bleeding. The iron fingers of Jones had torn away the skin as though it were the tender rind of ripe fruit. But Dave was ready and balanced when the other sprang up at him from all fours like the animal that he was, snarling and whining with pure fury of battle.

Now for the long left, the magic hand. It had stopped and dropped big Weaver. It had battered and foiled that monster, Jack Lumber. But would it avail against this human gorilla?

Dave let it go at a distance, his might behind it. It struck the mark. The other simply swayed to the side and kept coming in. Dave hit out again, desperately, and felt the full of his weight jar home, knocking his arm half numb to the shoulder. And still, though with shortened steps, Melvaney Jones came in at him, senseless to punishment.

Dave had not found the button with either blow. He sprang back. His shoulders landed heavily against the side of the rock, and he knew that this time he must hit with effect, or submit to another of those murderous clinches with a man who fought as an animal fights, for the life, and whose fingers were like the red-hot tongs of a blacksmith.

With the left he feinted, and with the left he hit, a shorter punch, and one that hooked down at the end. It bounced off the craggy ledges of Jones's chin and yet still he came on in. His chest struck the chest of the young man, but he did not instantly grapple. His weight seemed to sag forward. He caught at big Dave Reagan, but as a falling man clutches at a support.

Savagely Reagan thrust him away. A roundhouse swing came out of the atmosphere and landed with stunning force upon the side of Reagan's head. He ducked the coming of another, and, as he straightened, he hammered a good right solidly home.

Melvaney Jones reeled back on his heels. The inevitable left found his face, and knocked him, suddenly weak, clear to the farther end of the rock ledge. Dave Reagan followed. Doubt and fear had left him now, and he knew that he was the master of the situation. Following, he speared Jones with terrible force with the same invincible accurate left hand.

The head of Jones rocked back and clipped against the rock wall. He staggered. His knees bent. Another blow would have floored him, but that was not what Dave Reagan wanted—not yet.

He danced back, at ease, sure of himself. "They're going to get me, I suppose, Jones, but, before they get me, they're going to have the pleasure of seeing your hulk go down the flume. They'll see you go smash before they have a chance to enjoy what happens to me. Murder was what you wanted, and murder is going to be what you get. Look, Jones, I'm your master. Try to rush me. You see? I can hit you spinning. I can smash you to pieces, and pick you up when I choose and throw you into the river, as you knocked poor Gray Cloud. I tell you what . . .

Gray Cloud was worth a thousand such devils as you are. I wish that I'd let him tear out your throat when he had a chance before!"

Melvaney Jones, one hand against the wall, waited, head down, and from his bleeding face his eyes took note of the young man, of the river beneath them, and the death that was sure to come. Then, lowering his head, throwing up his arms as a guard against those hammering, stunning punches, he lunged suddenly at Dave Reagan, intent only on knocking him from the ledge, even at the cost of his own life.

CHAPTER FORTY-ONE

Too late, the young man saw what was in the mind of the other. He smashed out with all his force, and knocked the shielding arms from the head of Jones. The next blow would go home and stop the rush, but there was no time for another blow. The charging force of Jones was launched at him, low and terribly hard, and he could not avoid it with a side-step. There was no room for that on the narrow ledge. It had made a battle ground, before this, only because both the men were striving to keep their feet. Now, in an instant, Dave was knocked back.

"Jones, you're gone mad!" he shouted.

And then the white moonlight struck on his face, and he went spinning down through space. The clutch of Jones was still on him until he struck what seemed a flat surface of stone. He was half stunned. He only knew that icy cold had seized him— the cold of death and the other world, perhaps. He could not breathe.

It was water that he was falling through. His feet touched rock. He thrust himself strongly upward, and his head came above the surface of the stream with the brilliance of the moon striking on his face, and the life-giving air in his nostrils.

Above him, on the rim of the distant cliff, he could see fantastically small figures dancing against the sky, throwing up their hands, with the gleam of steel weapons in them. And then the current gripped him.

He had been in rapid water many times before, but never in

such a maëlstrom as this. It was not a gradual and strong laying hold. But when he came to the edge of the profoundly deep pool at the side of the creek, suddenly he was gripped and jerked out among the white riffles.

He struck out furiously. That hardly mattered. He was face down or face up, rolling like a log. He shoaled in shallow water, and stood up, waist-deep, and in the instant, he saw that he was not far from the little triangular island that split the sweep of the current like the prow of a ship. More than that, on the rock stood a lean, gaunt form—it was drenched with a continual dashing of spray, but he knew it was Gray Cloud.

Somewhere above and beyond this hideous life, there was a God, and he knew it. Then the hurling waters knocked him flat again. He tried to strike out for the rock. He was sure that he was bearing right down upon it, and then a side current pulled him away. With a broad sweep it wrenched him.

He saw the wolf come down into the water, shoulder-deep, and stretch out his snaky head, and, with a last effort, he flung one hand clear of the water, and as far toward Gray Cloud as he could reach. It was caught in the vise of fire that sent a thrill of agony shooting to his shoulder, to his heart. For Gray Cloud had indeed caught his hand, and with teeth that gripped to the bone, held him fairly against the pull of the water. He strained forward against the murderous pain. His left hand reached the rock, and in a moment he was kneeling on it—his arms around Gray Cloud, and the hot, red tongue of the wolf lovingly licking his face.

Over his head, like the crying of birds through a storm, he heard voices, and, looking up, he saw those grotesque forms that were silhouetted against the sky, dancing and waving their arms. They went through the motions of men who are cheering a strange and wonderful thing. But Dave's mind did not make head or tail of what he saw.

Another cry reached him, a moment later, from the water. When he looked, he could only see a great hand reaching out of the water, above the rock, and being swept away from it by the same current that had dragged him.

That was Melvaney Jones, being carried to his death.

He had been willing to murder Jones, not long before. But that black wish had been snatched away from him. It was a humbler and milder spirit that lived in the breast of Reagan again, and the blindly reaching hand whose body was invisible was too much for him.

His left hand, he used to grip the rock. With his right, he reached toward Jones, and saw the face of the man come to the surface, then, a face like that of a fighting bulldog, rather than the face of a man. But there was no wild terror in it, only wild determination to fight for his life to the last instant. And his life seemed to be gone, for his fingers swept down the current an inch from Dave's extended hand.

There was one way to make his reach longer. Keeping his left hand to hold on the rock, Dave thrust his body into the water again. And he felt a mighty grasp clutch him by the ankle. It was not like the grip of a hand, but the grip of a pair of fighting jaws bruising the flesh against the bone.

Over Dave climbed Melvaney Jones to the rock, and then he turned and helped to haul in Dave.

"Well," Melvaney Jones panted, "that was a kind of a close one, eh, what?" He was nearly spent with exhaustion, but he was as calm as ever. He kneeled there on one knee, with the spray still beating over him, and went on: "I try to murder you. I knock the wolf into the water. I knock the pair of us after him. He pulls you out of the water . . . you pull me . . . and there you are with a dead wolf and two dead men turned into three that's living." He laughed. Then, pointing upward, he said:

"They look kind of cheerful, don't they? Look at 'em yowling, will you?"

In fact, the men on the edge of the ravine, above them, were in a greater frenzy of excitement than ever.

"We'll jump ashore and go down the edge of the water," said the outlaw. "There's a safe and easy way up the cliff, about a half mile from here, I reckon." He set the example by leaping from the rock.

Reagan and Gray Cloud followed. But there Reagan paused.

Melvaney Jones turned back and gripped his arm at the elbow. "Look, Dave," he said, "will you trust yourself with me, now?"

The big fellow hesitated.

"I'm a hound and a wildcat, and a crook," said Jones, "but I ain't a skunk."

"No," Dave said. "I'll trust you, Jones."

"Good," the other said. "Come along this way."

CHAPTER FORTY-TWO

They sat again at the cabin where Reagan had seen Red Martin for the first time.

Dave's head was bowed. He was sick in brain and body from what he had been through, from hunger, from nerve strain, and finally from the exquisite pain of his hand. The gashes that the teeth of the wolf had left in his flesh were long and deep, and the great Melvaney Jones himself was dressing the hand with exactly the same care and method that he would have used on himself. But being himself without nerves, he poured in the iodine like water before he bound up the cuts.

"You'll get back to Granite Creek in time to have a decent doctor sew these here things up," Jones said.

"There's a doctor there by name of Robinson," said huge Jack Lumber. "What he can do with a needle is more'n your grandma could do in darnin' a sock. He worked on me when I was all kind of apart. I never seen nothin' like it."

"How's your face, Jack?" Jones asked, looking up suddenly, and with a grin.

The giant replied with equal mirth: "How's yours, chief?"

"Mine's worse than yours," answered Melvaney. "There ain't so much of it to spread the punches over."

They stood closely around the wounded man, all the riders who followed the fortunes of Melvaney Jones. Only, they took care not to crowd Gray Cloud, who sat at the knee of his master and watched every touch of the work of bandaging, sometimes favoring Jones with a low, deep-throated growl of warning, and again, twisting his head to stare up in the face of his man, as though asking for orders to hurl himself at the neck and the life of this tormentor.

But Dave with his free hand, stroked the wet mane, and said nothing.

"How did things happen?" asked young Pete Reagan.

"I go down on the rope," Jones began, "and find the wolf and Dave on a ledge, cut back under the face of the cliff, and I step off and give the wolf a bat with my gat, and he drops into the river. And what saves him, I reckon, is the same thing that saves us, later on . . . that big hole in the bottom of the creek. Doggone me, it must be about a hundred feet deep. Anyway, it kind of peeved Dave, here, when I socked the dog off the shelf. And he comes at me, meanin' trouble. I dodge, drop, pull a gun. He kicks my second gun out of my hand, and that's all I have with me. I don't have my whole armory with me for the job ahead. I get up and dive, and bring Dave down. I get on top, and fasten my hooks in his neck." He looked up and nodded with a grin of satisfaction. "You ain't goin' to swaller with no satisfaction for a couple of weeks, brother," he remarked.

Dave Reagan said nothing. He shuddered as he remembered.

"Once you got a fair hold, you must've choked him, and this here is only a ghost," Jack Lumber opined.

"That's what you'd think," said the chief. "But he's full of tricks, and the first thing I know, he's got his elbow under my chin and gives me a couple of jabs that bring out a flock of stars. Then he's up on his feet, and I go in to get a fresh hold. But what do I run into. Maybe you know, Jack."

"Yeah, I know. You run into a solid wall of lefts," Lumber said with a sort of gloomy satisfaction.

"It wasn't a solid wall. It was a fast-movin' wall," Melvaney Jones said. "It was like that left was hooked to my face with an elastic, and every time he pulls back his hand, it's gotta land. He hit me three times in a row harder than you could hit with a sledge-hammer, Lumber. And when I say it, I mean it."

"Yeah, I know you mean it," Lumber said, rubbing his swollen face tenderly. He added: "Sledge-hammers ain't as hard as his fist, and they ain't as heavy."

There was a general laugh, at this. And as the laughter quieted, the great Melvaney Jones remarked: "Now, when he got through slammin' me so that I was stopped, I takes a back step, and he follers, and that left is still in my face, and it makes me sick. Then he gets heated up, because I knocked the wolf over the side of the rock, and he says that a wolf like Gray Cloud is worth a thousand men like me, and he's goin' to kill me, and he meant it. So I thought that, since I didn't have a chance to live, so long's I had to die, I'd take him with me. So I swarmed at him, and the two of us went over the edge of the rock, and you all seen the rest that happened with your own fool eyes. Ain't I right?"

They admitted that he was right with a murmur of deep wonder.

Jones finished dressing the torn and wounded hand of his recent enemy, and arose from the task with a grunt. "Come here, Red," he said to Martin, and retired outside the door of the cabin, for a moment, to confer with him.

While he was gone, Pete Reagan asked: "You ain't goin' to change your mind and throw in with us, Dave, are you?"

"I'm not going to throw in with you," Reagan said, shaking his head.

"I'm kind of glad of it," said one of the other men, "because the stand-in that you've had with the chief, after tonight, it wouldn't leave much of a chance for the rest of us, I guess." He chuckled as he spoke. Then he went on: "When I seen the pair of you in the water, and then when I seen you reach down for

Melvaney, I thought you were goin' to give him a sock on the head to make sure of him goin' over the falls. And dog-gone me if you didn't stretch out and pull him out of the water, was all that you done." He grinned and shook his head with a joyous wonder. "I says to myself that that's the end of the good old days, and the gang busts up, is what I says to myself. We all had the same idea, but you fetched Melvaney through, which is what nobody else has ever had to do for him since the beginnin' of time."

This seemed to be the consensus of opinion.

Now Jones entered the cabin again, and with him came Red Martin, obviously gloomy and crestfallen.

Melvaney sat down, pulled out a scrap of paper and a soiled but unused envelope, and scrawled for some moments, making his writing extremely small. Then he sealed a fat package inside the envelope and handed the whole to young Dave Reagan.

"Dave," he said, "you take that to John Harvey Clinton, will you?"

"I will," said Reagan.

"And now you tell me, partner, what I can do to make things easy for you. Anything that I can do for you is goin' to be done. So long as I live," Jones went on, his voice growing suddenly somber and solemn, as he lifted his cut and battered face toward the light of the lantern, "so long as I live, whatever I can do for you, I'm goin' to do. I've had my ups, and I've had my downs. But the only gent that ever treated me white after I'd kicked him in the face was this one here . . . you, Reagan. Now you start in and use me, and you can't use me enough." He smashed his big hands together as he spoke.

There was a murmur of almost savage applause from the others. There was hardly a one of them who did not belong to the business end of a hangman's rope, but they could appreciate justice and manliness such as this.

Dave Reagan lifted his head and looked almost blankly around him. Then he said: "There's a cousin of mine here, with you, Jones."

"Yeah, there's Pete, and he's a likely kid, too," Melvaney Jones said.

"Well," said Dave, "if it's not too much to ask, I'd like to have Pete ride with me back to Granite Creek, and I'd like to try to persuade him never to come back to you."

Jones grunted. "You do your best by him. If there's any more that you think you can persuade to stay away from me, take 'em along, too."

"Only the one man," Dave Reagan said. "That's all I'll ask for. And a pair of horses to carry us to Granite Creek. That's all, if it's not too much."

"Too much?" Melvaney Jones said. "I'll see the gent that says that that's too much. But it's only the beginnin', partner. The day's goin' to surely come when I can do a lot more for you, and don't you mistake it. There's things and ideas on the inside of me that I never had before. And I got 'em all from you. You busted my face for me, and you let some new ideas into my head through the cracks."

They swarmed outside into the open night with Dave Reagan.

"I'm goin' to say good bye here," Melvaney Jones stated. "Some of the boys will see you down the trail a piece. And your cousin can go along with you to Granite Creek, and never come back, neither, if he don't want to. He ain't done anything that the law can hang on him, while he's been with me. He's rode on some parties, that was all, but he's never had no big hand in 'em. Pete, so long. You listen as hard as you please to what Dave says."

That was a strange party, with Jack Lumber holding the lantern up to the length of his vast arm, and staring with his little, inhuman eyes from face to face. One of those eyes was almost closed and surrounded by a great swollen, purple patch.

Dave Reagan shook hands all around, and he was given that same strapping bay horse that he had ridden away from the Todd Ranch earlier in the evening, at the side of the great Melvaney Jones.

The outlaw chief stood at the edge of the trail, waving his hand, talking noisily to the end. Dave and Pete Reagan moved their horses on through the brush, turned in their saddles and waved their hands, until the trees closed up behind them like files of soldiers, and gradually shut away the sight of the bandits who were grouped outside the hut.

But still their voices welled up, and rang with diminishing strength from the rear, and reminded big Dave Reagan of the times when he had ridden through those trees before, and the same voices had howled after him, like wolves after prey.

Chapter Forty-Three

It was the clear middle of the morning, when two tired riders came into the town of Granite Creek, and, crossing close to the turmoil of the labor on the dam, they reined their horses near the office of the famous John Harvey Clinton.

There they dismounted. Pete Reagan gripped the reins as his cousin walked up the steps and tapped at the door of the office.

"Come in if you got business . . . keep out otherwise!" shouted the familiar voice of the great Clinton.

Dave Reagan pushed open the door.

As he stepped in, Clinton shouted again, but in quite a different key.

It had been a face of brown, with rosy undertones, that had been before him on top of those same wide shoulders, before Dave Reagan went into the mountains on the perilous quest. Now it was a haggard, lean, and drawn countenance.

"Hey, you back already? You beat as soon as this?" demanded John Harvey Clinton.

Dave came to the desk and, without speaking, drew a slip of paper from his pocket.

"What's happened to your hand?" Clinton asked curiously. "Get it jammed in something?"

"Yes," Dave said, speaking for the first time. "I got it jammed inside the jaws of a wolf."

It was not often that Harvey Clinton was silenced, but this was one of the rare occasions.

"You know the writing of Ray Martin?" asked Dave.

"Yes, I know the writing," the other said, frowning. "Look here . . . you managed to find him as quick as all this?"

Dave Reagan stared down at the other. "Does that surprise you a lot?" he asked.

"Why, sure, it surprises me," Clinton said, losing force and conviction in every word that he uttered, and finding it very hard to face the eyes and the voice of the young man. For there was a gleam like that of burnished steel in the glance of Dave Reagan, and there was a hard, sharp clang of metal in his voice.

"Well," Dave said, "I found Red Martin, and I have his receipt."

He unfolded the slip of soiled paper—it was blood that soiled it—and laid it on top of the desk.

The other snatched it, and, with incredulous eyes, he read the writing and the signature. "Well, I'll . . . well, it was quick work, and good work, Dave," he said. "Mighty good work," he added, his voice growing weaker. He could not understand it. The rat-like activity of Red Martin, backed up by the entire resources of the great Melvaney Jones—how could such a scheme have been broken through so quickly by a single unaided man? His brain whirled now. . . . "Speaking about Mary, Dave," he said, "of course you understand that. . . ." He paused.

The hard, new voice of the young man insisted: "What should I understand?"

"Why," the engineer drawled, "the fact is, Dave, that while you were away, I was thinking . . . thinking. . . ." He stopped again. He began to feel as he had not felt since childhood— abashed by another human being.

"Hello!" called a voice at the door. That door was pushed open, and Colonel Tom Hagger stepped in.

"Stay out, Colonel . . . I'm busy!" Clinton exclaimed.

"Hello, hello," Hagger said. "Back so soon, partner?" He

started to shake hands, and then saw the bandage on Dave's hand. He looked up from it to the drawn, sober face.

"Hello," Dave Reagan said. "I'm glad to see you, Colonel." He turned back to Clinton. "There's another thing for me to give you," he said. He laid the bulky envelope on the top of the desk.

"Where'd you get this?" Clinton asked, frowning, and more ill at ease than ever.

"I don't know what's in it," Dave said, "but Melvaney Jones seemed to think that you'd like to have it." He turned back to Hagger. "Colonel," he said, "I have a few words to say to Mister Clinton in private. Do you mind?"

The colonel was still staring at the mention of the great Melvaney Jones. "Not at all," he muttered, and stole like a frightened boy from the room.

Then Dave Reagan said: "I took you for a right man, and an honest man. I'd never harmed you. I loved your daughter. That was all. And she cared for me. But rather than let me have her, you meant to smile in my face and have me murdered. Now that I know you, Clinton, I want nothing of yours . . . not your money, or your friendship, or your daughter. Because your blood is bad. It's low blood, and bad blood. Good bye!"

And, in a stride, he was at the door, and, in another stride, he was gone.

The colonel went down the steps with him. "What's the matter, Dave?" he asked.

"I want to find a doctor named Robinson," Dave said.

"He's the best man in town," said Hagger. "You come along with me, and I'll take you to him. But you seem to be raising a crowd, as usual."

"It's the last day of my life that I'll raise a crowd," Dave answered. "I'm going where crowds don't follow."

He went down to his cousin, still patiently holding the heads of the horses and shrugging his shoulders at the volleys of questions that were poured at him by the gathering throng of the curious, but the gray wolf was well-remembered, and they wanted to know what the master of the animal had been up to lately.

Dave said to Pete Reagan: "Pete, you go home and stay home. Take care of Cousin Bush. He's getting old. Be friends with Hank. If you have trouble, I've told you where you can find me in the mountains. That's all. Good bye."

With his left hand, he gripped the fingers of the other, and, leading the horse, with the wolf behind him, he went down the street with Colonel Hagger.

And the crowd followed as a flag follows the standard that it waves from.

It was a scant hour after this that John Harvey Clinton sat in his house once more, with a stricken look in his face, and confronted his daughter. He had told her a very strange story, in terse words. Now he spread a piece of penciled paper before her, saying merely: "I know that signature, and it's straight."

She read:

Dear Mr. Clinton: Dave Reagan dropped in on us. We thought it would please you if we put him under the sod, and we did our best to do it.

But he beat us.

He beat my best men. He beat all us put together. Then he beat me, hand to hand, which nobody has done before.

After that, when we'd run him with dogs, and run him with horses, and tried guns and knives on him and everything but poison, he fished me out of white water when I was drowning, and where I'd put him to drown before us.

Seeing that he's that kind of a man, I wonder what kind of a gent you are that wants him done in?

Right from now on, he's my friend. He played hard, but he played fair, and this part of the mountains won't ever forget him.

I've talked the thing over with Red Martin. He says with me that money for the scalp of Dave Reagan we don't deserve, because we didn't get it. And money for his scalp we wouldn't take, because his scalp is what we don't want.

I'm sending back the $10,000 that you gave the kid to carry to Red. I'm sending back the $10,000 advance that you paid Red, too.

Lemme tell you, in the wind-up, that no matter how many millions you got, there's some men that you can't put a price on.

If ever I hear that anything's happened to Dave Reagan, and the means of it is a little shady, I ain't asking any questions. I'm just coming for you, Clinton.

Yours truly,
Melvaney Jones

The girl looked up from the reading of the letter. She stared at the stricken face of her father. And he, waiting for the bitterness of her to find a vent in words, was amazed to see her face soften.

"I understand, Father," she said. "It was to keep me from the awful fate of marrying a country clod like . . . like Dave Reagan. Was that it?"

She smiled at him, and he was silent.

"He said that your blood was bad, and that means that my blood is bad, too," she went on. "But suppose that we go to hunt for him, and see if we can't persuade him to forgive us?"

He pushed back his chair. "Whatever you want to do, Mary," he said, "is bound to be right . . . because everything that I've done about that wolf and that man has been wrong from the start."

That was why, three days later, John Harvey Clinton, his son Jack, and his daughter Mary Clinton came up a long valley that narrowed and narrowed until it was only a meager ravine. And through the trees they presently saw the outlines of a log house.

"That's the place," whispered Jack Clinton. "Look, Father . . . built it all himself . . . with tools that he made himself."

"No one man," the cynic said, "could ever manage to lift logs as huge as those. It would take a strong tackle and whole teams of horses to move 'em."

The girl laughed. "He built an incline, and up the incline he hitched the logs, rolling them an inch at a time with a system of levers. And so he got them up, and when they were about ready to drop into place, then he'd level off the top and bottom sides . . . and there you are. It's all the work of one man . . . and a wolf."

"Aye," the engineer muttered, "and that's the kind of a man . . . I'd say . . . that's more of a wolf than a human."

They went on, without speaking. The ground where they rode was covered with a thick dressing of pine needles, and therefore the steps of the horses were noiseless, and as for the squeaking of the saddle leather, the noise from the creek and the whistling of a sharp wind covered all such minor disturbances.

So they came through the trees, and had clear sight of the cabin, at last, and of Dave Reagan sitting on a tree stump before it, with his arms folded, and his head bowed.

The girl slipped from her saddle, and held up her hand in warning.

"Go back, both of you," she said. "Go back, and don't let him see you. It may help a little, if he thinks for a moment that I came alone."

Clinton stared at her shining face, her trembling lips, then, with a characteristic grunt, he jerked the head of his horse and rode back, followed by his son. The trees closed behind them. They heard the loud, angry snarl of the wolf.

Then there was silence.

It lasted for what seemed hours to John Harvey Clinton, then the exclamation of his son brought up his head, and he saw coming through the trees the flash of the silver wolf, first, and then big Dave Reagan striding, and beside him, looking happily up to his face, the girl.

"It took her to handle him," Clinton said with another grunt, "but far as that goes, she could handle anything or anybody in the world. Now for a lot of fool smiling and grinning and congratulating. Well, since they're going to be married, I hope they'll live happy ever after. But, right now, I wish I were back on the job, and out of all this sticky sentimental stuff."

ABOUT THE AUTHOR

Max Brand is the best-known pen name of Frederick Faust, creator of Dr. Kildare, Destry, and many other fictional characters popular with readers and viewers worldwide. Faust wrote for a variety of audiences in many genres. His enormous output, totaling approximately thirty million words or the equivalent of five hundred thirty ordinary books, covered nearly every field: crime, fantasy, historical romance, espionage, Westerns, science fiction, adventure, animal stories, love, war, and fashionable society, big business and big medicine. Eighty motion pictures have been based on his work along with many radio and television programs. For good measure he also published four volumes of poetry. Perhaps no other author has reached more people in more different ways. Born in Seattle in 1892, orphaned early, Faust grew up in the rural San Joaquin Valley of California. At Berkeley he became a student rebel and one-man literary movement, contributing prodigiously to all campus publications. Denied a degree because of unconventional conduct, he embarked on a series of adventures culminating in New York City where, after a period of near starvation, he received simultaneous recognition as a serious poet and successful author of fiction. Later, he traveled widely, making his home in New York, then in Florence, and finally in Los Angeles. Once the United States entered the Second World War, Faust abandoned his lucrative writing career and his work as a screenwriter to serve as a war correspondent with the infantry in Italy, despite his fifty-one years and a bad heart. He was killed during a night attack on a hilltop village held by the German army. New books based on magazine serials or unpublished manuscripts or restored versions continue to appear so that, alive or dead, he has averaged a new book every four months for seventy-five years. Beyond this, some work by him is newly reprinted every week of every year in one or another format somewhere in the world. A great deal more about this author and his work can be found in *The Max Brand Companion* (Greenwood Press, 1997) edited by Jon Tuska and Vicki Piekarski. His next Five Star Western will be *Out of the Wilderness*. His Website is www.MaxBrandOnline.com.